PRAISE FOR *SHE LEFT*

"Readers who were raised on a steady diet of Agatha Christie will find much to love in *She Left*—the intriguing cast of suspects, the red herrings scattered through the story, and the sleuth who has to put it all together to get herself to safety. Grey's story is a satisfying riff on the classic mystery story structure that will keep readers guessing until the end."

—Eva Jurczyk, author of *The Department of Rare Books and Special Collections*

"*Knives Out* meets Lucy Foley's *The Hunting Party* in this tense, locked-room mystery. Be wary of invitations where everyone could be a suspect."

—Georgina Cross, author of *One Night, Nanny Needed, and The Stepdaughter*

"Deliciously twisty—Agatha Christie would be spellbound."

—M. M. Chouinard, *USA Today* bestselling author of *The Dancing Girls*

"Immersive and hypnotizing, *She Left* is the effortless summer read that will enthrall you from the first chapter. Suspense and mystery lovers will find each character to be convincingly suspicious, and the decades-past crime to be full of compelling unanswered questions. Start this in the morning because Grey's taut writing will drive you to finish this book in one sitting."

—Elle Marr, Amazon Charts bestselling author
of *The Alone Time* and *The Family Bones*

"In this engrossing mystery, a vividly drawn cast of characters, claustrophobic setting, and propulsive pacing will keep you flipping the pages until the final twist that will leave you reeling. Grey skillfully and lovingly plays within the rules of the genre while also bringing a fresh voice and perspective to the *And Then There Were None* premise that will delight not just Agatha Christie fans but fans of tense, clever, and goose-bump-inducing stories as well. Clear your calendar for the day, because this is a one-sitting read!"

—Brianna Labuskes, bestselling author of *A Familiar Sight*

"*She Left* by Stacie Grey, with its sharp writing, a cunning locked-room setting, and eerie atmosphere, reads like a modern-day Agatha Christie and has all the hallmarks of a can't-put-it-down thriller."

—Ashley Tate, author of *Twenty-Seven Minutes*

"In *She Left*, Stacie Grey combines a clever setup with all the excitement of a classic whodunit, complete with a compelling cast of characters (and suspects). The tension grabbed me from the first page and ratcheted up relentlessly with each scene."

—Elle Grawl, author of *One of Those Faces* and *What Still Burns*

She Left

She Left

A NOVEL

STACIE GREY

Sourcebooks, Poisoned Pen Press, and the colophon
are registered trademarks of Sourcebooks.

The characters and events portrayed in this book are fictitious or
are used fictitiously. Any similarity to real persons, living or dead,
is purely coincidental and not intended by the author.

Published by Poisoned Pen Press, an imprint of Sourcebooks
P.O. Box 4410, Naperville, Illinois 60567-4410
(630) 961-3900
sourcebooks.com

Cataloging-in-Publication Data is on file with the Library of Congress.

Printed and bound in the United States of America.
VP 10 9 8 7 6 5 4 3 2 1

For Lucy and Calvin
Maybe wait until you're older to read this one.

THE GIRL

Amy slammed the door behind her and stalked out into the night. She should have known. Obviously, she should have known. They would say they were her friends, but they weren't really. Not as long as Jenna was in charge.

She stopped in the shadow of the trees and looked back at the cabin. The problem was, they had all come up here in Chris's car, and right now Chris was leaning against Jenna's knee and laughing at how stupid Amy was. Plus, he'd had at least three beers, so even if there was a universe where Amy could go back in and ask him to drive her home, there would be too much risk of being caught in one of the holiday checkpoints that were all around town to catch drunk teenagers just like them. Amy should know—her dad was manning one of them right now.

So she couldn't drive. And she couldn't go back. And the cheap brick phone that was the only kind her parents would buy her didn't get any signal out here, so even if they weren't both working and she did have someone to call, she couldn't. Which meant that Amy only had one choice. She turned around and started walking.

It probably would have made sense to take the road. There were no streetlights this far from town, but the moon was almost full, and out in the open, there was plenty of light to see by. Plus, if anyone wanted to find her, that was where they would look.

But the road went all the way around the park, probably four miles. And anyway, Amy didn't want them to come find her. That would be pathetic, making herself walk all that extra distance, just because she was hoping they would be sorry. They weren't sorry; they were having a better time without her. She would go through the park, just to show them how much she didn't care.

It was darker than she had expected under the trees. Amy went slow at first, keeping her eyes on the path and listening carefully for the sound of anyone coming after her. A couple of times she thought she heard something—a footstep, or some branches breaking—but no one called her name.

Eventually, Amy's eyes adjusted to the darkness, and she was able to pull some of her attention back from the ground in front of her to the bigger picture of what she had done. There were only two weeks left in the school year, but that was enough. She could just hear them all laughing about how Amy Brewer got so mad about a dumb joke that she walked for miles on Memorial Day night, literally running home to her mommy. She could try to tell her side of the story, but who would care? She had been one of them; she got what she deserved. Amy thought about the I-told-you-so looks she would get from her former friends and almost cried. She couldn't imagine anything worse happening to anybody.

Any other time, when things were bad, Amy at least had sports to fall back on. People forgave a lot when you were scoring goals and winning races. But the soccer season wouldn't start until November, and she'd had her final track meet last week. As she walked, she wondered if it would still be possible to sign up for a summer team, maybe swimming? It was worth a try.

Her route took her through an open-space park, one of a dozen or so that ringed the suburbs east of San Francisco where Amy had lived her whole life. She had thought of it as a familiar place, ordinary and kind of boring, but it didn't feel that way now. It wasn't even the first time she had been out here at night, but this was no nature hike with the hippie lady from the ranger station. This part of the path hadn't been maintained, and trees leaned low over it, while bushes reached out to scrape her legs below her shorts. (Probably poison oak, Amy thought. Why wouldn't it be?)

That was bad enough, but the worst part was that every time she moved, she thought she heard another footstep from somewhere behind her or to her right. She would stop, and the noise stopped, too, and no matter how quickly she turned to look back, she couldn't see where it was coming from.

It's just the echo of my own steps, she told herself, but she wasn't convinced. Since when did bushes echo?

Then there was another sound, a very definite crunch, and Amy jumped. Did mountain lions hunt at night? She thought they might. Right now, night seemed like a time for hunting. She wanted to run, but she fought the impulse. Amy was pretty sure animals would chase you if you ran. They had to; it was just instinct. So she kept her pace steady and made herself look as tall as possible, stomping with every step to sound big and heavy.

Eventually, she came out from among the oak and bay trees into a eucalyptus grove. Here, the undergrowth vanished—she remembered the ranger telling them it was because the trees poisoned the ground below them. The ranger had also said the creaking noises were from the wind rubbing the branches together, but Amy had liked to make up stories about how they were doors opening in the woods. Now she wished she hadn't. She wasn't a kid anymore, and she didn't like to think about anything coming through a door right now, even an imaginary one.

The more she walked, the colder Amy got. She hadn't brought a jacket, and even though it was almost summer, the dry air didn't hold enough of the daytime heat for her shorts and belly shirt to be comfortable. There was an emergency blanket in her backpack, left over from her mom's Y2K supplies, but she didn't have to think very long to decide that even the small chance of someone seeing her hiking through the park wrapped in crinkly Mylar wasn't worth the risk.

Aside from the creaking trees, the park was quiet, but further away Amy could hear the pops and bangs of illegal fireworks going off all over town. That was why the mayor's office had decided to put on the official fireworks show, according to Amy's mom, who had to set it up. It was supposed to give people something better to see so they wouldn't go around scaring their neighbors' dogs and risking starting fires in the dry grass. From the way things were sounding, Amy didn't think it had worked.

Another blast went off, close enough that the ground shook. Amy stopped and looked around to see if she could spot where it had come from, but there was nothing in the sky, just the shrieking sound of whistlers in the distance.

In a weird way, hearing the fireworks made her feel better. It was a reminder that even though it seemed like she was in the wilderness, she wasn't really that far from people, and home, and all the parts of her regular life. She walked on through the cough drop–scented air of the eucalyptus grove and tried to imagine what that life was going to look like now.

———

"I get everything." Jenna had said it while she was looking straight at Chris, who was peeling the label off a beer bottle with his long fingers. He had just glanced over at Amy when Jenna made her declaration, and Amy almost hadn't heard her over his smile. But, of course, Jenna had gotten herself right back into the center of everyone's attention. She didn't explain what she meant by the comment; she didn't need to. Jenna was pretty and thin, and her dad was rich enough to buy her anything she asked for, and most things she didn't. She got everything, and she always would. Amy couldn't even remember what had brought it up; it was just the sort of thing Jenna said. And now, Amy thought, one of the things Jenna was going to get was the ability to ruin her senior year. It wasn't fair, but then nothing was.

Or maybe not. Amy slipped her hand in her pocket and wrapped her fingers around the small plastic bottle there, feeling its contents rattle as she walked through the trees. Maybe, just this once, Jenna was going to find out that she wasn't as untouchable as she thought she was.

Down out of the hills, the ground started to level off. The trail was more developed here, with signs reminding hikers to leash their dogs and cyclists to yield to horses, and the brush on either side was cut further back, so she didn't have to move branches out of the way or watch for leaves that would brush her ankles.

Still, Amy felt an uneasiness she couldn't quite shake. She had just about managed to convince herself that the rustling noises that seemed to follow her were nothing but the wind, and if anything had been stalking her, there was no reason for it to have waited this long, but there was still a prickling on the back of her neck that wouldn't go away.

As she made her way to the road, she was tempted to see if her phone had any signal yet. This probably wasn't the kind of emergency her parents had in mind when they bought it for her, even after seeing what it cost, but one of them would find a way to get out of work to get her, and then this whole stupid night would finally be over. But she didn't, partly because she wasn't ready to explain what happened yet, and partly because, in the only piece of good luck she had had all day, she had just gotten to the place where the park drive joined the main road when a late-night bus turned the corner and stopped. Gratefully, Amy climbed on, paid her fare, and sank into the hard plastic seat as two police cars flew by, blaring their sirens.

She was thinking about what she was going to say the first time someone asked her at school about what happened when her phone started chiming from the bottom of her backpack. Amy's first instinct was to lunge for it, and her fingers had wrapped around the plastic brick before she paused to think. The only people who were going to call her right now were the five she left back at that cabin. Maybe they wanted to play with her some more, or maybe they were worried she was going to tell someone and get them in trouble. Either way, Amy wasn't going to give them the satisfaction of answering.

She pulled her hand out of the backpack and folded it over in her lap to muffle the sound.

———

It wasn't far from the bus stop to Amy's house, which was one of the many ways it was different from where Jenna lived. The ranch-style stucco houses of the midcentury subdivision were all anyone needed to see to know this wasn't a rich neighborhood, but for once that didn't bother Amy. All she wanted was to get inside and forget this night had ever happened.

She was standing in the kitchen, holding a box of graham crackers, when someone started banging on the door. Still carrying the box, Amy walked slowly down the hall, unsure if she should even answer it. There was no peephole in the door, but there was a window in the hall bathroom next to it. Amy looked out, but all she could see was a hooded figure, banging on the door with one hand and holding something to their mouth with the other.

Then they stopped and started looking around on the front step. It didn't take long for the figure to find the key in the hollow rock (Amy's dad hated that thing), and before Amy even had time to run or lock herself into the bathroom, the door opened, and the figure swooped through and grabbed her.

"Oh, thank Heaven, thank Heaven!"

It was her neighbor, old Mrs. Andrews, dressed in one of her husband's oversized sweatshirts and clutching her cordless phone as she hugged Amy tightly to her generous bosom.

"It's okay, she's here. She's right here in the house," she shouted into the receiver. "Oh, honey, you had us all so worried!"

Confused, Amy pried herself out of the hug.

"Worried? Why were you worried? Did they tell you I did something?" That was a possibility she hadn't even considered, that the others would take it even further by trying to get her in trouble. This was worse than she had thought.

"Oh no, no, no. You don't know? Oh, honey, they're all dead."

1

Twenty Years Later

E xit at Douglas Pine Road in five hundred feet."

Special Agent Amy Therese Brewer put on her blinker and moved into the right lane to slow down, letting the rest of the cars roar past up into the Sierras. She didn't care much for the tone of the lady in her phone, but she didn't like to take her eyes off the road, and with no one else there to tell her where to turn, it was the best she had. In fact, despite the dramatic scenery of the mountains, the trip had been less than pleasant. For most of the way, the holiday traffic had kept her at a crawl, and the only station her rental car's radio seemed to get was a local news channel that spent the whole drive in a typically Californian panic about a potential late-season storm.

The next round of directions sent her down a series of local roads, at first wide and well-maintained, then growing narrower and rougher until she ended up on what was essentially a long driveway clinging to the side of a cliff, complete with sections that had washed out, leaving gaps in the asphalt that yawned over the mountainside. She slowed down, turned on her headlights, and hoped she wasn't going to meet anyone coming the other way.

Fortunately, she didn't. In fact, if it hadn't been for the electronic voice insisting that her destination remained just ahead, Therese might have thought no one had been down this road for years. (The cell phone signal was strong, at least, which gave her reason to hope she hadn't entirely left the civilized world.) So she drove on, distrustful but short on other options, resolving to get an actual paper map in the unlikely event she ever did something like this again.

In truth, she could hardly believe she was doing it now. Therese had spent the last two decades doing everything she could to distance herself from what had happened that night twenty years ago, starting with giving up her first name. Even at the agency, there were only a handful of people who had any idea about her connection to one of their most famous unsolved cases. That might be about to change after this weekend, but in a lot of ways that decision had been taken out of her hands.

The distance to her destination kept getting smaller, and there were still no buildings in sight. Therese was cursing her faith in technology when she rounded a tight bend in the road and the house rose up in front of her.

Therese supposed "house" was the right word; she couldn't think of a better one. But it seemed insufficient for the building she had arrived at, a huge wood-shingled structure sprawling across a ledge that looked to be carved in the mountain. It reminded her of the kind of national park lodges they built in the 1900s, when no one visited the wilderness without a butler.

The sun was beginning to go down, and around to the western side of the house, she could catch a glimpse of portrait windows shining gold in the setting light. Next to them there was the corner of a deck, which must have looked out over a spectacular view of the foothills and the valley beyond. The only flaw in the view was a swath of burned forest curving across the mountainside above the house: a stark reminder of the threats that the California wilderness had for even the most luxurious dwelling.

"TV money," she muttered to herself. "Got to be."

The invitation hadn't mentioned any television connection, but it had been vague enough on the specifics that Therese had come prepared for anything. The name and email address had belonged to a respected journalist, for what it was worth. After all, even respected journalists had to eat. But even if the piece Ms. Scott was putting together for the twentieth anniversary of what had come to be known as the Memorial Day Massacre was going to turn out to be pure exploitation, at least this time no one could accuse Therese of running away.

She parked her car next to a similar rental and took a quick survey of the other vehicles in the driveway. Three more had clearly come straight from the airport; the other six she judged as personal cars. One oversized truck that had never seen so much as a box of nails in its bed, one minivan that had been through the wars, two small SUVs—one with a lot of corgi-related bumper stickers—one high-end Tesla, and one absolute beater of a hatchback. It was an interesting assortment, this first glimpse of the people she was about to meet.

But Therese hadn't come here to spend the weekend with their cars. She walked up to the huge oak door and turned the handle.

——

There were plenty of things to be impressed by in the entry hall. The towering ceiling, the beams made from whole tree trunks, the striking geometric rug that stretched the length of the polished hardwood floor. But Therese wasn't looking at any of those details, because all her attention was taken up by what was on the walls.

Along the length of the hall were photos, blown up to ten times their original size, printed on cardboard stock, and hung from picture hooks. Smiling young faces, twice as large as life, crowded the space, a full-color window into the past.

Therese had seen the photos before, several times in the last twenty years, but not for a while now. They had been taken by Oliver that night, with his new digital camera that he was showing off, printed by the police to use in the investigation, and leaked to the press for what was bound to have been a pathetic amount of money. From there, the photos had appeared in every news story, magazine article, and breathless unsolved-mystery program that had featured the case, with special attention on the ones that featured Jenna, young and lithe and blond, and always smiling for the camera.

They were all from before it happened, of course. Oliver had likely died in the explosion, and when the camera was recovered, it was too damaged to have had any chance of recording what had come after.

Therese moved slowly down the line of photos, the weight of the duffel bag on her shoulder forgotten as she took in the details she hadn't noticed before. There was Chloe, trying to balance a paper plate full of Skittles on her fingertip—one of Josh's more innocuous dares. And in the next picture, Josh, posing with his fingers in sideways *Vs*, wearing the knit cap and hoodie that he thought made him look like Eminem in *8 Mile*, but on him it just looked sweaty.

And Jenna, of course. Her photos had the positions on either side of the stairs, angled slightly toward the door so they couldn't be missed. Just the way she would have liked it. In the photo on the right, she was standing in front of one of the cabin's windows, holding up a carved wooden candlestick. The place had been decorated in a kind of rural-medieval-vaguely-European style. Jenna had been making fun of the decor, picking up items and coming up with outrageous backstories for them, like the candlestick had belonged to Anne Boleyn, and the hideous "tribal" shield on the wall behind her had been the original inspiration for Tarzan. (More likely from an interior decorator from Tarzana, Oliver had said.)

In the photo on the left, Jenna was leaning against the kitchen counter, apparently unaware of the camera while somehow managing to give it every one of her best angles. Somehow, that was the picture that had made its way into most of the media coverage—it had even briefly featured on the cover of a self-published book about the deaths before Oliver's family had challenged the rights. Chris appeared on the edge of the photo, almost as an afterthought (indeed, many of the publications had cropped him out entirely), looking at her like a golden retriever who had been given an entire steak, and wasn't sure he was allowed to have it.

There was only one picture that had been taken after Therese had left the party, with Chris caught midspeech, looking like he was talking about something serious. Therese had spent a lot of time looking at that picture and wondering what he had been saying.

Not that there was any way for her to ever know. Based on the time stamps, that photo had been taken about three minutes before an improvised bomb made from a pressure cooker had gone off in the crawl space under the cabin, and approximately fifteen minutes before someone had come through with a knife and stabbed the survivors of the explosion to death.

2

Therese turned away sharply from the photos and nearly ran into the man who had been standing behind her.

"Quite the art display, isn't it?"

He was in his mid to late forties, dressed in a casually expensive outfit of chinos and a linen-blend sweater. His dark brown hair was worn long enough to brush his jawbone, and the tanned creases in his skin that spoke more of island vacations than manual labor.

Therese nodded.

"Not what I was expecting," she said. "I thought this was supposed to be a serious gathering."

"Me too. I'm afraid we may have been misled." The man smiled, and Therese was finally able to place his face.

"You're Adam Reynolds, right?" she said, feigning uncertainty. "Jenna's brother?"

"Half brother, but yes. And you." He made a show of studying her face. "You must be Amy? Our lone survivor?"

"I go by Therese now," she said. "My middle name."

Adam took the correction in stride.

"Of course. After everything, that makes sense. Gotta do something to escape the eye of Lord Google, right? Wish I could have changed my own name, now that I think of it. That would have saved a lot of trouble."

Therese didn't bother to ask what his troubles had been. She could imagine, and frankly, she wasn't that sympathetic. It might have been inconvenient to be related to a famous pretty, dead girl, but their shared father had been rich, rich enough that Jenna had talked disparagingly of how bored she was of the annual family ski vacation to Switzerland and occasionally mused whether her father was going to have to sponsor a building for her to go to USC, or if endowing a chair would be enough. That kind of money could buy a lot of not caring about what people said.

In Adam's case, it looked like it had bought a very fine wardrobe and enough peace of mind that he could seem comfortable at an anniversary gathering for his sister's brutal murder even with her photograph looming over them.

"I guess we've all changed a lot since back then. What have you been doing with yourself?" he went on, smiling like they were classmates reconnecting at a reunion.

"Oh, not much," said Therese. "Got a government job, getting by. You know how it is."

He probably didn't, all things considered. Therese used the "government job" line occasionally, when she didn't want to deal with the reactions being an FBI agent got her. She liked it because it had the advantages of both being true and sounding boring enough that people rarely wanted to know more. Still, before Adam could ask any follow-up questions, she shifted her bag on her shoulder and looked toward the stairs.

"Do you know what the situation with the rooms is? I'd like to get settled in before I meet everyone else."

"Oh, sure. It was first come, first served, but I'm afraid you're the last one here, so I'm not sure what's left. Probably one of the two bedrooms at the end of the hall—the view is great, but they share a bathroom."

Therese grimaced and silently cursed the traffic that had held her up. She hoped her neighbor wasn't the type to take long showers.

As if he was reading her mind, Adam added, "By the way, we're on a well here, and it's been running pretty low this year, so if you could try to keep your water consumption down, it would be a big help."

"We?" Therese asked. Up until now she had been under the impression that he was a guest too.

"Yes, well, as a matter of fact, the house is mine." Therese didn't even bother to hide her confusion, and Adam hurried to explain. "Not the pictures, obviously. God, of course not. But the house, it's been in our family for decades. I had it fixed up a couple of years ago, and since I haven't been using it, it's let out as a vacation rental."

"So did Ms. Scott contact you about holding this event here? What did she tell you about it?"

"Nothing. The rental was handled through my usual agency, and I had no idea about it until I got the invitation. I guess she must have liked the idea of something connected to our family? Anyway, I didn't mind being able to come somewhere I was familiar with. Though, I've got to say, this wasn't exactly what I had in mind."

"Me neither."

—

The house was aligned parallel to the cliff, with the front door and main staircase at one end. The stairs were wide enough for a team of horses to walk up, if you were having that kind of party, each tread cut from a single smooth board. Therese didn't think you could even get lumber like that anymore—probably because all those trees had been cut down to make fancy staircases.

She also didn't think whoever had designed them had imagined that people would be carrying their own luggage. She was in good shape and had packed light, but even so, she was breathing heavily when she made it to the second floor.

"Must be the altitude," she muttered, defending her honor to the empty hallway.

Here, the bare wood of the entrance and stairs gave way to plush carpet so thick that it curled around the edges of Therese's sandals and brushed the sides of her feet. Against the wall next to the staircase, there was a side table with a carved wooden box on it behind a sign that said, "necessities." She opened it to find it was full of phone-charging cables, mostly for out-of-date models.

The only light in the hallway came from wall sconces, set far apart, with low-wattage bulbs, giving it a dim, twilit quality. Marching down the hall in a not-quite-symmetrical arrangement were ten doors, five on each side. They had the same old and substantial look as the rest of the house, but Therese was relieved to see that they had all been fitted with gleaming modern dead bolts.

Only one of the doors stood open, all the way at the end of the hall, where Adam had suggested she would find her room. The only surprise was that it wasn't the one facing the uphill side of the mountain—Therese had assumed the rooms with the views would be the more desirable. It wasn't until she had put down her bag and opened the curtains that she was able to guess why it had been left.

From the outside it was clear that the building's foundation was firmly anchored in the mountainside, but that perspective wasn't available from the second floor. From here, the house appeared to be cantilevered out straight over the cliff, with nothing between the interior of the room and the dark trees below but a plate glass window that went to the floor. Therese wasn't afraid of heights, but even she found it unnerving.

She considered closing the curtains, but it was still light out, and Therese didn't like giving in to fear. So she left them open and let herself get used to the view while she took in the rest of the room.

The decor was about what she would have expected from the rest of the house—fancy lodge crossed with a high-end hotel. The bed was only a queen, with a standard comforter, but there was a

Pendleton blanket folded at the foot and, at the other end, enough decorative pillows to build a decent-sized fort. The other furniture in the room—a desk and chair, dresser, bedside tables, and a chest holding extra blankets and pillows—were all blond oak, solid and well-built. The effect was decidedly old-fashioned, but the abundance of outlets showed a care for modern needs.

Speaking of needs, a second door led into the bathroom, which was unimpressive but entirely adequate. The door to the adjoining room was locked, which meant Therese would have to wait to learn anything about her neighbor, but at least they had a certain amount of sense in common. It wasn't much, but in her current situation, she would take any source of connection she could get.

As she washed her hands, Therese caught a look at herself in the mirror and was briefly distracted by her reflection. It should have been no surprise how tired she looked—she had been up early to catch her flight, and her height made sleeping on the plane a challenge. Combine that with the long drive up the mountains, and it was no wonder her eyes looked like two burned holes in a blanket, or that her long brown hair was more limp than wavy. She did the best she could with the comb she had packed and tried not to wish she had brought a better supply of makeup.

It was funny, she thought, how little it took to bring the old insecurities flooding back. In her normal life Therese had no problems with her confidence—she knew she wasn't exactly stopping traffic, but she could get attention when she wanted it. (Which, admittedly, wasn't very often.) But she arrived at this place and suddenly she was too tall, her shoulders were too wide, that layer of fat on her stomach was a huge bulge, and her clothes were obviously cheap and unstylish. None of it was true, and it wouldn't matter if it was, but it seemed like only took remembering the past for her brain to start following its familiar old tracks.

It was foolish even under normal circumstances, and particularly ridiculous now. She was here to confront the terror of her past, but not that part. Therese set down the hairbrush and turned away from the mirror, and as she headed back into the bedroom, she focused her thoughts on the one guest she had encountered so far.

She remembered meeting Jenna's half brother a few times at their father's house—a good-looking guy about a decade older than his sister who had mostly seemed annoyed by their teen-aged antics. In her memory he was someone impossibly adult and sophisticated, which was amusing in retrospect because he would have been in his late twenties and still living at home. Not surprising he would be here, she supposed; she had a vague memory that their father had died not long after Jenna did, and Jenna's mother, well, she wasn't the sort of person you would want to rely on for anything.

The part about the house belonging to their family was interesting, though. Therese wondered how much credibility she should give to the idea that Adam hadn't known what the event was about ahead of time. And she was surprised she hadn't heard of the house back in the day—it wasn't like Jenna not to have mentioned a valuable property. On the other hand, they were a long way from the more fashionable locations on Lake Tahoe, and as glamorous as Therese found the place, it probably didn't have much about it to interest an attention-loving teenager.

On a typical day, anyway. This weekend, Therese suspected it was going to see enough drama to satisfy the most discerning connoisseur of the genre.

3

Therese was on her way back down the stairs, wondering if she was ever going to see any of the other guests, when one of the doors in the entrance hallway opened and an older woman came out, drying her hands on the edge of her shirt.

"They never have decent towels in these places," she grumbled, then looked up and saw Therese.

"So. You're here," she said, with an emphasis on the *you*.

"I am here," Therese agreed mildly. "Therese Brewer. I'm sorry; I don't think we've met?"

"Changed your name, did you? Figures." And with that the woman turned and proceeded down the hallway, leaving Therese with little option but to follow her and the whiff of stale cigarette smoke she left in her wake.

Past the stairs on the uphill side of the house, there was a small breakfast room, then some sort of lounge, and what looked like a library. On the other side of the building, Therese and her silent guide passed double doors to a formal sitting room that was heavily outfitted with taxidermied animals. The one thing the rooms all had in common was that they were all empty—for all the evidence she had seen of her fellow guests, so far the people themselves were mostly proving elusive.

Except for one. While she registered the layout, Therese searched her memory for the other woman's face. Not one of her friends' parents, but she did look familiar. Maybe somebody's aunt? A teacher? She was probably in her sixties now, which would have put her in her forties then. Twenty years was a long time, and people did change, but this woman didn't look much like someone who had. She was short and slightly overweight, with black hair streaked with gray, and was dressed in a black pantsuit. It seemed oddly formal for the setting, but Therese supposed she couldn't claim to know what was appropriate. Maybe everyone else would be dressed like they were going to a coworker's funeral, and her jeans and cotton button-down would look out of place.

She didn't have to wait long to find out. Halfway down the hall, her guide made an abrupt right turn through a pair of double doors into a large dining room, with an enormous table and crystal glittering behind the bar, and more stuffed dead animals decorating every available niche. The woman made a sharp right at the grizzly bear and passed through another set of doors and into a more brightly lit room beyond. Hearing voices, Therese paused and held back, not wanting anyone's first impression to be her trailing behind like a lost dog.

She hesitated next to a rattlesnake frozen midstrike and

registered the boarded-up windows that suggested this room had once had an exterior wall. So far she had avoided confronting the purpose of this trip, and her own reasons for making it. But she couldn't put it off forever; after all, she was here. So, giving the dead serpent a sympathetic nod, she headed toward the sound of the voices.

Unlike the rest of the house, the huge open-plan lounge she entered looked like it had been built in the last couple of decades. The pale hardwood floors were clearly manufactured, and one entire wall was lined with windows, with French doors that opened onto the deck she had seen from the driveway. To her left there was a kitchen—all granite countertops and stainless-steel appliances around the expected island—and two more doors, one to the outside and another back into the main body of the house.

Therese realized she was calculating her methods of egress and checked herself. This wasn't that kind of trip.

The room was full but not crowded. Three women and six men were scattered around on the pale leather furniture in an array of defensive postures, legs crossed and hands folded. Aside from the two people she had met so far, she didn't recognize any of them.

The gathering generally resembled a party, with the guests arranged in conversational poses, some holding wineglasses or beer, some with water, but no one looked like they were having any fun. As Therese entered they all fell silent and turned to look at her, and she felt like the entire room had experienced a sharp intake of breath. Therese stood in the doorway for a long painful minute, wondering what kind of madness could possibly have caused her to agree to this, and fighting a powerful urge to turn and run.

But she couldn't do that. Not this time.

It was Adam Reynolds who broke the spell.

"Ah, there she is," he said, rising from his spot on the sofa. "Did you find your room okay?"

"Yes, no problem." Therese came down the short set of steps into the room. "It's got quite a view."

As she spoke, she searched the faces of the women in the room, her curiosity deepening. True, it was often the case that people's public photographs didn't represent exactly what they looked like, but none of the ones she had seen of Angela Scott, the journalist who had sent the invitation, had resembled the woman she had followed into the room, or someone well into her seventies with wild gray hair, or an Asian woman.

"I'm sorry if I've held things up by being late," Therese said carefully. "Is our host around?"

From the looks exchanged by the other people, it was clear she wasn't the first to bring up the subject.

"She seems to have been called away," said one of the men, a pudgy guy about Therese's age with curly dark hair and an ill-conceived goatee. "We were just talking about it. She left a note, though, and a nice-looking spread for dinner."

He gestured toward the kitchen, where the scent of Mexican food wafted from foil catering trays laid out on the counters. It had been a long time since lunch, and Therese's stomach responded with a rumble, but food was the furthest thing from her mind.

"She's not here?" she said, trying to keep the alarm out of her voice. Of all the ways she had thought this weekend could go badly, that wasn't one that had occurred to her.

The other guests had clearly had more time to consider the possibilities.

"I still think it's a trick," said a Black man who looked to also be in his thirties. "This reporter gets us all to come here, then just happens to be called away, leaving us to talk among ourselves. What do you want to bet she's got this whole place wired with cameras and microphones, catching everything we have to say? We could be starring in a reality show right now, for all we know."

"California is a two-party consent state," Therese said automatically. "She wouldn't be able to use anything she got that way."

As soon as the words were out of her mouth, she regretted them—what kind of person knows that off the top of her head? But fortunately, no one seemed to care; they were too interested in making arguments of their own.

"Like that ever stopped someone in the media," the shorter of the two older men said darkly. He was sitting a bit apart from the rest of the group, clutching a beer that looked like it might not be his first. Despite the fact that his dark hair was more gray than not, he was dressed in a T-shirt with a pair of luridly drawn cartoon women and a pair of baggy gym shorts that fell below his knees. "They just do whatever they want and pretend they didn't know."

Adam set down his empty wineglass, looking bored and mildly amused. "Well, it doesn't matter what she knows or not; I can tell you that's not what's happening here. There's no way there are any hidden cameras or microphones in this room, or any of the others. And even if there were, there'd be no possible way for them to be broadcasting anywhere. I don't know how much of the standard rental information she forwarded to you all, but there's no internet connection here."

"No internet?" said Therese, aware that she sounded like someone who had just learned she was expected to go a week without running water.

"I'm afraid not," said Adam, who had clearly had this conversation before. "Getting the lines run all the way out here was going to be obscenely expensive, and satellite is all that and unreliable as well, so considering that we get fairly good cell phone reception these days, it didn't seem to be worth the investment. None of which really matters right now, except to say that I am confident that our conversations are not currently being broadcast to living rooms across America."

"Why would we be saying anything, anyway?" goatee guy argued. "I don't even know any of you people. For all I know, none of you is who you say you are, and you're all actors."

"What, to trick you?" said the other older man, a white guy who Therese thought might look familiar. "You really think you're that important?"

That sounded like it had the potential to be the start of a fight, or an opportunity for Therese to get some of her own questions answered. She went for option two.

"Speaking of not knowing anyone, other than Adam here, I

haven't been introduced to any of you yet. My name is Therese Brewer—back in high school I went by Amy." She turned to the woman she had followed into the room, who had so pointedly refused to introduce herself earlier. "And you?"

The woman pressed her lips together in a thin line, and for a moment Therese thought she was going to uphold her commitment to the silent treatment. But then her face relaxed, and she very nearly smiled.

"Sonia Fletcher. I suppose it's been awhile; you don't remember me."

That was true, and it wasn't. Therese hadn't recognized her, and even now struggled to remember her face, but she had no trouble placing the name. Sean Fletcher had been a classmate of hers since seventh grade, but she had never given him much thought, until he was caught after the murders with a box of bomb-making materials hidden under his bed. He confessed to the crime. That should have closed the case, but his apparent lack of knowledge about what had happened after the improvised shrapnel bomb went off under the cabin had left a lot of questions, and his death by suicide in his jail cell left them unanswered.

Not that the police had seemed very bothered by the possibilities. The rest of the world might have been convinced that Sean Fletcher had been a pawn of the "real killer," but the men in charge of investigating the case insisted there could be no one else, and with the death of the alleged murderer, the case was closed. Which went over with the public about as well as expected.

Throughout the ensuing media circus, Sean's mother could

always be counted on for a quote about how he hadn't acted alone or possibly done it at all, and when the conspiracy theorists settled on the girl who claimed to have left the cabin just before the deaths as their favorite suspect, Sonia had been happy to contribute her own insinuations.

Well, Therese hadn't come here because she was expecting a good time.

"My name's Wendy Zhao," the Asian woman said, unprompted. "I went to Saint Jerome's; I don't think we ever met. By the way, I think we're sharing a bathroom. I hope you don't take very long showers."

"I hope none of you do," Adam said before Therese could reply. "We're on a well here, and the water heater has seen better days. If everyone could remember their drought training and try for Navy showers, we'll all be a lot happier."

"Aye, aye, captain," goatee guy said, then turned to address Therese. "Victor Aguilar. We were in school together, but I doubt you remember me. But feel free to lie if you want to."

He was right, and Therese might have been polite about it, but the way he smirked at her drained her sympathy. In fact, that was the thing about him that was familiar.

"A friend of Josh's?" she said, and his sneer turned into smug delight.

"You do remember!"

"No. Lucky guess." Through everything, Josh had been her least favorite of all of them. Jenna might have been objectively the worst, but at least she had style. Josh had been nothing but a hanger-on, ready to join any form of cruelty as long as it marked him as one of the insiders.

On the other hand, he had died a horrible, violent death, and that made any complaint Therese had about his personality seem petty. But that didn't mean she had to like his friend.

Wendy watched the exchange with dry amusement. "I'll save your guessing and confirm that my family was friends with Chloe's," she said. "But you probably already assumed that one."

Therese was embarrassed to realize she had. Not that she thought of Chloe as only having other Asian friends—in fact, Therese couldn't remember any. Chloe had been Jenna's right-hand frenemy—not quite as rich and just as pretty. In their largely white suburb, her Chinese heritage had made Therese think of her as "exotic," and looking back she wondered if her race was the reason Chloe had found it necessary to accept second-tier status.

Therese thought she had long since evolved past that kind of thinking, but the fact that her brain had automatically made the association with Wendy embarrassed her; that it turned out to be correct was beside the point.

She muttered something about not having known many of Chloe's other friends and turned back to the group. She settled on the taller older man who she had thought looked familiar. Her memory must have been working in the background, because now his identity sprang immediately to her mind.

"And Detective Moll, of course. I'm sorry I didn't recognize you right away. Are you still with the force?" It was a silly question—the man had to be well past retirement age by now—but she couldn't think of anything else to say, and it seemed like a harmless enough question. For some reason, though, Moll looked uncomfortable, and someone else in the group snorted a derisive laugh.

"No, I retired a few years ago," he said shortly. "How's your father doing these days?"

"Very well, thanks. He's retired, too, and he and Mom just bought a camper van, so they can take their dog on trips. I'll be sure to tell him you said hi."

In fact, Moll and Therese's dad had hated each other's guts. She'd never known why, just that her dad had thought the detective was a brownnoser and a lousy investigator, and had been convinced that Moll had blocked a promotion he was after. Not that that had meant anything to the people who were convinced Therese was the real killer, being sheltered from prosecution because she was a cop's daughter.

There were still four people she hadn't met, but the rounds of introductions were starting to get awkward. Therese wasn't exactly upset when the small man in the gym shorts lumbered to his feet and glared at all of them.

"I've had enough of this. You all can keep playing kindergarten class if you want, but I'm going to get another beer and have some of this food before it gets cold."

No one else said anything, but they must have all been as hungry as Therese was, because one by one they got up to follow him. Therese fell into step with Adam.

"About this host of ours, did her note say when she was going to be back?"

Adam shook his head. "No, just that she might be gone for a while, and we should eat dinner and not wait for her. I can show you the note; it's around here somewhere."

"I don't like it," said Wendy, echoing Therese's thoughts. "This whole thing was shady enough from the beginning, and now she's not here? And none of us has even met her?" She looked at the can of seltzer in her hands and then set it down on the counter, seemingly making a decision. "I'm not staying. Whatever is going on here, it can happen without me."

Sonia Fletcher snorted. "You think you're going to find a hotel room in the Sierras on Memorial Day weekend? Maybe if you want to go all the way back to Sacramento, but good luck with that."

"She's got a point," said one of the men Therese hadn't met yet—a younger guy with sandy-brown hair and a round open face. He had already piled his plate with tamales and chips, and was negotiating an overloaded taco onto the edge of it as he spoke. "Anyway, I didn't come all this way to turn right around without seeing what was up."

His grammar was questionable, but his logic was sound, even if Therese suspected some of his unwillingness to leave was related to his desire to get at least his share of the food. She was hungry, too, but the truth was it was her curiosity that was keeping her there, far more than the inconvenience of finding another place to sleep or the fear of driving at night.

Curiosity, and the concern for what would be said about her if she ran away again.

4

Whatever their own reasons, the rest of the guests seemed to also have decided against leaving, and as they lined up at the counter to fill their plates, the conversation turned to what they knew about their host. Like Therese, none of them had spoken to Ms. Scott in person; all correspondence had gone to the same email address that had sent the original invitation, proposing an in-depth piece about the murders, centered on the twentieth anniversary of the events.

"And it really was her email," said Wendy, who hadn't quite lost her wariness. "I checked on the *Atlantic*'s website."

"I wouldn't have done it at all, except that I read the piece she did on that oil rig fire in the Gulf. Really impressive stuff. My husband has a couple of her books—he's been a fan for a long time. She just doesn't seem like someone who would do something shady." That was the Black man Therese hadn't met yet. She noticed that the mention of a husband drew a sneer from the short guy in the gym shorts.

"So," she said as she waited behind him for her turn with the guacamole. "Since I already have a reputation for profiling, should I go ahead and assume you're here for some connection to Oliver?"

He smiled and set his food down, offering his hand. "Not much of a guess, since three of the victims and the killer are all accounted for. Joseph Boden. Please don't call me Joe. And yes, Oliver and I dated for a while on and off back then."

Oliver hadn't been the only gay kid in their school, but he had been the best looking, with his porcelain skin and white-blond hair. (Naturally blond, as he liked to remind Jenna when her roots were showing.) His sexuality was no secret—Oliver had organized a mini Pride parade for Spirit Week, painted his nails (shocking at the time), and talked openly about his celebrity crushes. He had also implied there was more to his social life than they knew, and as she looked at Joseph, a fragment of conversation floated back up in her memory.

"Were you his friend in San Francisco? We were never sure you were real."

Joseph picked his plate back up, looking away as he laughed. "Well, the jury's still out on that one. But I did live in the city back then."

With that, he edged away from her, so Therese let him go and turned her attention to her dinner. There were still three people in the room she hadn't yet identified, but she had learned as much as she needed to know for now: that their host, wherever she was, had sought out one person connected to each of the victims, as well as a handful who had other connections to the case. She was wondering who would have been invited in her place if she had refused when she looked up from her enchilada and realized she had company.

"Hi." It was the sandy-haired young man she had noticed tackling the food earlier. He had already emptied his first plate and was on to a second course of tortilla chips topped with all three kinds of salsa available, plus some of the meat for the tacos.

"I didn't get a chance to introduce myself before," he said as he unselfconsciously scooped up a bite of his improvised nachos. "I won't even try to make you guess, because there's no way you'll remember me. I'm Gil Morley, Chris's cousin. We came to a couple of your games. Me and my family, I mean."

"Of course." Therese did remember him, but she wasn't sure how to say it. Her recollection was of a chubby, overly talkative preteen hanging onto Chris like a shadow. Now he towered over her, six-foot-four if he was an inch, looking like he didn't need to wait for anyone to tell him he couldn't come along. Therese wished she could have come up with a friendlier memory for him, but the best she could do was to settle for the obvious. "You've changed a lot."

The younger man grinned and took another bite.

"Yeah, around sophomore year I hit a real growth spurt. My mom had to get a Costco membership just to keep up with how much I was eating," he said through a mouthful of crumbs. "But you were gone by then." He said it as a statement of fact, not a question, but Therese felt the need to explain anyway.

"Yes, we moved to Florida. My aunt and uncle were living there. Are you still in the Bay Area?"

It was an innocuous question, but a cloud passed over Gil's face before he answered.

"No, Seattle," he said shortly. "Hey, remember that game where you scored three goals in five minutes? That was really something. My mom was afraid I was going to pass out, I was yelling so hard."

Therese smiled. She did remember it, the highlight of her soccer career. An unusually hot day in October, the sun in her eyes, but everything had just seemed to fall into place. Whenever she got the ball, a hole in the defense opened up; every kick landed perfectly, that last second of spin sending it past the goalie's fingertips. Her team had already been doing well that season, but that was the game that got people talking about the state championship. It was also the event that put her on Jenna's radar and got her invited to a late-season pool party, the first place she had met Chris.

"That was a great game. I didn't realize you were there." What she meant was she hadn't realized Chris might have been there too—even after all this time, the thought that he might have been present for her triumph gave her a warm feeling.

"My mom coached youth soccer, so we went to a lot of games," Gil explained. "And Aunt Rachel—that's Chris's mom—she and my mom are twins, so we all did things together. Chris used to always come, too, because he wanted to be a college coach, and he thought he should know all the sports."

That brought back a memory so clear it almost took Therese's breath away. "We used to talk about that. How he saw himself as being there to make other people better, and asking what I found in my coaches that worked for me and for my teammates. He was really serious about it."

It had been a surprise to her back then. Therese had had plenty of coaches, from youth sports and school teams, but she had never thought about what their motivations might have been. They were just there, like the teachers who blinked out of existence as soon as you left the classroom.

But Chris had made it seem like coaching was a thing a person could do to make a real difference in the world, and his square jaw, high cheekbones, and gray eyes with their shockingly long eyelashes had only made him sound that much more convincing. Therese had been aware of Chris since the first time he had sat down across from her in freshman chemistry, but she had never been able to get up the nerve to talk to him until they reached for the same can of soda in the poolside cooler.

It was generally accepted knowledge that Chris and Jenna were an item, if not officially dating, ever since Jenna's last boyfriend had graduated and moved to New York. Therese had been sure there was no way she could compete, but the way Chris had smiled at her that day had done a lot to inspire her fantasies. And when it became clear that belonging to Jenna's social circle had its costs, the thought of losing the access to his attention was part, if not all, of what kept Therese around.

Gil was a good-enough-looking guy in a wholesome, all-American way, but he didn't seem to have much of his cousin's charm. In fact, the resemblance was so slight that Therese assumed their mothers must be fraternal twins. But he was a link, and talking to him was the best time she had had in the whole weird day.

"I didn't realize Chris came from such an athletic family. Did you play any sports in high school?" she asked. Again, she had meant it to be the most innocuous of small talk, and again she ran into some unseen wall.

"No, well—no. None of our teams were very good by the time I was in high school. Not that it would have…anyway. What about you? Your new school must have been pretty glad to have you on their teams when you moved. Do you play anything now?"

Now it was Therese's turn to dodge a question.

"Actually, I didn't really keep up with sports. You know, senior year, new school and everything. These days I mostly just run, do some rock climbing."

"Oh, sure. Makes sense. I guess it's not a good idea to hold on to that old teenage glory anyway, is it?" His weak smile and quick acquiescence made Therese wonder if Gil had guessed the real reason she had abandoned the things she had loved best for her entire childhood. It had been all that had been keeping her going, those two months in her aunt and uncle's guest room while her parents had the house packed up and looked for a reasonable rental property in the hot sticky swamp that was their new home—as soon as she knew what school she was going to, she would sign up for any team that would have her. Varsity, JV, club, whatever; the only thing that mattered was that she would be able to show how she could contribute, and then she would have a place in their world.

But then she had been googling the different programs, and the names and pictures of the athletes were all over them, not just on the school websites but in local papers and blogs, and she had realized that using her middle name wasn't going to be enough. If she ever wanted to live again, Amy Therese Brewer was going to have to vanish.

But she wasn't going to explain all of that right now, and if Gil hadn't guessed it on his own, then there was no harm in leaving him wondering.

Speaking of wondering, she had some more immediate questions in mind.

"How did you end up coming here?" she asked. "Did Ms. Scott contact anyone else in your family?"

"No-o," Gil said slowly. "At least, I don't think so. Aunt Rachel doesn't get out much these days anyway, not since she and Uncle Henry split. Last I heard, he was living somewhere out in Montana. She could have gotten in touch with him; I don't know."

Therese didn't know either, but she would have liked to. She was becoming curious about how the people in attendance had been selected. Having never written a magazine article about a long-ago tragedy, she couldn't say for sure, but her sense was that she would want her subjects to be as intimately connected to the event or victims as possible. So while she wasn't surprised at her own inclusion, a long-ago friend or younger cousin of one of the victims didn't strike her as fitting the brief.

Still, whatever her thinking was in terms of her guest list, their absent host's taste in Mexican food certainly showed good culinary judgment. The tortillas were fresh, the salsas were spicy, and the carnitas had that mix of crisp edges and soft insides that Therese just couldn't seem to find in DC. If she had any complaint, it was the touch of bitterness in some of the sauces but, as Gil excused himself to seek out another beer, that didn't stop her from going back for seconds. The food must have come from one of the taquerias in the foothills, she thought. There was nothing but tourist traps this high in the mountains.

Therese wandered over to look out the windows. The sun was going down, and the west-facing orientation of the room offered a full view of the sunset over the mountains and pretty much nothing else.

"So, you want to know who we all are, huh? I bet you were going to ask me next."

In fact, Therese had not been planning to do anything of the sort. The small man in the gym shorts, who had just appeared beside her, was the least appealing person in the room by a wide margin, though the way he was leaning in and leering at her made it clear he didn't think so. Their height difference meant his eyeline was just about at her chest level, and he was making no secret of enjoying that. He was the sort of guy Therese had dealt with plenty of times, in both her personal and professional lives, and usually the only question was how high they were going to jump.

But she didn't think it would be a good idea to start the weekend like that, and she could deal with him later if she had to. So Therese forced the sort of smile the man probably saw a lot and never understood, and said, "I'm just trying to get a handle on what kind of angle our host is going for. We've got all the victims accounted for now, so how do you connect to the case?"

There was something about that phrasing he didn't like—or maybe it was just that Therese wasn't able to get all of the interrogator out of her tone—because he drew back and looked at her suspiciously.

"All business, huh? I thought you were supposed to be the nice girl. Where I come from, they at least ask you your name."

"We must come from different places," Therese said, stepping back slightly and angling her head down so she could make steady eye contact. The man puffed up in offense, and he started to say something when Wendy Zhao came over to take charge of the situation.

"His name is Mike Swift," she said. "He's the jail guard who delivered the care package to Sean. The one that had the rope in it."

"It wasn't a rope," he said sulkily. "And how did you know all that? I didn't tell you."

"Cord, whatever. It's still hard to imagine how you could have thought it was a licorice string." Possibly aware that the boy's mother was in the room with them, she quickly changed the subject. "As far as knowing who you are, what did you think? Someone I knew got murdered, and I wasn't going to follow every part of the case? I've got binders with pages for all of you guys. Except you," she said, turning to Joseph. "I didn't know about you, no offense."

"None taken," Joseph said, sounding amused. "If there was ever a situation where I don't mind being the invisible gay, it's this one."

Victor looked intrigued and a little flattered. "You had pages for us? All of us?" Josh's friend had been focused on constructing a perfect mini taco, but now he straightened up and brushed the crumbs out of his goatee.

Wendy gave him an appraising look. "Well, you got more like a paragraph. To be honest, I can't really figure out why you're here."

"Oh, yeah? So maybe you don't know as much as you think." He crossed his arms and affected a look that was probably supposed to be mysterious or menacing, but the effect was spoiled by him bumping his paper plate with his arm and needing to rescue it before his meal tumbled to the floor.

He was met by a loud, abrupt laugh from the corner of the room, where the older woman with the wild gray hair had settled in with a plate that looked to be filled entirely with the various salsas.

"You know things, do you? I bet you do, kiddo, I bet you do." She gave him a smile that included more amusement than teeth, and Victor, looking confused and embarrassed, turned away from Wendy and went back to his meal.

Everyone else stared at the smiling woman, an unspoken question hanging over the room, until Adam went ahead and spoke it.

"I'm sorry, but I think I missed what your role was in all this, Ms.—?"

It wasn't an obvious joke, but there was something about it that the old woman found hilarious, and she responded with an odd hiccup-y laugh for so long that Therese was worried she might have to perform CPR. But their fellow guest managed to pull herself together after a couple of minutes and, wiping the tears from her eyes, looked up at Jenna's half brother with a startling shrewdness.

"Me? Oh, I'm the crazy lady in the woods!"

———

Back in her room—dinner finished and excuses having been awkwardly made as the guests came up with reasons for why they would rather be alone with their cell phones than share the current company any longer—Therese reflected on the range of the people who had been invited for this peculiar event.

Some, like her and the police detective, made a certain amount of sense. Whatever the truth might be, it wasn't hard to see how the argument could be made that they might have information that could shed new light on the case. Even the prison guard and Mrs. Fletcher offered some opportunities, considering that her son was the only person known to have contact with the presumed real killer, and there was some chance that that person, if they existed, might have colluded with the guard on duty in some way to get the critical piece of rope into Sean's jail cell. And Adam, well, apparently he owned an appropriate venue, and the fact that he was almost as photogenic as his sister couldn't hurt magazine sales.

But Chloe's friend? Josh's neighbor, Chris's cousin, and Oliver's boyfriend? Therese didn't doubt that the deaths had loomed large in their respective lives, but she had a hard time imagining they would have anything to add after all this time.

She would have liked to know when they were contacted, if it was after all the more likely subjects had turned down the invitation, and what explanation they had been given that got them to come. But Therese had spent enough time asking questions— too much more of that, and people might start suspecting her own motives.

Then there was their final mystery woman, who had turned out to be no real mystery at all. There had, in fact, been a "crazy lady in the woods," a homeless addict who was living in the park at the time of the killings, who claimed to have seen someone (or two people or maybe more) approaching the cabin that night. She had been questioned extensively by the police and the media, but her story had changed every time she told it, and well, she was a homeless addict living in the park, so her testimony wasn't given much weight. Her name was Lorelei Hughes, and she currently lived in Fresno, where she worked at a produce market.

Therese set her phone down on the table by the bed and lay back into the pillows. The energy that had gotten her this far had all drained away, and she found she could barely keep her eyes open. For a while, Therese tried to fight it, to stay awake longer and think more about what she had gotten herself into and what she needed to do, or at least read a few chapters of the book club book that she had been determined to get through this weekend. But the book had been chosen by the horror-loving member of her club, and after ten minutes of trying to read about giant mosquitoes, she gave up and rolled over, tucking the blankets around herself. It had been a long day of traveling and uncertainty, and what she needed now was a good night's rest. Everything else could wait for the morning.

As she drifted toward sleep, though, a thought pushed its way to the front of her fogged brain. Ten guests, ten occupied rooms. Where was their host supposed to be staying?

THE BROTHER

The master suite was reassuringly familiar; comfortable in more ways than one. Stretched out in his grandfather's armchair, Adam thought about all the other parties he had been to in this house, and decided that, for weirdness at least, this one had to rank in the top two. He picked up the heavy crystal tumbler he had filled from the stash in the locked cabinet in the library and swirled it, watched the brown liquid slosh over the ice cubes, then downed it all in one gulp. He'd have to make sure no one saw him going in there, he thought. That Victor kid looked like the type who would drink a hundred dollars' worth of Scotch just to have something to throw up, and their prison guard friend would probably steal everything he could carry if he knew it was worth taking.

He might do that anyway, which was why there was a deposit and a credit card required for the rental. Adam hoped their host, wherever she was, had a decent credit limit.

Adam picked up the coaster he had been using and examined its surface. There was a burn mark down the middle, a straight line ending in a hole that went all the way through to the other side. He held it up to the light and smiled at the memory. Now that had been a party. Back when people really knew how to have fun. None of these sad little men and women standing around eating chips off paper plates and trying to figure out who was the most important. There had been the time when they had had to lock the doors to the deck to keep Ari's new girlfriend from trying to prove to all of them that she really could fly, or when they moved all the furniture out of the dining room to try and turn the floor into a skating rink. God, he missed those days.

Though, if he was being honest with himself, Adam wasn't sure even he knew how to have fun anymore. There had been a point in his life when mornings were something that happened to other people, and there was always plenty more where everything came from, and now look at him, yawning at nine thirty and worrying about how much he could bill for damages to Great-Aunt Dixie's hideous self-portrait. Was this what it meant to get old? Adam wasn't a fan.

But it was better than the alternative. And that was why he was here, wasn't it? He owed Jenna that much, at least; some remembrance of the life she never got to have. He wondered what she would think of this crowd. Not much, probably, though she might be interested to see how her friend Amy had turned out.

He wouldn't blame her, Adam thought as he reached for the bottle he had set on the floor. There was something to be interested in there.

THE MOTHER

S onia Fletcher pulled the drapes across the window, carefully over-
lapping the edges so the view couldn't seep through. She didn't
know what had possessed her to choose a room on this side of the
house; she was terribly afraid of heights.

But that didn't matter. She had been afraid of a lot of things in her
life, and none of them mattered now. Not when the worst had already
happened. Worse than the worst. Who could care about anything when
they had that in their memory?

She went back to the bed, sat on the edge that faced away from
the window, and wished she could have a cigarette. But of course
there was no smoking allowed inside, and she didn't want to get
started on the wrong foot. She would just have to find another way to
calm herself down.

The room was nicer than she had expected. Nicer than anywhere
she had stayed in a while, in fact. Since the divorce, money had been
tight, and anyway, nothing was fun. The trip to Las Vegas with her sister's

family had been a complete disaster; she didn't think they would take her with them again even if she wanted to go.

Which was fine. And so was this place, Sonia thought, as she pried off her nice shoes and slid her feet into the slippers that had been Sean's last Christmas present to her. She had avoided wearing them too much, not wanting to face the day when she couldn't wear them anymore and even that final connection to him was gone, but she reached for them at times like these, when she needed to feel like he was with her.

And he was, she was sure of it. They were doing this together. She nestled herself into the pillows and thought about how much he would like them. Sean had always loved soft things, especially when he was a baby. She picked up one of the pillows and squeezed it, remembering how he had banged his stuffed rabbit on the sides of his crib for hours, just for the fun of it.

She had thought that coming here might help in some way, maybe give her that "closure" that her sister was always talking about. But she could tell already it wouldn't; there was no such thing. It was actually worse, seeing all these people who had just gone on with their lives while her dear sweet boy was forgotten in the grave.

Forgotten, except for the people who had never known him but thought they did. She had seen them on their internet sites, drawing pictures that made him look like the Devil and talking about him in their made-up videos. The ones who hated him were bad enough, but the others… Sonia shuddered. It made her sick when she thought about some of the stories they wrote about him. Utter perversion—that sort of thing shouldn't even be legal.

That was what she was here to fix. She was the keeper of the truth, and the truth was what was going to be told. If it made some people unhappy, that wasn't her problem. She hadn't been happy in the last twenty years.

5

Therese rolled over and reached for her phone. It was morning—she wasn't sure what time, but from the way the light was pouring through the crack in the curtains, she guessed she must have overslept. That wasn't like her, particularly with the time zone change, and she was annoyed with herself.

And she was even more annoyed that she couldn't find her phone. At home it had a charger it sat in next to her bed, and she could lay her hands on it without opening her eyes. But here everything was in the wrong place, including the bedside table where she had left her phone before collapsing into sleep.

At least, that's what Therese thought she had done. Now, as she ran her hand back and forth on the table's surface, she cursed the carelessness that was going to make her get out of bed to find it.

Ten minutes later she was still cursing, and this time she meant it. Her phone wasn't on the table, and it hadn't fallen on the floor. It wasn't under the bed, or on the dresser, or in her suitcase or handbag. In short, it wasn't anywhere in the room, and what had started as an inconvenience had now become a problem and was approaching crisis status.

Both doors, to the hallway and the bathroom, were still locked, as she had left them when she went to bed. The lock on the bathroom door was simpler than the dead bolt to the hall, but neither looked like they had been picked or forced.

She was examining the bathroom door when the door from the other room opened and her neighbor, Wendy, looked in, blinking sleepily and looking worried.

"Oh, hi," she said. "Hey, you aren't going to believe this, but I can't find my phone. And my car keys are gone too."

———

They gathered back in the open-plan lounge, a shabby, sleepy, and unshowered group all eyeing each other with suspicion. Almost everyone from the previous night was there; only Sonia Fletcher was missing. Therese was about to suggest that someone should go to look for her when she was distracted by Gil Morley going to the refrigerator and helping himself to some of the leftover food.

"I'm not sure that's such a good idea," Therese said as Chris's cousin raised a forkful of carnitas toward his mouth. Everyone turned to stare at her, including Gil, his bite of pork frozen in front of his jaws.

Therese went on, "Did anyone else find that you slept unusually well last night? Because I don't know about the rest of you, but I'm typically a pretty light sleeper, and I was out like a light.

Enough so that someone was able to come into my room without waking me."

Gil lowered his fork and looked at it suspiciously. "You think we were poisoned?"

"I'd say drugged, but yes, that's my theory." Therese was aware that her attempts to keep her work habits out of her voice were starting to fail, but she had bigger things to worry about right now.

Joseph frowned. "I was unusually tired last night. I thought it was the altitude," he said. Therese had been surprised when he arrived downstairs in sweatpants and a Radiohead concert T-shirt, then annoyed at herself for her surprise. What had she expected, an all-ABBA wardrobe?

"So did I. I was so tired, I didn't even take my contacts out." Of all of them, Victor Aguilar looked like he was suffering the most, to the point that Therese wondered if he had tried some sleep aids of his own. His curly black hair was in a serious state of disorder, and there were spots of toothpaste crusted in his goatee.

"But who would do that?" asked Wendy. "And why?"

Therese didn't answer her immediately, and when she did, it was Adam she was looking at. Though his hair was clearly unwashed and unbrushed, Jenna's brother was wearing a fresh linen shirt and white chinos, looking more amused than concerned about their predicament. But maybe that was just his resting rich-guy face.

"I don't know, but I'd guess it would be someone who had keys to all the guest rooms. I think they'll have to tell us why," she said in his direction.

Adam looked up at her, surprised. "What, me? No, I'm just as confused as anybody. There are spare keys to all the rooms, but they're stored in a lockbox in the library, and the code is sent to the renter, you know, for emergencies."

Most of the guests took that in with various looks of concern, but Mike was nothing but angry.

"The renter? So that journalist bitch is hanging around here somewhere, stealing our stuff?" he asked and looked around like he expected someone to answer. The night's rest clearly hadn't done much to improve his demeanor—or his appearance, unless you could see the appeal in greasy strands of hair and extra wrinkles in yesterday's oversized outfit.

From the way he looked at the other man, it was clear Joseph didn't. "If she was even here at all. None of us have ever talked to her, and the only evidence we have she was even here is a note that was left before anyone else arrived," he said. "How do we know this whole thing wasn't a setup from the beginning?"

"Oh, well done. A gold star for the young man."

The group had been so intent on their conversation that no one had noticed the final member of the party had arrived. Unlike the rest of them, Sonia Fletcher had taken the time to get ready before making her appearance. Her hair was freshly washed and set, and her outfit— another pantsuit, this one in red with a floral-silk shirt—had the look of something she saved for special events. She was carrying a boxy black leather briefcase of a style Therese hadn't seen in years.

Sonia strode into the middle of the room, nodding at each of the guests in turn, with something like glee in her eyes. When she got to Therese she stopped, aware, perhaps, of the younger woman's own stare, hard and cold. For a moment her resolve faltered, but the moment passed.

"Well," she said, deliberately turning away from Therese. Then she tugged on her suit jacket and smiled, like she had been looking forward to this. "I suppose you're all wondering why I brought you here."

"You brought us?" Adam said. "What are you talking about? Where's Angela Scott?"

"I don't know where your journalist is. Probably at home eating breakfast. None of you realized that wasn't her you were corresponding with, did you?" Sonia was looking very pleased with herself, and Therese almost couldn't blame her. She had thought of herself as a professional skeptic, always on guard and hard to fool, and here she was, taken in by a suburban mom with a briefcase and a grudge.

Therese wasn't the only one struggling with this new information.

"You tricked us into coming here?" Joseph said. "How? Why?"

"The how doesn't matter right now, and the why should be clear to all of you." Everything Sonia said sounded stiff and stilted, like she had practiced it a few too many times in the mirror. She rotated slowly, holding the briefcase awkwardly against her chest, and took a deep breath before continuing. "I'm sure you all have a lot of questions. I will answer them all, but only—"

"Did you steal our phones?"

"Where are my keys?"

"What they hell is going on here?"

Wendy, Gil, and Adam all spoke at once, interrupting her well-rehearsed speech. Sonia looked annoyed, but she stayed silent until the hubbub died down.

"Are you all finished? As I said, your questions will be answered, after I have gotten what I came here for."

"You took our stuff? What kind of fuckin' nut are you anyway?" It had taken Mike a little longer than the rest of them to catch on, but once he did, he stuck to the essentials. "Give it back now, you crazy bitch. I don't care what you want."

Sonia turned to him slowly.

"No, I'd guess you don't. You don't care about anyone or anything other than filling your own pockets. Even if it means a boy dies and a murderer gets away."

Mike sprang up from his chair, his fists clenched.

"You can't—"

"I can do whatever I want! And you all had better listen to me, or you're never going to get your things back," Sonia shouted back at him, apparently unfazed by the implied threat. Therese didn't know if she was crazy or just confident, or both.

"Okay, so tell us," Therese said, coming from where she had been standing near the kitchen island to place herself between the two of them. "That's what you want, right? To tell us something? So go ahead. We're going to listen to you now."

She gave a pointed look to the rest of the group, with a particular focus on Mike. He looked like he was about to object again, but Adam started to move toward him, and Detective Moll, who had been standing in the kitchen, taking sips from a glass of tap water and squinting like he had a headache, came over and placed a hand on the former guard's shoulder.

"I don't like this any more than you do, but we're in a tight spot here, and I think things are going to go a bit smoother if we let the lady talk." He guided Mike back to his seat and looked at Sonia. "So, we're listening, for now."

"I'm sure you are, Detective. In fact, I think you're going to be very interested in what I have to say."

Confident that she had their attention now, Sonia returned to her spot in the middle of the room and resumed her speech.

"Last night"—she pointed at Joseph—"you called my son the killer. And the rest of you are thinking it. But he wasn't; he couldn't have been. None of you knew Sean the way I did. My boy was no murderer, and that is a fact."

"Except the part where he built a bomb and used it to kill people," Gil muttered, before catching Therese's eye and lapsing back into silence.

Sonia paid no attention to him.

"Sean was a caring, sensitive boy, something the likes of most of you would never understand. But someone did understand him, and that person used their understanding to trick him into contributing to a terrible thing, and then to kill him."

"Ma'am," said Moll. "Your son committed suicide in prison. There was an investigation; no one else was there when he died. He also confessed."

"Suicide!" She laughed in a way that sounded like it hurt. "Sure, it was suicide. With a rope that no one knew how it got there, except there was a box in his cell that nobody sent."

She turned back to Mike, who had suddenly grown even smaller as he shrank into his chair.

"You were on duty that day, weren't you? No one would have gotten into that cell without you seeing them, and anything in there you must have delivered. So how much was it? How much did they pay you to make sure my son would never speak to anyone again?"

Mike opened his mouth to respond, then snapped it shut.

"I've got rights," he muttered. "I don't have to talk to anybody without my lawyer."

"That's what they told you to say, isn't it? Well, your union isn't here to cover for you this time." She gestured theatrically to encompass the rest of the group. "None of you have anyone here to protect you."

That sounded ominous enough that Therese felt like it was time for her to step in. "Protect us from what? What do you expect us to do for you?"

Sonia gave her a look that was hard to interpret. For a moment Therese had an uncanny feeling that Sonia was seeing through her, that the other woman knew what she couldn't have known. But Sonia looked away again and went on.

"I just want answers to some questions about what happened that night, and before and after."

Joseph moved slowly toward her, holding his hands out, palms up, and spoke in a calming tone of voice. "Of course you do. We all do. But trapping us here isn't going to help you solve anything. Twenty years is a long time, and there's no reason anyone is going to know more now than they did then. And why us? Most of us had nothing to do with what happened."

His eyes might have flickered in Therese's direction at that, but she was so relieved to have someone be a calming voice that she didn't even mind that much.

Unfortunately, none of it had any effect on Sonia.

"I have reason to believe that all of you have something to contribute to the question, and maybe one of you even has the answer." Sonia looked around again. "And as for why now, well, perhaps I can convince you."

She was still clutching the briefcase, holding it close to her body like she expected someone to try and snatch it away. Which wasn't a bad bet, considering how many of the people in the room must have thought their phones and car keys might be in it.

Therese wasn't one of them. Whatever Sonia was up to, it had been far too thoroughly planned to end in anything as simple as that.

She was right, unfortunately.

Sonia set down the case on a table in the middle of the room and opened it with a flourish. Despite their generally expressed disdain, the rest of the group automatically drew closer, craning to see the contents. But all that was visible was a pile of black cloth, and for a moment Therese wondered if Sonia had gotten her bags mixed up and was accidentally showing them her laundry. But she wasn't done, and when she was sure she had their attention, she pulled back the top layer of fabric.

"I suppose you know what this is?" she asked, in a tone so dramatic that Therese might have laughed, if she didn't suspect that she did, in fact, know.

"It's a knife," Gil said. "A big one."

The description, though accurate, was an understatement. The weapon was laid diagonally across the briefcase—the only way it would fit. The blade alone must have been a foot in length and the handle was long enough to be gripped with two hands. It had the look of something that had been buried for a while and half-heartedly cleaned, but the stainless-steel blade said it was no ancient relic.

Therese hadn't seen it before, but she suspected that, if things had gone differently that night twenty years ago, she might have.

"I think she would like us to think it's *the* knife," she said carefully. "Which, if it is, she should be giving it to law enforcement." She glanced at Moll and amended, "Current law enforcement. Not making it part of whatever kind of personal stage show she thinks she's putting on here."

"Thank you for the legal advice, Agent Brewer; I'll keep it in mind." Holding the case with the knife awkwardly in front of her, Sonia only seemed to have grown more confident. She was smiling now, apparently oblivious to the near-universal expressions of skepticism and distaste around her. "In the meantime, I think you can all understand now why you need to answer my questions."

"Like hell we do."

6

Gil stepped away from the knife and addressed the rest of the group.

"That knife might mean something to someone here, but it doesn't scare me. And the only thing I'm interested in right now is where my phone and keys are." He looked around the room. "It's not like she could have taken them anywhere. They've got to be in this house, and if we search we can probably find them in under an hour."

"And if you can't?" The suggestion seemed to amuse Sonia.

Gil didn't answer, having already left, so Joseph was the one to respond. "I don't know about anyone else, but if we can't find them, I plan to start walking. But I'll tell you one thing: there's no way I'm spending another night here."

On his way out the door, Joseph paused to look back at the other guests.

"I'm going to start with the public areas. If anybody wants

to help, we can work on getting into her room." He looked back at Sonia and tried his calmer voice one more time. "Unless you would be willing to give us the key?"

He plainly didn't expect her to agree, but to everyone's surprise Sonia merely smiled.

"No need," she said. "It's unlocked. Feel free to search away, and when you're done, you can come back here and we'll talk."

"When we're done, I'm going to be leaving," Joseph corrected her. "One way or another."

Sonia might have had another retort lined up for that one, but before she had a chance to say anything, Joseph turned and left the room too. Most of the rest of the party followed him, some talking about how they planned to split up the search, some glancing back nervously to see what Sonia would do. Soon only Therese and Adam were left.

"I wish you would reconsider this—whatever this is," Therese said to Sonia. "However you thought it was going to go, you've got to see it's not going to work."

"Do you think so?" Sonia said. "Well, maybe you're right. But maybe not."

She was still maintaining her look of enigmatic self-satisfaction, but for a moment Therese thought she saw the facade beginning to crack. She tried to think of something else to say, some sort of encouragement that might bring the other woman around, but there was a crashing sound from upstairs and the moment was lost.

"Come on," said Adam, touching Therese gently on the arm.

"She's obviously made up her mind. The others have the right idea—let's find our keys and phones, and the police can deal with her."

Reluctantly, Therese followed him from the room, pausing on her way to take one more look at the knife.

———

The noise turned out to have been the headboard from Sonia's bed falling over. By the time Therese and Adam got to her room, it was on its way to being thoroughly searched. Every drawer was emptied, the bedclothes stripped, and Sonia's suitcase and clothes were spread out across the floor. Mike and Gil had the one chair in the room turned over and were probing the bottom of the upholstery, while Joseph, Lorelei, and Wendy went over the mattress, looking for any sign of an opening.

"Any luck?" Therese asked—pointlessly, given the scene.

"Nothing so far," said Gil. "By the way, you were right about her having drugged us." He pointed to three pill bottles lined up on the empty dresser. "It looks like she was stockpiling her prescriptions for months. She must have planned this a while ago. But I guess she wasn't bluffing when she said we wouldn't find our stuff in here."

Wendy stood up from where she had been prodding a lump in the mattress. "Or maybe that's what she wants us to think," she said, before turning to Adam. "Are there any secret doors or passages in this house? You would know, right?"

Adam shook his head. "I would, and there aren't. Just a lot of regular nonsecret rooms. Which I'd like to suggest we try searching before anyone starts pulling up the floors."

"He's got a point," Mike said. "Art, that is, Detective Moll, already went to look outside, to see if she might have buried them somewhere. Maybe that's the right kind of idea. If we all spread out, we can search the whole place."

Joseph threw up his hands in exasperation. "That's what I said in the first place. And then all of you guys followed me in here."

Mike sneered at him. "Yeah, well now we're going to do it the other way. You want a trophy or something?"

"Let's take it easy," Adam said. "We all want the same thing. Whoever came up with it first, I think splitting up to search is what we should do. I'm going to look in the shed where we keep the snow gear; maybe someone else can check around the cars. She can't have left herself without a way to get out if she needs to."

That met with general agreement, but Therese wasn't so sure. There had been something about Sonia's attitude that suggested she was all in on this plan of hers, whatever it was. Which led to some uncomfortable thoughts about where their possessions might be, and made Therese wonder if Joseph's idea to start walking wasn't such a bad idea after all.

Wasn't a bad idea for someone else, anyway. Therese had done enough walking away for one lifetime.

Instead, she joined the search, choosing to focus her efforts on the taxidermied animals in the formal living and dining rooms. It was an unpleasant task, running her fingers through the dusty fur and feathers, and over the plastic tongues, but the way she figured it, that made them better hiding places. But the only things Therese found were some old paper napkins and a long-forgotten bag of marijuana, probably left there by vacationing teenagers who hadn't gotten the chance to go back for their stash.

Josh had claimed he was going to get some pot and bring it that night. It was funny—Therese had forgotten that detail until just that moment. He hadn't, of course. Josh's SOP was to claim he could do just about anything that he thought would get him attention, positive or not, but there was always some sort of complication outside of his control that prevented him from following through. It was a bit of a mystery how he had landed a coveted spot with that crowd—he wasn't rich or particularly good-looking, or amusing in anything but the most basic way. But every court needs a fool, and Josh had had an instinct for cruelty that Therese suspected had been appealing to Jenna. Not to mention, he knew full well how tenuous his position was, and his willingness to take any sort of abuse from the rest of them reflected that.

Including from you, Therese reminded herself as she ran her hands around the base under a bighorn sheep. It was hard to get too judgmental about something she herself had been part of, and harder still when she was the only one left alive.

That brought her back to the knife. The explosion hadn't killed them all, not right away. Chloe had even been able to call 911 from her cell phone before—

Before the knife. Or "bladed weapon of unknown origin," as the police report called it. That was what had finished off the injured survivors, their throats methodically slashed as they lay in the rubble of the cabin. It was a big part of why the story had been so sensational and widely reported on, and why it had been so important to find the bus driver who could testify that Therese's clothes had been clean and unbloodied when she had picked her up.

And now it seemed Sean had had the weapon the whole time. It was odd that his mother should think this might somehow prove his innocence, when it seemed to Therese it did the opposite. Sean had always been the obvious choice for the killer, what with him having built the bomb and his car being seen in the area. And, of course, the confession. It was only the fact that when he gave his account of what happened that night, he got several crucial details wrong that raised the question whether he had truly acted alone. And, of course, the circumstances of his death by suicide had done a lot to inspire the conspiracy theorists of the world to new heights of creativity.

But what if that had been the plan all along? If Sean Fletcher's main goal had been to become famous in death, he couldn't have done a much better job. After all, school shooters were a dime a dozen these days, but make some intentional mistakes in describing how you stabbed your classmates to death after blowing them up, and a person could get at least three *Dateline* specials out of it.

As theories went, it wasn't great, but Therese had heard worse.

For example, she didn't know yet what Sonia had in mind, but she was willing to bet it would make less sense than anything Therese had come up with. She couldn't see Sonia from the dining room where she was, but a whiff of cigarette smoke suggested she hadn't gone far. Therese wondered if she should go and try to reason with the woman—maybe away from the antagonism of the rest of the group, she could make her see how badly this was likely to go. She had the impression that the older woman thought once she separated them from their keys and phones, they would be in her power, and that everyone else was as obsessed with the crime as she was. But that clearly wasn't the case, and what worried Therese was how much else Sonia might have gotten wrong.

That was when she heard the scream.

It went on for too long and stopped too suddenly, and before Therese even started running toward the source of the sound, she was already sure of the worst. She arrived in the lounge a few seconds ahead of Gil, who followed her in through the dining room. No one else was there, though hurried footsteps were approaching from the rest of the house.

"Did you hear that?" Gil asked. "What was it?"

"I don't know," said Therese. "But I think we should check the balcony."

The sliding doors near the kitchen were standing open, but the outdoor area was empty. The only sign that anyone had been there was a lingering smell of cigarette smoke and a cheap plastic lighter lying on the ground. Therese approached it carefully and looked over the edge. As she leaned, she was acutely aware of how low the railing was, some building code work-around, probably in order to preserve the view. But it wasn't out she was looking; it was down, and she saw what she had known she was going to see: a crumpled body in a red pantsuit and a bright floral blouse.

"What happened? Who was screaming?" Joseph was the

next person to arrive on the scene, followed closely by Wendy and Victor.

"It was Sonia. She fell." Therese's words were short and clipped, her mind everywhere else.

The others crowded around her at the railing, and for a moment Therese had a vision of them all going over en masse. But she didn't step back, not until she was sure of the other thing she thought she had just seen.

"How did it happen?"

"Did she jump?"

"I knew that bitch was crazy."

The last comment was the signal that Mike had arrived, standing next to Adam with his arms crossed.

"What the hell was she even thinking?" he asked.

"We might be able to find out," said Therese. "She just moved. I'm going down there."

7

Y"ou can't do that. She must be fifty feet down," Adam said.

"Twenty, and I have to try. If she's still alive, I need to help her."

Therese was already gauging the slope of the mountainside below them. From the deck it looked almost vertical, but from the way the shrubs were growing, she judged it to be steep but manageable. It wouldn't be the easiest climb she had done, and she didn't relish the thought of doing it freehand with a badly injured woman to bring back up, but there was no choice. She expected the others to argue, but instead help came from an unexpected source.

"Do you want climbing gear? Because I saw some in a closet," Gil said. "It looked like it was in pretty good shape." Therese looked at him appraisingly. Chris's cousin looked hopeful, but nervous, and while nothing about him suggested a natural climber, his height and apparent strength wouldn't be unwelcome. "Yes, that would definitely help. A second person would be useful too. Have you done any climbing?"

Gil laughed nervously. "I, um, I went to a birthday party at one of those gyms, and I thought I was going to get into it, so I bought a bunch of the stuff. But I didn't. Get into it, I mean."

"Well, this seems like a good time to start." Therese headed back into the house. "Show me where you found the gear, and we'll see what we can do."

"Hey, wait a minute." Apparently, Mike had recovered from the shock of seeing the fallen woman and refocused on the real problem, which was that he wasn't the center of attention. "What's with you giving orders all of a sudden, lady? Who died and made you the queen of this place?"

"Nobody's died yet, and I'm hoping to keep it that way," Therese said, barely breaking her stride as she followed Gil through the lounge. But as they reached the door, she changed her mind. There was no point in not bringing it up now. "And I don't know what royalty has to do with it, but the U.S. government has made me an FBI agent, and that makes me in charge in a place where a crime has been committed."

"Crime? Why do you think there's been a crime?" Wendy asked.

"Because," Therese said, "the knife is missing."

———

Therese could hear a hubbub of conversation rising behind them as she and Gil left the room, and she filed it in her mind under "deal with it later." That Sonia had survived the fall was pure luck, and there was no telling how long she had. The only chance was for Therese to get to Sonia soon enough that she would be able to tell her where she left the phones, so they could call for a medical evacuation. Or at least tell her who else was on the balcony when she went over the edge.

Gil led Therese to a closet in the front hallway, where there was indeed a good collection of climbing gear. It looked pristine, as little used as Gil's probably was, and Therese wondered if in this case it was Adam who had failed to take up the hobby. (She also had questions about the advisability of stocking it in a rental property, but that wasn't her problem.)

"This looks all right to me," she said after checking the ropes, harnesses, and clips and handing half of them to Gil. "Come on, I think it will be faster if we go back and take the stairs."

When they got back to the lounge, it was clear that out on the balcony an argument was well underway. Therese was aware of a number of voices addressing her, but she blocked them all out, leading Gil across the room toward the door that led out from the kitchen. Outside of it was the staircase Therese had seen earlier, leading down from the far end of the balcony.

"Did you want to say anything to them?" Gil asked as Mike let loose a string of invectives at their retreating backs.

"One thing at a time. They'll keep; she won't."

"Right, sure. You know, you really are just the same."

That stopped Therese in her tracks.

"Excuse me?" She looked at the young man and was surprised to find him turning red.

"You know, back then. When you were on the soccer team. This is just exactly what you looked like when you were lining up to shoot a goal."

For a moment Therese was at a loss for words. Then she remembered where she was, and her hands tightened around the coils of rope.

"Yeah, well, most of them missed. Let's keep moving."

———

The stairs led from the kitchen down to a path that wrapped around the building. The way the house had been built into the hillside had left it with a small lower floor—not quite a basement but bigger than a crawl space, with a door in the middle. Therese made a mental note to check it later, if they needed to. More critically, she also registered a change in the weather. The previous day's bright sunshine was gone, replaced by a gray leaden sky and rising wind. Therese's pace sped up as she made her way down the path.

It wasn't hard to find where Sonia had gone over the edge—a manzanita shrub growing angled out of the mountainside had been almost totally uprooted at the spot. Therese looked down the slope to where Sonia's crumpled body had landed, caught in some sturdier undergrowth. It was further than she had estimated, probably more like thirty feet than twenty, but that didn't make much difference to Therese's thinking. Once you've decided to do something impossible, it doesn't really matter if it gets a bit harder. The thing that did matter was that Sonia moved again, lifting her arm slightly and inadvertently shifting her precarious position.

Impossible or not, she had to do it now.

"Okay," she said to Gil. "Let's do this. I'll set an anchor on one of the pillars here; they should be strong enough. While I'm down there, you stay up here and belay. Have you done that before?"

"I, um, I took a class, and the instructor showed us how. But he said we weren't supposed to do it on our own yet." Gil looked like he was seriously regretting having agreed to help Therese. And if she was being honest, she didn't feel great about it either.

"He was right, but we're doing this anyway. I'll get everything set up; all you need to do is maintain tension on the rope and pay attention to what I tell you."

"I understand," Gil said, and Therese hoped he did. She was breaking about eighty climbing rules here, but she didn't have a choice. *Sometimes,* she thought, *you do what you can and hope for the best.*

It took longer than she would have liked to deal with the unfamiliar gear, and Therese had to force herself not to rush the process. From the balcony above them, she could hear the voices of the other guests—arguing, encouraging, and offering useless suggestions—and the sound of footsteps coming down the stairs told her some of them weren't willing to remain passive observers. So she was relieved for more than one reason when the last carabiner clicked into place before anyone reached them.

"Are we ready?" Gil asked. He was trying to sound cool, but his voice couldn't quite manage it.

"As we'll ever be. Let's go."

The first couple of feet of the climb was fairly easy, just

maneuvering down a gentle slope and keeping the gear from getting caught. But then the terrain changed abruptly, going from a shrubby hillside to a sheer rocky cliff face for at least twenty feet before the angle softened again to where it could support the tree that was currently supporting Sonia.

Therese chose her hand- and footholds with care, calling out instructions to Gil above her. But his practice at the climbing gym must have served him well, or he had been downplaying his experience, because his response with the rope remained steady.

It took her about fifteen minutes to reach the point where Sonia was lying. Up close, her injuries were worse than Therese had feared. From the angle of her leg, it was clearly broken, probably snapped when it had caught in the tree that was holding her now. That would have been bad enough, but worse were the deep gash on her forehead and the blossoming patch of blood that was spoiling the pattern of Sonia's blouse. Under normal circumstances, Therese never would have moved a person in that state, but these circumstances were not normal.

By the sounds of voices above her, interrupting Gil and shouting their own commands, it was clear that the other guests had all come down to join them. That wasn't going to make anything easier—Therese only hoped she could manage to work fast enough to do what she needed to before one of them decided to help.

She eased herself down until she was close enough to reach the woman and began gently sliding the straps from the extra harness around her. As she worked, Sonia cried out. Willing her voice to be calm, Therese leaned in near to her face and spoke to her.

"Sonia, can you hear me? We're going to get you out of here, okay? But we need your help. You have to get to a hospital, and we can't do that without our phones. Where are they? Where are the phones?"

She had hoped Sonia's instinct for self-preservation would be strong enough to get her to answer, but it wasn't clear she had even heard her, much less understood the situation. Sonia's eyes stared blankly past Therese, unfocused and seeking a point in the distant sky.

"It was on the wall," she whispered, as bubbles of blood formed at the corners of her mouth. "The picture."

"The phones? Is that where the phones and keys are?" But Therese's questions went unheard and unanswered as Sonia's eyes glazed over and her body went limp. Therese fumbled for her wrist and found the pulse, but it was weak and fading. Even as she hurried to finish strapping the woman in and called for Gil to help her pull her up, she knew it was hopeless. It wouldn't matter if she had a phone in her hand right now; no medevac would be there in time.

By the time she made their way back up to the level ground, Sonia's body hung limp and heavy, a literal deadweight. Still, Therese laid her out on the path and attempted CPR, wincing every time her mouth touched the bloodied face. Eventually, it was clear she was doing no good, and she sat back on her heels.

"She's dead," she said to the others, who had all gathered on the path. "I think her internal injuries must have been pretty severe. She probably hit a couple of times before she got caught in that tree."

She was aware that she didn't have the full attention of her audience. Mike was starting to look a little green, and Victor was already retching into the bushes. Wendy was clutching Adam's arm, and even Art Moll, who should have seen enough of this sort of thing on the force, couldn't seem to quite bring himself to look at the body. Of all of them, only Lorelei was the only one who seemed to be feeling more sorrow than disgust, leaning over to gently close the dead woman's eyes.

"Poor thing," she said. "Sometimes you want something so much, you can't see how anyone else figures into it."

8

Lorelei's eulogy, such as it was, seemed to be enough to lift the spell of horror over Sonia's body, and Gil came forward and offered Therese a tissue to clean her face.

"You were able to talk to her for a minute there, right?" he asked. "What did she say? Did she tell you where the phones and keys are?"

Therese shook her head. "Just mumbling. I couldn't understand it."

"What are we going to do now?" Even Wendy appeared to have gotten over her squeamishness and looked directly at the body for the first time. "We can't just leave this out here."

Mike snorted. "Why not? It's not doing her any good. And once the coyotes get through with it, there won't even be that much to clean up."

"You're disgusting," Joseph said. "How do you even live with yourself?"

"Better than you do, sissy boy. Maybe you should try being with a woman instead of being one. Might make you some kind of man."

Gil glared at the former guard. "Like the kind who takes bribes to bring a kid rope to hang himself? Really manly history you've got there. You know, it sounded to me like Sonia might have known something about what you did. Did you come out here and make sure she couldn't tell anyone else?"

"She knew nothing, and neither do you." Possibly aware that was not the best way to protest his innocence, Mike abruptly changed the subject. "Anyway, I was all the way on the other side of the house. You were right here, weren't you? Maybe you're the one who didn't want the lady to keep talking."

"That's enough," Therese said. "We can leave those kinds of questions to the police when they get here. For now, we need to store the body in a secure place and get back to finding our phones and keys."

As she spoke, the wind whipped her hair across her face, and she looked up at the sky where clouds had been piling up as they talked.

"Walking out is still an option, but the way things are looking, I think it's going to have to be a last resort."

"So you're in charge now?" Victor asked. "How did that happen?"

"Do you have any other suggestions?" Therese said mildly. "I'm sure we'd all be happy to hear them. I just want to get us organized so that we have the best chance of getting out of here,

and leave the question of Ms. Fletcher's death to the relevant
authorities."

But Victor wasn't the only one who was having trouble with
her earlier revelation. Even Adam, who had been a figure of calm
up until now, was eyeing her suspiciously.

"And that's not you?" he said. "What's this whole deal with
you being an FBI agent? Did you know what was going to happen
here? Are you even really Amy Brewer?"

Therese smiled. "No, I didn't, and yes, I am. I think you're
giving the Bureau a little more credit here than they deserve. I
came for the same reasons the rest of you did—I thought there
was going to be a journalist writing a story about the deaths, and I
wanted to make sure I had a chance to speak for myself. As for my
career." Therese shrugged. "I grew up in a law enforcement family.
If you have any ideas about what else might have driven me to a
life of monitoring the communications of domestic terrorists, you
can take it up with my therapist. In the meantime"—she looked
down at the body at her feet—"if no one objects, I think we had
better search her."

———

Joseph volunteered to help, revealing that he was a medical doctor:
a psychiatrist, to be precise.

"I would have offered to help with the resuscitation, but you
looked like you had it under control," he said as he started at
Sonia's head and Therese worked her way up from the feet.

"How considerate of you," said Therese, but she wasn't actually mad. Of all the guests, Oliver's onetime boyfriend seemed to be one of the most clearheaded about their situation, and Therese had a feeling she was going to need all the allies she could get. And if that meant stepping in and helping when and if Joseph gave in and gave Mike the beating he so deeply deserved, well, she didn't think that would be too difficult for her.

Certainly, it would be easier than running her hands over a still-warm corpse, sliding her fingers into places they had no business being in a futile search for anything that would help them to escape this place.

No sign of anyone's car keys or phones was found on Sonia's body, not even her own. That was about what Therese had expected—Sonia would hardly have been so confident if she had made it that easy. Equally unsurprising was the lack of any sign of the missing knife. The one thing they did find was a ring of house keys, with the address of the rental agency helpfully printed on the tag. Only the key to the front door was labeled, but the ten identical smaller keys were almost certainly for the bedrooms. That would be a problem to be considered soon, but for the moment Therese had something else on her mind.

"These four extra keys, what are they for?" she asked Adam.

"Let me see." He took the ring from her and frowned at it. "This one is to the door by the kitchen, and this one is for the garage. Some people insist on having an indoor place to park, you know. And this is for the shed where we keep the snow shovels and stuff, so this last one must be to the basement."

"Which we haven't searched yet," Therese said. "And if

nothing else, at least it should make for a temporary storage spot for the body."

This time no one objected when Therese took the key ring back from Adam and turned to the small door in the wall behind them.

The door stuck a bit, like it didn't get used much, but even before she found the light switch, Therese was sure someone had been here recently. Boxes and pieces of broken furniture took up most of the space, and dust lay thick over almost everything, except the clear spaces on the floor where some of the larger boxes had been shoved aside to make a path. Therese followed it, and the rest of the guests trailed behind, chattering hopefully about finally having solved the mystery of Sonia's hiding place. The space was cool and musty, with a ceiling low enough that even Wendy had to duck under the beams.

"Why else would someone come down here?" Victor said. "She must have thought it was the perfect spot."

Therese wasn't so sure, but she saw no point in arguing. It was just a little too easy, and that was making her uncomfortable.

"At least it should be a decent place to put her body. It's cool enough, and no animals are going to get in here," said Art, who had been surprisingly quiet up until then. Of all of them, he was the one Therese had most expected to push back against her claim of authority. In her experience, cops, even retired ones, tended to think they belonged in charge of any emergency situation.

Unless he had some reason to want to avoid a conversation about his career? Now that she thought about it, Therese seemed to remember there had been something about Art's retirement from the police force that wasn't entirely aboveboard. It had been a few years ago, and her dad hadn't wanted to discuss it when it came up, but now she wished she had pressed for more details.

The path of shifted boxes led them more than halfway back through the basement to an area where one of the bare bulbs that lit the space had burned out. It was dim and shadowy, and Therese instinctively reached for her phone so she could use its flashlight, cursing quietly when she remembered. As it happened, they didn't need the additional light. The pressure cooker was plenty visible even in the gloom.

It sat on the concrete floor in a spot that had been cleared out among the boxes, free of dust and sealed around the lid with heavy tape. Even so, a person might think it was the sort of thing that would be stored in a basement, but that person wouldn't be someone who had almost been killed by one twenty years ago.

"That crazy bitch," Art said, sounding almost admiring. "I guess her kid didn't get it from anywhere strange."

"What is that? Is it something of Sonia's?" Victor must not have been as up on the details of the murders as the rest of them, or maybe he just wasn't much of a cook, because he moved in closer to examine the pot.

"It's a pressure cooker," Therese explained, her voice tense. "Like the one that was used for the bomb under the cabin."

"Oh? Oh!" Realization struck, and Victor jumped back. "What are you all standing around for? We need to get out of here!"

"It probably won't—" Therese started to say, but Victor was already well on his way to the door. And honestly, she didn't disagree with his reasoning.

"Maybe we should all—" she began again, but this was not to be her moment for finishing sentences.

"No! Not again! This ends now!" Gil surprised them all by darting forward and grabbing the cooker, tucking it under his arm like a football, and running for the door.

"Stop! Gil, no!" she shouted, but her voice was lost in the sound of the others saying versions of the same thing, except for Wendy, who had dived to hide behind some boxes. At the sound of Gil's approaching footsteps, Victor turned, screamed, and lunged for the open door, knocking into Lorelei, who had stayed outside. They landed in a pile on the doorstep, and Gil leaped over them. As soon as he gained a stable footing on the other side, he raised the pot over his head and threw it down the mountainside.

Therese might have said something then, but there wouldn't have been much of a point, and anyway, it would have been drowned out by the sound of the explosion.

"Jesus! Is everyone here just fucking crazy?"

For once, Therese had no argument with Mike's position.

"That was incredibly stupid," she said to Gil, once they had all gathered outside again and it was clear that the only injury was a bad splinter Wendy had picked up from the old cabinet she was hiding behind.

"What? Was I just supposed to leave it there to blow all of us up? What if it was on a timer? Maybe it was always going to go off right then, and I saved all of us. Risking my own life, even."

Gil looked so hurt Therese couldn't bring herself to explain the reasons why she found that unlikely. Besides, she had just spotted some bits of the shrapnel that had made it all the way back up onto the path, and the thing that had been a passing thought earlier solidified into a fully-fledged concern.

There were tiny shards of glass, twisted chunks of mostly black plastic, and many fragments of circuit boards, more than even a relatively sophisticated bomb would have needed, which she was willing to bet this was not.

Mike noticed her interest and came to look over her shoulder.

"Let me guess, you're also a bomb squad expert? Don't worry, everybody, we've got Girl Wonder here to take care of us!"

Therese ignored him, her attention drawn to a larger piece of thin metal that had been wedged into the ground just below the level of the path. She pried it up, being careful to avoid the sharp edges, and wiped off the dirt as the first fat raindrops hit her head.

"Ooh," said Mike, who had a real problem with knowing when to shut up. "Is that a clue? Are you going to solve the whole case now?"

"Not exactly," Therese said, turning over the piece so that everyone could see the stylized apple etched into its back. "But I think we found our phones."

9

It was a subdued and dejected group that filed back into the house as the first drops of rain started falling. There had been a few desultory returns of the suggestion that someone should try hiking out, but the temperature was dropping fast, and some of the rain hitting the windows was looking suspiciously like sleet. They had gathered back in the kitchen and lounge, where the view showed nothing but a solid wall of clouds.

"After all," said Victor, who had been in favor of the plan until someone said he would be a good candidate to go, "we're fine here. Plenty of food, water, electricity. Someone is bound to figure out something is wrong when they can't reach us, and they'll call the authorities."

Wendy glared at him from her spot on the sofa. "Yeah, and only one person has been thrown down the mountain so far." Ever since she had found a piece of her phone case stuck in the shingled siding of the house, Wendy had been taking a very negative view of their situation.

"Nobody pushed her; the bitch jumped." Mike had found some more beers in the refrigerator and had already drunk two, which hadn't done much to improve his outlook or personality.

Joseph, for one, was clearly fed up with him. "And I suppose she tossed the knife over first? Just to see how far it was?"

"Why not? Everything else she did was to screw with us. Bitch was crazy, remember?"

"I don't think so. And believe me, I'm an expert on crazy." Up until then, Lorelei had been so quiet that most of the group had forgotten she was there. Now they faced her, with various expressions of interest and distrust.

"With all due respect, do you really think all that could have been the actions of a sane woman?" Art said. "Her son's death obviously did a number on her, and now we're paying for it."

He had stayed outside longer than the rest of them, searching fruitlessly for some usable fragment of a car key while the rain came down, and his thin hair was still plastered in random lines across his scalp. He ran his hand over his head, trying to smooth them, but only managing to rearrange them into a different disorder.

"Who could know what was going on in her head?" he went on. "I don't care for the way he puts it, but Mike may be right."

Lorelei shook her head. "I didn't say she was sane, but there's crazy and there's *crazy*, you know? And the way it looked to me, she wasn't that kind. All the work she did to stick us all out here, she wasn't doing it to throw herself a surprise going-away party. I don't like thinking one of us is a killer any more than the rest of you, but facts are facts."

And there, she had said it. The thing all of them had been thinking but no one wanted to put out in the open. If Therese had been betting, she wouldn't have put her money on the former homeless drug addict as the person with the best grasp on their situation, but life was full of surprises, and Therese could find time to think about that later.

At least, she hoped she could.

At the moment, she was a lot more interested in who had been where when Sonia went over the edge, but before she could start asking questions, Adam changed the subject.

"Well, whatever the facts are, it looks like we're here for at least one more night. So how about we table this conversation for now and see what we have in the way of supplies? I don't know about anybody else, but I didn't have much for breakfast, and we're well past lunchtime. Once we all get something to eat, we might be thinking more clearly." Adam didn't specify what they would be thinking about, but it didn't really matter. Once again, he was playing peacemaker, something he did well. It might have been related to the house being his giving him a sort of surrogate-host role, but it probably had more to do with the fact that he was the kind of rich good-looking white guy people were used to taking orders from.

"Now that you mention it, I am pretty hungry." On the subject of things people did a lot, Gil gave the impression that was something he said on a regular basis. Every time he had been near the kitchen, Chris's cousin had instinctively turned toward the refrigerator, with the expression of a young man who hadn't had the ravages of an adult metabolism catch up with him yet. The rest of them just seemed relieved to have something to do that wasn't standing around arguing, and the party shortly broke up into sub-groups to tackle the question of food preparation.

Therese found herself in the pantry with Lorelei, going through what had been left there. Just off the new kitchen, this room must have served that function in the building's previous life. Back then, food preparation would have been a job for servants, and unlike the new one, this kitchen was no showpiece. The wooden counters were narrow and heavily scarred, the windows small, and the whole place was barely larger than the bathroom Therese was sharing upstairs.

Still, there was more than enough space to hold the sorts of things that got left behind at rental houses, and Therese was amused to note that the tastes of the people who could afford to stay in this one were no more glamorous than what she was used to.

"Do you suppose this is still any good?" Therese asked, peering into an almost-full package of instant grits.

Lorelei grinned, exposing a mouth that had slightly less than half its original teeth. "Anything's good if you're hungry enough. But I don't think we're going to get to that point, do you?"

"No, of course not." Therese put the box back on the shelf. "I'm not sure what we would do with that anyway. But Victor was right, even if we don't decide to make it out on foot, someone here must have somebody expecting to hear from them, who knows where they are."

"Someone? So you wouldn't say it's you? No disrespect intended, but I thought the Feds kept some kind of eye on their people."

"None taken. If I don't show up next week, they'll probably start asking questions, but I said I was going on vacation, and I didn't exactly advertise what it was for." Therese grimaced. "Not a lot of people know about…about me being part of all that. It's one of the reasons I wanted to keep my job out of the conversation when I got here."

In fact, it had been one of her main concerns about coming in the first place, when she had thought all she had to worry about this weekend was what was going to be written about her in that mythical magazine article. Her reasoning had been that any reasonably determined journalist was going to be able to find out where she had ended up, and if she was here, she might at least have a chance to try and convince her to leave out the details. In fact, she liked and respected her colleagues at the Bureau, and the ones who did know about her history had never held it against her. But she had spent so much time dodging recognition that it was almost second nature to her now. She hated to admit it, but part of Therese had actually been relieved when Sonia had announced her scheme. It wasn't great to be trapped in the mountains by a crazy person, she had thought, but at least she wouldn't have to read yet another story about herself.

There would be plenty of stories now, of course, whether or not Therese was around to read them.

Not that any of that was Lorelei's business. "So I don't want to count on me to get us found," she went on. "But certainly, if it goes on too long, they'll try and find me, and they have the resources to do it."

Even as she said it, Therese wasn't so sure. That is, she was sure the FBI would take a missing agent seriously enough, but she hadn't told anyone where she was going, and it would be some time before it was worth tracking her down through plane tickets and car rentals. Her friends and family were used to her dropping out of communication occasionally, and the less said about her dating life, the better. Her best hope, she thought, was that someone else in the house had left something more than a couple of houseplants behind at home to be worried about them.

"What about you?" she asked, hoping the question wouldn't be seen as insensitive. "Is there anyone who's expecting to hear from you?"

"Like a husband and five little kiddies waiting around the dining table? Nope, afraid not. Somehow that's not how things turned out for my life." Whatever else Lorelei might have been, she wasn't easily offended. "Funny enough, you might say it was all those deaths that saved me. You know, they tossed me in jail for a while, which was pretty bad, but with all the publicity, some nice folks in Fresno found me a spot in their rehab place, and I've lived in the area ever since. Been working part-time at the produce market, and I've got a room in a house with some other people from the program. It's not much, but I get by, you know?"

"Oh, well, that's good. I'm glad."

Based on appearances, Lorelei wouldn't have been Therese's first choice of the guests to have seen their situation improve in the last twenty years, but she supposed it was all relative. Along with the missing teeth, there were signs of Lorelei's former life in her gnarled fingers and scarred arms, and in the deep wrinkles that spoke to a lot of time spent in the sun. She was short and thin, swimming in her outfit of well-worn twill pants and sweater that was twenty years out of style. But she seemed to have taken their situation more in stride than anyone else, and now as she sorted through the cans, she was humming the *Green Acres* theme song.

It had never occurred to Therese to wonder about what had happened to Lorelei, the only person besides her who might be considered a witness to the events that night. The police had found her—they described her at the time as a "vagrant/addict"—living in a makeshift tent about a quarter mile from the site of the ruined cabin, and arrested her on general principle. Initially, they had even put out word to the media that she was the one who had committed the crime, and when it became overwhelmingly obvious she couldn't have done it on her own, downgraded her to a "potential accomplice."

At the moment, the older woman appeared to be considering the possibilities contained in a jar of peaches and a couple of cans of condensed milk, which didn't strike Therese as particularly homicidal, unless you were concerned about your sugar intake.

"What did you see that night?" Therese asked abruptly.

"I've been thinking about that lately," Lorelei said. "Ever since I got the email from that journalist lady. Except that I guess it wasn't from her, but I didn't know that. It's hard to remember sometimes, in between all the things the police told me I must have seen and done. Boy, did they have some ideas! And it gets into your head, you know? Especially when you haven't been eating much, and you're having some withdrawal. I wasn't high that night, by the way. I know everyone thinks I was, and I don't blame you, but I had run out a couple of days back. So I won't say I was doing great, but I knew what planet I was on, you know? And I would have noticed if I'd killed a bunch of people with a knife!"

She laughed, and Therese obligingly chuckled along. It wasn't funny, but she was interested to know what Lorelei really knew, not filtered through the medium of police reports. And maybe it was a little funny.

"Did you hear the explosion?" Therese asked, as she picked out a can of tuna and added it to the "not expired" pile.

"Hard not to. That was what woke me up, I'm pretty sure. I thought at the time it was just someone setting off some fireworks where they shouldn't. Which had me worried enough, because a fire out there would have been bad news for me. So I was kind of looking around, which is why I saw the guy."

"Guy? You know it was a man?"

"Ha! Nah, I'm just old. Thought it was a guy, but too dark and too far away to be sure. Anyway, like I told the cops a million times, before and after they started making up stories for me, all I saw was someone walking up the hill toward where that little house was, going pretty fast but not running. Then later maybe I heard steps coming back, but I'm less sure about that. I'd decided there was too much going on in the area for me to hang around, so I'd gone back to pack up my things by then."

"And…the screaming?" Therese had long since decided the explosion she had felt shaking the ground on her walk through the forest was the bomb going off, but she had never been sure about the other noises. It wasn't clear if the victims had been conscious enough, or if she had been close enough for it to be possible for their screams to reach her. But aside from the big questions, it was the one thing she really wanted to know. Had she heard her friends' last cries of pain and mistaken them for shrieking fireworks, or was that just another trick of a memory that tried too hard to fill in the blanks?

Unfortunately, Lorelei wasn't able to help her.

"Well…I did hear things. But you've got to understand, back then I was hearing a lot of things. That's part of why I got to doing the drugs, you know; it helped keep them quiet. So I might have heard your friends, but I can't say for sure. My head wasn't a real reliable place then." She flashed the toothless grin again. "Still isn't sometimes. But at least I know how to handle it now."

That was supposed to be another joke, and once again Therese laughed dutifully. This time, though, she was thinking about how little she knew about psychiatric meds, and specifically how they might interact if someone was unwittingly given a dose of sleeping pills. Could Lorelei have been hearing something when Sonia was out there on the balcony? Trapped in an unfamiliar place, with a cocktail of drugs doing who knows what in her brain, might something have made Lorelei think the best thing to do was to push their captor off?

Therese didn't want to suspect her. She didn't really want to suspect anyone. But that wasn't smart, and if there was one thing Therese needed to be right now, it was smart. She could work on being nice some other time.

"It's weird, but it should do for now." Lorelei was talking about the haul of foods they had assembled, nodding appreciatively at the pile of nonperishables. "It's amazing how much people can leave behind. It's like they don't even know what it's worth."

THE GUARD

All the young people were talking about food, and Mike was bored. These weren't the kind of folks he would normally hang out with, and he was sure they thought the same of him. Bunch of stuck-up assholes, no idea of what real life was like. There was nothing they could say that he wanted to hear, anyway. The Asian girl was cute, but she was only interested in the rich guy, which was typical. That's what they were all like, wasn't it? And the other one—hoo, boy. Probably never even had a man, the way she liked giving orders. Mike thought he knew what she needed to straighten her out.

He could have told them all a thing or two, not that any of them would listen. Even Art: they had met a couple of times back in the day, and the cops had always treated him decent. They knew who was on their side and who wasn't. But now here was their boss, sitting back and letting some lady Fed walk all over him.

Not that he hated all of them. For a rich guy, that Adam kid wasn't all bad, even if all that hair made him look like a girl. Just went to show, you couldn't always judge people by their looks. Mike prided himself on his ability to judge people.

That crazy bitch Sonia, for example. He knew from the first time he saw her that she was going to be trouble. He remembered her from back then, now that he thought about it—always showing up and shouting questions, all about what had happened to her kid. Like it was any of her business. Anyway, that guy killed a bunch of people; she was better off that he was dead. He probably would have done it again if he got the chance. Who cares if he took himself out and saved the rest of them the trouble?

The other young dude, the Mexican-looking one with the little beard, said something, and all three of them laughed. Mike didn't catch what it was about, but he was pretty sure they were looking at him. He glared back at them and got up to see what was left in the kitchen. He would have liked another beer, but he wasn't about to go over there now.

The funny thing was, he thought, as he reached into the pack of lunch meat he had scavenged from the refrigerator for himself and peeled off a slice with his fingers, he could tell them all some things they would like to know. Information he'd had all these years, that no one else had ever found out. He'd always figured it was his business and no one else's, and anyway the downside for him was too much. But he was ready to retire now, and maybe the past wasn't as past as he had thought it was.

There had been some good money in it back then. He wondered how much more there was where that had come from.

THE WITNESS

It was still raining. Having brought her ingredients from the pantry into the kitchen, Lorelei paused to close her eyes and listened to it, trying to judge the storm by its sound. It was something she had learned to do a long time ago, when she lived her life by the weather. This one sounded like it was settling in to go for a while, and it was probably going to get worse before it got better. Most things did, in Lorelei's experience.

The kitchen was nice, at least. Shiny metal appliances, smooth granite countertops, and a big stove that looked like it had hardly been used. Lorelei took a moment to take it all in and appreciate the kind of luxury she usually only saw on TV. Really, the whole place was a lot fancier than she was used to, and she wished she had more of a chance to enjoy it. The closest thing she had had to a vacation recently was a couple of years ago when she and her housemates, Ruth and Patti, had rented a boat for Ruth's sixtieth, and they had spent a long weekend at the lake, cruising around and camping on the shore. Parts of it had been nice, but Lorelei had decided camping wasn't her idea of fun. Too much like the old times.

It was funny, though; she had spent less time thinking about those days that weekend than she was now. Not just because people here kept talking about what happened that night, though that was part of it, obviously. *It's more about the way I feel*, Lorelei thought. *I'm the person nobody wants around.*

Not that any of the rest of them seemed to be any happier. Those poor kids, Lorelei thought, and then wondered if she meant the ones who died or the ones here. Of course, these people weren't kids anymore, but they felt that way to her.

More than just kids, they felt like scared kids. Even before the morning, when that woman had pulled her silly trick, she could sense their fear and uncertainty. And why not? For them, that night was probably as bad as their lives ever got. Before, they would have just been normal kids, with their normal kid lives, and after—well, then it was after. Not just another event in an eventful life. She felt a lot of sympathy for those young people, whatever they thought of her.

Not the two older men, of course. Lorelei's life experiences had been such that anyone involved in law enforcement was considered a cop, and Lorelei had no time to worry about cops' feelings.

Of course, on that basis she also ought to think about the FBI woman as one, but Lorelei wasn't very concerned with consistency. At least she was trying to take care of people, for what it was worth. Probably something to do with what happened that night. There was something worrying the young woman about that, Lorelei was sure of it.

She wondered if any of them thought she did it. Probably they did. There were times when Lorelei herself wasn't so sure. Not the part with the bomb—where would she have gotten a bomb? But sometimes she thought a lot about knives, even though she didn't like them, and the truth was there were parts of that night she didn't remember.

Then again, there were parts of a lot of nights she didn't remember, and she can't have been killing people in all of them. It wouldn't be practical.

10

Therese had brought her share of the haul out of the pantry, leaving it in the kitchen where Lorelei had already joined Gil and Joseph in working through the contents of the refrigerator, selecting the packaged items and discarding anything that could possibly have been tampered with. There didn't seem to be space for Therese to join them, and she wasn't much of a cook anyway, so she looked around for something else to do.

Most of the others were fanned out across the living room. Mike was sulking in one chair with a beer, and Victor was standing by the window, staring at the weather. As Therese scanned the room, she had the sense that all three of them were intentionally avoiding her gaze.

That was fine; she didn't want to talk to them either. Wendy was setting up some glasses and a bucket of ice on a side table—a kind of a bar, though it could barely have been past two in the afternoon. Aside from their brief interaction in the bathroom,

Therese hadn't had much chance to meet her neighbor, so she went to join her.

"How are you doing?" Therese asked.

Wendy jumped like she had been shocked. "Oh, um, yeah. Not good, I guess. I was just trying to remember the last time I backed up my phone."

It wouldn't have been the first thing on Therese's mind on a day that had included wild accusations, violent death, and an actual bomb, but she supposed everyone had their own priorities.

Aside from her phone contents, Wendy's priorities seemed to include grooming. Therese wasn't sure when on this insane day she could have found time to do her hair and makeup, but on Wendy both were pristine, her black bob smooth and glossy and her pink lipstick drawn into a precise cupid's bow. She had changed into an outfit of white skinny jeans and a striped sweater, and she presided over the makeshift bar like she had dropped in on her way to brunch.

It was exactly the sort of look Chloe might have been wearing, if she had lived long enough for her preppy high school style to grow into the modern adult version. Therese didn't know what had drawn her classmate to a wardrobe of pleated skirts and Lily Pulitzer minidresses—in truth it would never have occurred to her to ask. At the time, it seemed like a natural result of Chloe's environment, like dusky feathers on a desert bird.

Chloe's mother had been a successful Realtor, instantly recognizable in her pink suits and gold BMW. Her daughter had affected embarrassment at her mother's extravagant style, but her rebellion had never extended as far as to skip their shared shopping trips, or to turn up her nose at the Burberry purses she got for her birthday. It had been too long since Therese had even an academic interest in luxury brands for her to know if Wendy's clothes would have met with her long-ago friend's approval, but though they didn't look much alike, stylistically the resemblance was there.

And it seemed like they might have had one other thing in common. Chloe's favorite thing to watch had been cable TV true crime shows—she had known more about the cold cases of the day than some of Therese's own coworkers did now. And if Wendy's own account was to be believed, she had carried on her friend's interests in her own way, keeping detailed records of everyone connected to their own famous crime. Which was exactly the sort of information Therese was interested in.

"I wonder if you can help me with something," she said. "Last night you mentioned you'd been keeping a folder on all the people connected to the crime and the victims. I'd been wondering why a journalist would invite some of the guests here, and it doesn't make much more sense to me now that we know it was Sonia. Do you have any idea what she was thinking, based on what you know?"

From the way Wendy was looking at Therese, it was clear she didn't trust her, but she also wasn't immune to flattery. And in Therese's experience, people who followed crimes loved nothing more than talking about what they thought they knew.

"Well, I'm not sure," Wendy said, in a way that suggested she had some ideas. "I mean, you're obvious, and Mike and Art. And I guess Adam, since it was his family that owned the cabin."

"And Lorelei was a potential witness and suspect," Therese added. "But what about Gil, or Victor, or Joseph?"

"Or me?" Wendy may have been trying to sound breezy, but her tone had picked up a guarded edge. "I guess it depends on why she wanted us here. If it was just people who knew the victims, or if she thought there was something special about us. And actually..." her voice trailed off as she seemed to really consider the question for the first time. "Actually, there might be something to that."

"How so?"

"Well...I'm not sure I really want to say." Wendy looked suddenly pleased with herself, and at that moment Therese would have bet money that she was having thoughts of starting her own investigation.

Therese did not think that would be a very good idea.

"The more we can share information, the safer we'll all be," she said, firmly ignoring the voice in her head reminding her of Sonia's final words. (*What picture? What wall?*) Regardless, Wendy was unmoved.

"Oh, I know. I just need to think about things a bit. I wouldn't want to start saying things that could be taken out of context."

"Now, if more people followed that advice, the world would be a happier place," said Adam, who had come into the room, carrying two bottles of brown liquor.

"I feel like I should fess up," he said as he set the bottles down on the table Wendy had prepared. "There's one key that wasn't on that ring. I don't come up here often these days, but when I do, I like to have some supplies ready, and well, let's say these aren't part of the rental package. But I had a feeling we could all use something uplifting right about now."

On the one hand, Therese could see all kinds of potential problems with this plan. But on the other hand, she could really use a drink.

Clearly, she wasn't the only one. Wendy gave Adam a full-power smile, stepping between him and Therese to hand Adam a glass with some ice. "Thank you so much, Adam, that's so generous of you. Can you pour me one?"

It was more flirting than Therese might have considered appropriate for the situation, but then she could hardly call herself an expert in that. And no one else seemed interested in anything but what was in the bottles.

"My man!" Gil came over to examine the labels and gave a low whistle. "Wow, you really brought out the good stuff, didn't you?"

Victor was equally impressed. "Count me in. It's dead-o'clock somewhere, right? What, too soon?"

Despite what Victor might have liked to imagine, his joke didn't raise shock so much as distaste from most of the other guests. The only person who laughed was Mike, though Adam split the difference with a weak smile.

"I can see why you and Josh were friends. You have the same sense of humor," said Therese. She hadn't liked Josh then, and she had no intention of tolerating his imitator now, so her tone had made it clear that she didn't intend it as a compliment. Still, she didn't expect the intensity of Victor's reaction.

"I do *not*. He and I—look, we weren't even friends, okay? I don't even know why I'm here."

Joseph, who had been working in the kitchen on some sort of dough, set it aside and came around to help himself to a drink. "You're here for the same reason the rest of us are. Because a crazy woman sent you an invite, and you couldn't turn it down. Let's not pretend that any of us are above this situation at this point."

Nobody seemed to want to argue with that, and even Victor lapsed back into silence. Therese was thinking about what an odd group they made, when it occurred to her that one of them was missing.

"Where's Art?" she asked abruptly. She had assumed the former detective had just been on a bathroom break, but it had been a while, and he hadn't returned. Which might just mean it was time to break out the room spray, but recent events had her jumpy.

"He went out to try to hot-wire the cars," Victor said, still sounding annoyed. "I don't think he really knows how, though. He said he thought he could figure it out."

"In that case, good luck to him," Joseph took a sip out of his glass and looked over at Therese hopefully. "I don't suppose that's one of your areas of expertise?"

She shook her head. "If it was, I would have been out of here hours ago, and to hell with my rental car agreement. But I'll go and check on him now, just to be sure."

"I'll come with you," Adam said. "I've been wondering if maybe all the computers in my car might be good for something here."

Adam set his glass down on the table next to Wendy with barely a glance at her, and if he noticed her disappointment and anger at her failure to hold his attention, he gave no sign of it. Therese almost felt bad for Wendy, but then, she didn't even own any white jeans.

———

Adam's car was the Tesla, of course. Therese wasn't even surprised that she wasn't surprised. While he tried to figure out how to get inside a car that didn't even make the door handles available without an electronic key, she looked around at the other vehicles.

Her own rental car was still where she parked it, locked up tight and looking just like the cheap American sedan it had been when she left it. Of all the times not to forget her phone in the cup holder, Therese thought, as the cold rain pattered on her head and ran down the back of her shirt. But there was no point in regrets now. She considered breaking into the car—she was confident she could manage that much, and at least it would be dry—but without a plan for what to do next, it didn't seem worth the charges to her insurance.

"Do you really not know how to hot-wire one of these? I thought that was the sort of thing they taught you in the FBI," Adam asked, looking up from where he was trying to pop out a door handle with his fingernails.

"I wish I did, but no," Therese assured him. "Some specialized field agents get extra training in that sort of thing, but tell you the truth, I'm mainly a desk jockey. I can't start a car without a key, but if you ever need anyone to comb through the text messages of domestic terrorists, I've got it covered."

Adam laughed. "I'll keep that in mind. Too bad, though. And it's also too bad that our detective friend doesn't seem to have had much more luck."

Therese agreed. There was plenty of evidence Art had been there—a broken window and some damage on the driver's side of one of the SUVs, a couple of wires pulled out under the steering wheel of the elderly subcompact, which looked like it was mostly held together by forlorn hope. But where was Art now? The rain had let up a little, but it was still coming down in a steady drizzle, and there was nowhere obvious nearby where a person might take shelter while he thought about other ways to try to start cars.

"Maybe he went inside to warm up?" Adam gave up after a couple of half-hearted attempts to get into his car. "Could be he didn't want to come right back and tell everyone he failed."

"Could be." Therese looked toward the side of the house, where the path they had been on earlier connected to the driveway. "I just want to check one thing."

———

They heard the former detective before they saw him. First as a scrabbling sound in the underbrush, like a large animal going after a smaller one, and then, as they approached, as a voice from somewhere down the slope.

"Hey! Hey, is someone up there? Can I get some help here?"

When they had gone inside, Therese had left the climbing

gear coiled up under the shelter of the balcony, still attached to the pillar, just in case. Now the ropes led from there and disappeared over the edge of the path, shifting under what seemed like a significant amount of tension.

Therese approached the edge, Adam trailing behind her. Between the shouting and the movement on the line, the signs weren't pointing to another worst-case scenario, but it had been a hell of a day so far, and Therese was running low on optimism. So when she looked over, to about ten feet down where Art was hanging sideways on the line he had seriously tangled, the humor of the situation was initially overwhelmed by her relief.

Then, in an attempt to pull himself up, Art managed to flip himself over so that he dangled upside down like history's worst Cirque du Soleil audition, and it was all she could do to keep herself from cracking up.

"What…happened?" Therese asked in a strangled voice, while behind her Adam made a series of hiccuping noises that also sounded a lot like someone trying to suppress laughter.

Art grabbed on to the rope and tried to right himself, smashing his face into the hillside in the process.

Finally, he got himself turned around well enough to look up at them. "I was looking for any keys that might have survived the explosion. But the rain made it difficult," he said with as much dignity as he could manage in the situation. Which, as the rain plastered the long hairs of his comb-over across his muddy face, wasn't much. "I think I could use some help."

This time, Therese wasn't going down the mountainside. She

took hold of the rope near where it went over the edge, and Adam grabbed on behind her, and together they were able to haul Art back up onto the path. The man himself was more trouble than Sonia's body had been—hanging limp for most of the time, except when he would suddenly decide to "help" by thrashing around and tangling the ropes in the shrubbery. By the time he had belly flopped onto the path, the three of them were soaked to the skin, and Therese's hands were rubbed raw.

Finally unwound from the ropes, Art couldn't seem to manage to do anything more than glare at his rescuers.

"Well," he said at last. "Thanks. I'm going inside now, gonna dry off. I'll let you know about what our next steps should be."

He squelched off, dripping mud. Left behind, Adam and Therese looked at each other, and Adam shrugged.

"I guess he'll tell us our next steps then," he said with a laugh.

Therese had a lot of thoughts about that, but none of them were going to be productive to share. So she joined him in laughing and said, "At least someone has it figured out. Right now all I know is the others had better not have finished all of the whiskey before I've had a chance at it."

11

When Therese and Adam got back inside, they found that the party had moved into the dining room, where the rest of the group was eating underfilled lunch meat sandwiches and canned fruit salad. The good news was there was still some whiskey left, and the bottles and glasses had been brought into the room and set up on the sideboard. The bad news was everything else.

The remaining guests, minus Art, were seated around the table, where they seemed to have divided themselves into three general factions. On one side, Joseph, Wendy, and Gil were seated in a line, facing off against Victor and Mike at opposite ends on the other side, with Lorelei by herself in the tall chair at the foot of the table. The dark wood-paneled room gave it the feeling of a dysfunctional board meeting, with the taxidermied deer heads and mounted fish on the walls standing in for the portraits of the founders.

Everyone in the room seemed to be talking at once, and there was no way of telling what exactly the conflict was about, only that everyone involved was taking it very seriously.

"Why don't you shut up?" Victor said, to a visibly agitated Gil.

"Look, I'm sorry," Gil said. "I didn't know it was such a touchy subject. You can't even laugh about it after all this time?"

"Why should I laugh? Everyone else has been laughing at me for two decades. You think I'm just going to give in to jerks like you, and like him?"

Victor tried to go on, but his words were lost in the general hubbub. Both Art and Joseph were trying to tell the others to calm down, while Mike tried to get a word in to make his own point about them all being crazy or stupid. The only island of calm was Lorelei, who had found a fruit basket and was eating a banana. None of them seemed to have registered Therese and Adam's damp arrival.

"What are you even talking about?" Joseph asked when the noise died down. "What video?"

Therese brushed a wet strand of hair out of her eyes and tried to fade into the background as Gil picked up the story.

"It was an early viral video, might have been one of the first ones I saw. This guy comes out a door, and someone pours water on him, and his shorts go totally transparent." As he said it, Gil seemed to realize he wasn't making a great case for his side of the argument, and his face fell, leaving him looking uncomfortable. "I thought it was funny. I was like, twelve. Anyway, I never knew who it was, but Wendy says it was Victor."

"Thanks a lot for that," Victor said bitterly to Wendy, who was looking pleased with herself.

"I said I had folders on everyone, remember? That's pretty much the only thing that I found about you. It's the first hit for your name in Google, you know."

"Oh, I know. Why did you think it was something you needed to have in your folder? I know what people were saying, but I'm not a perv. I didn't—I had no idea it was going to happen, okay? So what's the point of bringing it up now?"

Therese thought she had an idea, but Wendy was on a roll, and Therese wanted to see where she was going with this.

Wendy did not disappoint. "Because Josh took the video, didn't he?" she said. "That's the whole reason I had you in the file. Josh had a Friendster page, and he posted a link to the video there, with your name. He didn't say he took it, but when I looked you up and saw you lived near him, I figured he must have, and that put you in the circle of connections. Otherwise you weren't very interesting."

"Oh, great, thanks for that." Victor looked around the table, and then up at Therese and Adam, stopped near the door where they had entered, waiting for him to go on. He dropped his head and sat quietly for a moment, and then gave a resigned little shrug.

"Fine, whatever. Yeah, it was me in the video, and yes, Josh took it and shared it. Josh and I had been friends since we were little. He was my next-door neighbor. And we got along pretty well, even though he'd always been kind of mean. But when we got to high school and he got these new friends, he stopped wanting to hang out with me at all. Then one day he called and said there was a party at the pool, and I was invited, but when I got there it was just him and a kids' swimming class going on. He said the party was starting soon; the other people were just coming from somewhere else. And I should have known something was up, but I'd been having trouble making friends, and I really wanted it to be real, you know?"

He had looked up from the floor, searching their faces for approval, and Therese nodded. She certainly did know.

"Josh told me we were going to play some kind of game, and we had to wear special swimsuits to show what teams we were on. So he gives me these yellow trunks, and I go get changed. And then, when I come out of the dressing room, he sprays me with some water. Which you know, ha ha, I'm already going to the pool, so it's cool. Except that when they got wet, the trunks went totally transparent, and I didn't know until the little kids started yelling and laughing."

"You can hear them in the background of the video," Gil said helpfully. "That's what made some people think it might be faked. Like, it was just too perfect."

"It was real enough," Victor said, with feeling. "It took a lot of explaining to convince the swim teacher not to call the police. It didn't help that Josh was nowhere around by then. But he'd gotten what he came for."

"The video," said Therese, who felt like she could enter the conversation now. "Josh was really proud of himself for that."

"Right. It wasn't like now, with everyone having their phones all the time, but he had a little digital camera, and he sent the video to a blog about pranks, with my real name, and it got shared around a lot. You can just imagine what my senior year was like after that."

"At least you were alive to have one." Joseph had been listening to the conversation with quiet interest as he finished off a sandwich. "I don't mean to be rude, but it sounds like you might have had a reason to hate Josh and his friends at that time."

"Yeah, maybe I did, so what?" Still clearly stinging from having to share his story, Victor responded with annoyance, before the implication of what Joseph was saying must have caught up with him.

"Wait, you think I killed them all? Over a prank? You can't be serious." He looked around for support. "Is everyone here crazy?"

"Nobody's actually accusing you of being the murderer." Gil must have meant it to sound reassuring, but the way his voice rose at the end of the sentence made it come out as more of a question.

"Except Sonia, and she's dead. If you think about it, she was kind of accusing everyone here." Wendy, on the other hand, obviously wasn't done with causing trouble. And Therese wasn't going to oppose her this time.

"She did, and she is," Therese agreed. "I know we've all been avoiding the topic, myself included. But since it looks like we're going to be here at least another day, I think it's time we face it."

She walked over to the makeshift bar that had been relocated to the polished mahogany sideboard and poured herself a (small) drink. This was the moment she needed to take charge of the situation, but she caught a glimpse of herself in the beveled glass of the cabinet doors and grimaced. Therese prided herself on her lack of vanity, but even for her, the rain-matted hair and smears of mud on her face were taking the casual look too far. But she was just going to have to roll with it, because there were some things that needed to be said.

"So now you're the one accusing us?" Victor said, spitting out sandwich crumbs that landed in his goatee. "Are you going to get everyone arrested if they say anything to you that's not true? I've heard how you Feds work. You can say anything you want to trick people."

"I'm not here in my professional capacity." Therese didn't like to admit it, but the quick warmth of the drink hitting her empty stomach was already making it easier for her to respond calmly. "And I'm not accusing anybody. My point is that Sonia thought she had reasons to suspect all of us, myself included, of either being involved in the deaths or having information about them. I'm not saying she was right, but I'd be lying if I said I wasn't curious about where she came up with some of those ideas. But mostly I think we need to confront the possibility that there's at least one person here who was afraid of what she might have known or been able to find out. And that person might still be dangerous."

"What do you mean?" Mike said. "You think there's a psycho here who's going to kill all the rest of us? And I thought that Sonia bitch was nuts."

"That's your answer to everything. Don't you have any other lines?" Gil rolled his eyes and picked up another sandwich.

"Therese knows more about this sort of thing than any of us. I think we should listen to her."

"Of course you do," said Victor. "And what do you have to be worried about? You and Adam are the biggest guys here. What are the rest of us going to do to you?"

Adam smiled. "I don't know about Gil, but you may be overestimating me. I think what Therese is trying to say is that, whatever we personally believe, it can't do any harm for all of us to treat this like a hazardous situation."

He joined Therese at the bar and poured himself a neat glass of whiskey. His hair was still wet from their trip out in the rain, and it was curling as it dried, which spoiled his slick man-of-the-world look a bit, but in a good way.

And Therese wasn't the only one who noticed it. Despite the fact that her glass wasn't quite empty, Wendy got up and came over to join them, wedging herself between Therese and Adam with an "excuse me" and a smile that only went to one of them. For a moment Therese felt a familiar flash of anger—this again? Just the same as then?

But no, that was twenty years ago. She wasn't that person anymore.

"That is what I was getting at, thank you," she said to Adam, making room for Wendy between them like it was the most natural thing in the world, then turning to address the rest of the group. "Look, go ahead and think whatever you want about me, about Sonia, about all of this. But please, stay alert, and maybe we should all agree that the balcony should be off-limits for the time being."

Therese hadn't expected the suggestion to go over well with everyone there, and she was right. Gil looked shocked and Lorelei concerned, while Victor was clearly unhappy, and Mike's lips moved as he tried to come up with some sort of insulting retort. But it was Wendy, stepping away from the bar to face her, who started the resistance.

"It's nice of you to be so worried about us," Chloe's onetime friend said, her voice dripping with sarcasm. "But shouldn't we be the ones warning each other about you? After all, none of the rest of us were there that night and just happened to have a reason to walk out right before all the rest of them got killed. Do you really expect us to sit here and let you tell us what to do, when if anyone here is going to be the killer, it's you?"

Therese wasn't exactly surprised by the accusation—she knew she was going to have to confront it as soon as she accepted the invitation. She had given a lot of thought to how much she was and wasn't going to tell, and up until now she hadn't come to a firm decision.

"That's a reasonable question," Therese said, meeting Wendy's eyes with what she hoped was a friendly and lightly amused gaze, until the other woman looked away.

She went on, addressing the room in general. "I imagine a lot of you have at least thought it. Lord knows at least half the internet seems to have. To tell the truth, that's why I've kept it to myself. What could I possibly have to gain from feeding that beast? But I think it's pretty clear we're beyond that now."

Therese helped herself to a sandwich from the platter. Her

fingers left dents in the soft bread that slowly filled back in as she set it on a plate and looked around for a place at the table.

She chose a seat on the side with Victor and Mike, and the sound of the heavy chair scraping across the floor as she pulled it out was like thunder in the silent room.

"Obviously, there's nothing I can say that will prove to you I had nothing to do with what happened that night," she began, before taking a bite of her sandwich. It was ham and processed swiss cheese, with too much mayonnaise, but until she tasted it, Therese hadn't realized how hungry she was. It was all she could do to keep from scarfing the whole thing down, and to hell with appearances. But at least for now, she needed to be in control. "The best I can do is tell you what I know, and let you decide for yourselves."

From across the table, Gil frowned like he couldn't quite understand what she was doing, and Joseph looked amused but interested. Mike was making derisive noises to one side of her, while Victor sulkily ate another sandwich, and down at the end, Lorelei smiled and peeled another banana.

Adam came around and took the seat at the head of the table, leaving Wendy standing awkwardly at the bar.

"I can't speak for everyone," Adam said. "So I'll just say I never suspected you exactly. But you have to admit it raises some questions, the way you left right before it happened, and never explained."

The way he said it was almost apologetic, and Therese knew she was never going to get a better opening than that. So she took a deep breath, a bite of her sandwich, and a sip of whiskey, and dove in.

"You want to know what happened in that cabin? Why I left? Fine. It was—look, you know how Jenna was. She had her sense of humor, and it wasn't always nice. I don't think there's anyone here who'd be surprised to hear that." She looked at Adam, who nodded sympathetically. "So, the track season had just finished for me, and I'd maybe put on a couple of pounds. I'd been trying to diet, but coach made me cut it out. Jenna figured out I was self-conscious about it, and she started saying things like how I shouldn't have eaten the pizza I'd had. And that kind of escalated, until she got Chloe to help her, and they tried to make me throw it up."

Gil hadn't struck her as the type to be easily shocked, but his jaw dropped open, unfortunately exposing a half-chewed bite of food.

"What? How?"

"The usual way. I don't think either of them wanted to actually reach into my mouth, so they both were holding me, and Jenna told Chloe to force me to stick my finger down my throat. It wasn't a very well-thought-out plan."

"And?" Wendy asked. "What did you do?"

"I bit Chloe's hand and kicked Jenna in the shin." Therese smiled grimly at the memory. "That was one thing they were right about—I was bigger than them. And anyone who thinks girls' sports are kind and gentle hasn't seen what goes on under the surface at a water polo match. But I think at best you could call it an empty victory."

"Why?" asked Victor, who seemed oddly invested. "You

beat them, didn't you? They weren't going to try something like that again."

Therese considered attempting to explain to him what it meant to be a teenage girl, but something about his expression, both blank and angry, told her there would be no point. He reminded her too much of Josh, hooting and shouting about jello wrestling that night, and fair or not, she wasn't going to bother.

"A person can win and still lose," was all she had to say about that. "Anyway, at that point it was clear there was no place for me there, so I left."

It was more detail about that than Therese had ever told anyone. Even now, after all these years, she could feel her face getting hot with the shame of it. The laughter, the feeling of the hands on her arms and mouth, the ungovernable anger that had taken hold of her. Everything seemed like it had started then, and nothing had been the same since. She lifted her head, ready to take on the others' responses to her revelation.

"That's it?" Wendy said.

12

I mean, seriously? A little joke, and you just stormed out?" Wendy looked around with incredulity, like she expected everyone else to agree with her. They didn't exactly do that, but Therese noticed that no one was rushing to argue the point.

"It seemed like a big deal at the time. And it's not like I knew what was going to happen after I left," Therese said, suddenly sullen.

"We didn't find any bite mark evidence on any of the bodies," said Art, who had come into the room while Therese was telling her story. He had changed into clean clothes, but there was a scrape on his nose from where he had run into a shrub on his way back up the mountainside. It might have been her imagination, but Therese had the impression that he was avoiding looking at her or Adam as he helped himself to a heavy pour of the whiskey.

"Well, it's not like I broke the skin. Chloe was surprised, and she let me go. This wasn't some kind of knock-down, drag-out fight. Just some kids doing stupid kid things."

"I can't believe Chris would have let that happen," Gil said. "I thought he liked you."

Therese gave him a pitying look. "I thought so too. More to the point, so did Jenna. And I think Chris didn't mind being the center of attention."

"So the whole thing was just you fighting over a boy?" Victor asked. At this point, it was safe to say that the conversation was not going at all the way Therese had imagined.

"We were seventeen. What did you think it would be, a heated political discussion?" she said, annoyed. "Anyway, that was the point when I figured out the friendship Jenna was offering wasn't worth it and never would be, and if I didn't leave, then I was signing up to take her abuse forever. Obviously, I didn't know what was about to happen."

"Or so you say. How do we know it wasn't something totally different that you made up so you could leave before the bomb went off?" Wendy must have gotten over her initial disbelief, because she was back on track with the accusations. Therese didn't mind, actually. This was what she had been prepared for.

"You don't. Obviously, everyone else who was in that cabin is dead, and I have no way of proving I wasn't involved. All I can do is tell you as much of the truth as I know it, and hope the rest of you will do the same." Therese took a careful look at all the other people around the table, trying to gauge how seriously they were going to take what she had to say.

"Sonia knew something about what happened at that cabin, or thought she did. She tried to play a lone hand, and now she's dead. I don't know if anyone here is at any similar risk; all I ask is that if you think you know anything, you share it now. And even if you don't, be careful and stay alert."

Finally, Therese thought she had managed to put the seriousness of their situation into words that everyone could grasp. Naturally, it was Mike who had to argue.

"Sure, let's all play pretend that the crazy lady was a master detective, and we've all got to hide from her killer. Is that the kind of game they have you do at FBI school? No wonder you Feds can't find your ass with both hands."

Joseph had been quiet for a while, looking like he was lost in thought, but that brought him back from wherever he had been. "You're pretty invested in this idea that Sonia didn't know anything about anybody. Which is kind of funny, don't you think?"

"I don't know what you people think is funny. It doesn't sound funny to me." Mike was trying to maintain his bravado, but the way he crossed his arms and tucked his head down looked more like a defensive position.

"Not ha-ha funny," Joseph said. "More like interesting, because you did deliver the package with the rope her son used to kill himself. The one that didn't come through the normal prison mail? And I don't think you ever told anyone where it came from."

"I don't have to tell you anything! I've got my rights!" Mike half rose from the table in his outrage.

Victor had finished his latest sandwich, and he perked up at this new front in the hostilities. "Yeah, you've got your rights.

I wonder what else you got?" he said, leaning to look around Therese at Mike. "Sonia thought she could make you talk, and now she's got her head smashed in. That's a lot of dead people around for you to still not be saying what you know."

"I didn't—I don't have to tell you anything." Mike looked around the room, and for a moment, Therese thought he might have hesitated, though she couldn't see where his eyes rested. "What I know is my business, and I'm going to keep it that way."

"He's right, you know," Art said, getting up to refill his glass. "You think we didn't talk to him back then? We were satisfied with his information."

Wendy made a sharp, angry sound that might have been a laugh.

"You're pretty easily satisfied when it comes to one of your people, aren't you?" She turned and addressed Therese. "Maybe you don't know, because you moved away, but did you ever hear about how this great detective lost his job?"

"Not exactly, no," Therese said.

"A cop was beating up his wife, and when she finally left him, he went and found her, shot her five times in the face with his police gun. Blam, blam, blam, blam, blam." She looked straight at Art as she spoke, enunciating each shot carefully. "And then the killer went back to his cop buddies, and they helped hide the gun, and then they found a guy working in a restaurant near where he dumped the body and framed him for it. It was only because the victim's family hired a private investigator that the truth came out at all, and our noble public servant here was the ringleader of the whole thing. So his punishment is, he gets to retire, take his full pension, and now he's here, still covering for his guys." She gave Therese a meaningful look. "That's what they do."

"I see." Therese nodded, ignoring Art, who was attempting to protest. She spoke directly to Wendy, but her words were addressed to all the guests. "My father was a cop, so you must think the same courtesy was extended to me. That I killed my friends, and the police helped to cover it up. That didn't happen, but I understand I can't convince you of that. All I ask is, if you're going to suspect me, you should apply that same suspicion to everyone else. Which is why I'm a little disappointed that no one seems to have remembered that I have these."

Therese took the ring of extra room keys out of her pocket and held them up for everyone to see.

She waited until she was sure that all of the other guests understood what she was saying, and was gratified to see that at least some of them looked abashed when they understood the implications.

Not all of them, of course.

"So, what, are you going to keep those so you can check up on us, make sure we aren't killing each other?" Mike asked. "Cause if you wanted to come into my room, all you had to do was ask."

Therese didn't dignify that with a response. "The question is what to do with these keys. I suggest we divide them up, with everyone getting the key to their own room. We can leave the ones to the common spaces out, unless someone has a burning desire to hole up in the basement." She tossed the ring down on the table in a definite motion and stood up. "I'll be right with you, as soon as I have another sandwich."

———

In the end Therese decided to take her sandwich to go. Adam took charge of the key ring, and everyone else seemed ready to make up for their earlier lack of concern by insisting they got their own keys as soon as possible. That was easier said than done, because none of them were labeled, so the only way to figure out which went where was to try each one in turn.

Upstairs, the group moved in a tight knot from door to door, with each person taking their key as soon as Adam found the one that fit. Some, like Lorelei, Art, Gil, and Joseph, immediately retreated to their rooms, with or without an excuse or a claim they would be down soon. The others stayed on—Adam to help with his knowledge of the house, Wendy to help with Adam, Mike and Victor for reasons of their own, and Therese because hers was the last room on the floor. The keys were all nearly identical in appearance, and some of the locks stuck, but she was at least relieved to find that no one had decided to save money by keying all the doors the same.

They finally made it to Therese's room, and a quick check confirmed that it was in the same disarray as she had left it. The others were talking about going back downstairs, with emphasis on the idea of seeing what else Adam might have in his liquor collection, and she knew she should join them. But on the other hand, she didn't want to. She was still wet from her last outing, tired from hauling two people up a cliff, and drained by a list of reasons too long to admit to. What she wanted was to stand under a hot shower until her fingers wrinkled, and even the way Adam looked at her when he said he might have the ingredients for some cocktails wasn't more appealing than that right now.

Besides, she thought, with Wendy back downstairs with him, she would have the bathroom all to herself. Was this what getting old was like?

—

Five minutes later, with the doors locked and triple-checked, the water was blasting onto her back, and Therese knew she had made the right decision. More than anything right now, she needed some time to think. About the present situation, but also about the past.

It wasn't always at the front of her mind, but that night had been a constant presence in Therese's life for the last twenty years. In the immediate aftermath, with the move to Florida and the endless media repetitions of the story, she had thought it was something that would blow over. That if she just kept her head down, things would eventually go back to normal. But that had never seemed to happen. Every time Therese thought she might have a chance to let her guard down, there would be another book, another TV show. Eventually she gave up, and secrecy about her past became her default. It made friendships hard and relationships harder, but every once in a while, something would happen to convince her it was the right choice.

Like just eight months ago, when she had given in to her mother's urging and signed up for a dating app. Her matches had been the usual parade of duds, creeps, and fine-but-not-feeling-it guys, but she had been pleased with herself for doing something like a normal person, and had even met a couple of men who seemed promising and didn't even panic when they learned about her job. One of them, Rob, had been particularly charming, a fellow rock climber and bluegrass fan who laughed at all her jokes, and she thought she might be on her way to her first serious relationship in years.

Until she was doing some due diligence before their third date and discovered that "Rob" was actually "Erik," an aspiring host of a true crime podcast, who had lately been promising his listeners "a new angle on a favorite case that you won't believe."

That was it for the dating thing for a while.

In a way, it was Rob who convinced her to come on this trip. Not in person, of course. As soon as she canceled their date, she blocked him on every platform and dropped a word to a member of her book club who worked for the SEC about some undisclosed crypto promotion on his podcast. But the way he had gone so far woke her up to the fact that she needed to take control of her story. So, when the email came in, allegedly from a reputable media organization, Therese decided it was time to accept that she would always be the girl who left, and to stop letting her desire to get away from that define so much of her life.

Therese washed the streaks of dirt off her arms while she thought about that.

Even her job—making it into the FBI had been more than tough, and her dad had been absurdly proud when she had achieved it. But despite it being the culmination of a long-held dream, Therese had never felt fully like she belonged there. That was on her, Therese decided as she ran the washcloth over her face, noticing as she took it away that some of Sonia's blood was still under her chin. If she got out of this place—and right now that felt like a real "if"—she was going to give her whole self to what she did, and to hell with people and their ideas.

Which would be a lot easier to do if she was able to figure out what had driven Sonia to gather them all here, and most importantly, who had killed her over it.

Mindful of the water she was using, Therese turned off the shower and reached for one of the giant fluffy towels. The luxury felt incongruous with her situation, which Therese knew was silly. She was going to be thinking about murder anyway; she might as well be nicely dried. If anything, it helped to clear her mind.

Early in her career, she had fallen into the common trap of thinking the only way to engage with an investigation was to run around asking as many questions as possible and getting in everyone's face. But time and experience had taught her that was mostly a good way to make mistakes. Hunting for answers was important, but so was taking the time to think about what the right questions were.

So, what did she really know?

Sonia had planned this weekend well ahead—the way she had stockpiled the pills proved that. However badly she had miscalculated the risk to her, there had been a method to her actions. And she must have had a reason behind her choice of guests. Maybe there was some truth to what Wendy had said, about each of them having a reason to want to kill some or all of the people in the cabin. Unfortunately for Sonia, at least one of them had one to kill her.

The idea that Sonia had died by suicide wasn't worth entertaining. Lorelei might not be the most perceptive person in every situation, but Therese thought she had been right on the money with her assessment of their host's behavior. Whatever Sonia had thought she was doing here, she had clearly believed she was going to be around to witness it.

And Therese was equally certain her final words had been more than the garbled mutterings of a brain close to death. Sonia had been trying to tell her something, something that was more important to her than getting the help that might have saved her life.

It was on the wall. The picture. What wall? What picture? There were the blown-up photographs that someone, presumably Sonia, had installed before they arrived. At first, Therese had thought it might be a clue to their belongings being hidden there, but Gil's explosive discovery had put that to rest. But she still needed to search them, and she would have to come up with some excuse for looking—Sonia's last words were something she intended to keep to herself for the time being.

It wasn't the only thing she was withholding, of course. Telling the story of what had happened that night had been easier than she had thought, even if it hadn't gone exactly as she'd anticipated.

Not cathartic exactly, but surprising, to hear herself putting those memories that had haunted her for so long into words, and how trivial it had all sounded, even to her. Of all the things she might have thought she would encounter this weekend, murder aside, the idea that her long-held trauma might have been essentially silly was the least expected.

As for whether it had accomplished what she had wanted to with regard to the others, that was still an open question. No one had argued with her, but they hadn't opened up about their own experiences either. Still, there was nothing she could do about that except try to set a good example, for as far as she was willing to go.

She hadn't told them everything, but what she had told them was the truth.

13

Therese was sitting on the bed in her room, wrapped in a towel and staring out the window into the storm. Coming out of the bathroom, she had realized that she hadn't closed the curtains and almost retreated out of modesty, before realizing there was no way anyone could see in unless they were hanging out in one of the windswept treetops with binoculars. So she kept the towel mostly to keep from getting the comforter wet and allowed herself to enjoy a few minutes of peace.

She had accepted the idea that one of her fellow guests was probably a five- or now six-time murderer. Now the obvious question was, which one?

A brother, a cousin, a friend, a neighbor, a boyfriend, and a drug-addled vagrant. All groups that had produced killers in the past, and would in the future. There were also Art and Mike, two men involved in the investigation, but without any connection to the victims that she knew of. Therese wasn't a great believer in coincidences, so she wasn't considering them for the original killings, but that didn't leave them out of the running for Sonia's death. Sean's mother might have known about something they had done—either in the investigation or in that jail-cell delivery—that would incriminate them, something bad enough that it was worth it to one of them to make sure she didn't continue the conversation she had been determined to start.

But what about the others? Of all of them, the only one Therese had really gotten a chance to know so far was Lorelei. Therese was surprised to realize that she liked the woman, and found herself feeling oddly protective toward her. Also, Lorelei could most easily be profiled as the killer—the crazy person driven to violence by drugs or madness was a cliché of fearmongering— which by itself made Therese unwilling to believe in Lorelei's guilt. (Which was no better of a reason than suspecting her because of it, Therese reminded herself.)

The next most obvious person was Adam, if only because he had the closest connection to one of the victims and would have been familiar with the layout of the cabin. He was also the only other guest Therese remembered clearly from those days, and there was nothing she could think of that was suspicious. She had seen him a few times at Jenna's house, and he had always been nice enough to his sister's friends, in the way of an older sibling who had better things to do and possibly a hangover. And Jenna, who loved to talk about how much various people hated or were jealous of her, never made any such comments about her half brother.

Not that his name didn't come up. Jenna had enjoyed telling

stories about Adam's exploits on the party scene and the trouble
it got him into with their father, but none of them had involved
violence that Therese could remember.

And if a brother was a long shot for a suspect, a cousin was
hard to even imagine. Gil was the only other person here who
Therese had ever met before, though his memories of that time
were obviously much clearer than hers. That wasn't surprising—
how many teenagers paid attention to their crush's preteen relative? But it was useful to remember that, as much as he seemed
the same age as the rest of them now, back then he was only a
kid, and what had happened in that cabin hardly seemed like a
child's crime. Particularly not a child who would grow up to be as
simple and ordinary as Gil seemed to be. Therese knew all the stories about the mass killer next door who was "just a regular guy,"
but she viewed them with skepticism. In her experience, there
were usually plenty of signs; people just didn't want to admit they
hadn't been paying attention.

One of those signs was free-floating anger and generalized
animosity, which would describe Victor well enough, though on
the balance of the evidence, Therese was inclined to think he was
just a jerk. But Josh's prank was a motive of sorts, particularly if it
was part of a larger pattern of mockery and abuse. In a certain sort
of mind, those things could build up to a motivation for serious
violence.

Did Victor have that sort of mind? Did any of them? Wendy's
focus on the crime could be the ordinary tabloid fascination she
said it was, or it could point to something more sinister. Whatever

reason Sonia had for inviting her, it wasn't because there was no one around who had been closer to Chloe. A brief internet search before Therese had come had confirmed that Chloe's parents were still alive, retired and living in the huge stuccoed McMansion where Chloe grew up.

Therese had only visited it once, when Chloe had invited her to come over and get ready before one of Jenna's parties. It had been antiseptically clean—from the cream-colored furniture that looked like it had just come from the store to the pale travertine tiles that made her nervous that even her bare feet might be too dirty to step on them.

Chloe had never mentioned any other friends then, but she wouldn't have, unless they had been rich enough for her to brag about the vacations they had invited her on. And Therese hadn't gotten to know Wendy very well yet, but she didn't have the impression she was the yachting-in-the-Med type. Though, considering the play she was making for Adam, maybe she wanted to be.

Therese chided herself for the thought. Things were bad enough without her sliding into cheap misogyny. Adam was a charming, good-looking guy; there was no need to call anyone a gold digger.

And on the subject of relationships, one common element in a lot of mass killings was an aspect of domestic violence, and there was only one guest who had been in a relationship with one of the victims. At least, that was what he claimed. Aside from occasion-ally mentioning his "friend" in San Francisco, Oliver had never said anything about having a boyfriend. There could have been a lot of reasons for that, and that Oliver was being abused wasn't anywhere near the top of the list, but Therese had to consider all the possibilities.

She liked Joseph—from what little she had gotten to know of him, he seemed to be pleasant and intelligent, and of all the guests he had had one of the most sensible responses to their situation. (Namely, to focus on getting out.) But he was the one who had suggested they split up to search the house, and he had waited until Sonia was well past saving to mention his medical background. Therese couldn't imagine Joseph shoving Sonia over the railing and then sprinting away, the knife in his hand, but that didn't mean it couldn't have happened. Investigating a crime based on how you wanted things to be was a bad, if perennially popular, approach.

So what was a good one, then? If Therese was an investigator on this case, in a situation where she had access to none of the usual resources, what would her next steps be? Follow up on Sonia's last words by searching the area around the pictures, she supposed.

Then there was the question of the knife. Dried and dressed, Therese went to the window and looked down at the rain-soaked mountainside. It was certainly possible that the weapon was down there somewhere, tossed away by a person who was afraid of what it might tell about them. But if that was what had happened, it would have been the careless choice—the guests in the house might not be able to find it there, but a police search certainly would, and that was likely to happen once they finally were able to contact the authorities. The riskier, but ultimately more sensible, solution would have been to pick it up before pushing Sonia off the deck, then escape down the stairs to hide it somewhere on the property to be retrieved and disposed of later. There was still a chance it might be found, Therese thought, but it was probably better to assume it was gone for good, or at least for now.

So, while it was still fresh in her mind, Therese found a piece of paper and a pen and did her best to draw the knife from memory.

She started with the blade. Therese had not spent a lot of time over the last twenty years thinking about the details of the weapon that had been used that night—had put some effort into not thinking about it, in fact—but what she might have imagined wasn't that. The knife Sonia had shown them had been absurdly, impractically large, not a straightforward way of committing multiple murders, unless you thought you might also have to kill an elephant.

It took Therese a few attempts to draw the blade in the shape she remembered it—an inch and a half to two inches wide, curved but only at the end, with a deep channel running about halfway up the length. Hardly practical for any purpose—she wondered where it could have come from. The distinctive design might have been the reason the weapon had to be hidden, but in that case, why use it at all? There was no shortage of knives in the world.

Setting aside that question for the moment, she moved on to the design on the handle. This part she was less sure about: it had looked damaged, and she had been distracted by the blade, and the dirt and possible blood on it. But she had the impression it had been highly decorated at some point, with straps of fabric or leather wrapped in a crisscross pattern around metal studs. Again, an impractical and showy detail. Therese had a feeling there was something important there, but its meaning was just out of her reach.

She finished the drawing and held it up to examine it, remembering her ninth-grade art teacher's comment that she "lacks a clear sense of proportion." *You have no idea, Mr. McClinton*, she thought. But Therese thought the sketch would at least be enough to give her colleagues at the agency something to look into, if they were interested after all this time.

In fact, Therese hadn't been entirely honest with the others about her reasons for her choice of career, not that they needed to know. She loved her father, but she had never wanted a life like his, writing traffic tickets and rousting drunks from under the freeway. It was only when she met the agents who had come to interview her about the attack—which, in the post-9/11 moment it had happened, was initially thought to be a terrorist incident—that she realized there was more to law enforcement than the locker-room culture of her local PD. She wanted to wear a suit and ask every question like she already knew the answer, and after some work, that was what she did.

What she hadn't anticipated was how much the job was going to demand of her. Not in terms of time or effort—Therese had never been afraid to work hard, and she enjoyed most of it, aside from the paperwork. But where her colleagues were able to give their whole selves to the job, Therese always found herself holding back, resisting the idea that being an FBI agent was central to her identity.

That position, thought Therese, was already filled.

She studied the picture for a while longer, but there wasn't much more the sketch was able to tell her. It was an unusual-looking knife, but hardly so distinctive that it might lead straight to the killer, particularly not without the actual item in hand. The most interesting thing about it was that it had been in Sonia's possession. Interesting, at least, if you were going to assume Sean hadn't acted alone, because if he did, then there wasn't much to think about—Sonia really had killed herself, and they were all just waiting in the rain for someone to notice they hadn't been answering their cell phones. But if he had gotten the knife from the other killer, the one who set him up to die by suicide in jail, then he must have had other contact with that person.

And if he had left any evidence from those interactions behind, it might have ended up with his mother. How much had she known? Who had she told?

14

The oversized photos were printed on poster paper and glued onto cardboard backings. It took very little time for Therese to determine that there was nothing hidden on the wall behind them, and peeling up the corner of one to check for writing on the back of the sheet turned up nothing. She was moving on to the next one when Joseph came down the stairs.

"Already tearing up the place? I thought we would have a couple of days before we got to that point."

"Just checking to see if Sonia left anything here that might help us," Therese said. "She must have brought these and set them up, so there was a chance she might have used them to hide something. But no luck so far."

"Well, it was worth a try, I guess." He walked over and joined her in front of the photo she was holding, one of her, Oliver, and Chloe on the small couch in the cabin. "I haven't looked at these in a long time. God, he was cute. And so young."

"They all were. We all were." Therese wondered what Joseph was thinking. She had known Oliver was gay even before she had met him—he had founded his LGBT group during their sopho-more year, and he tried to get the school administration to give them Harvey Milk's birthday as a holiday. But his insinuations aside, he had never admitted to being actually involved with anyone, and the discovery that he was jarred her memory of him.

How much had she even really known these so-called friends of hers?

Of course, that was assuming that Joseph was telling the truth. Therese had no reason to believe he wasn't, but she wasn't in a very trusting place right now.

"How did you and Oliver meet?" she asked.

"At a Model UN event. His team was Poland; mine was Italy. We formed a politically inaccurate alliance over climate change and met up later for dinner. After that we hung out, talked all night. It was amazing." He looked back up at the picture of the smiling boy. "He was my first real boyfriend. I don't think either of us had any idea what we were doing, but that's kids for you."

"Why didn't I ever meet you? Were you guys long-distance or something?" Therese asked. What she really wanted to know was why Oliver had never mentioned him by name, but that seemed like a cruelty too far.

Still, Joseph didn't miss the question behind the question.

"Nope, I was just over in the city. I did come around to a hang out with Oliver's friends one time, might have been before you made the inner circle. Anyway, once was enough for me." He gave her a shrewd, appraising look. "I should probably watch what I'm saying here. Federal agents don't go around asking questions just to make conversation."

"I mean, sometimes we do. It's been at least a month since I arrested someone for lying to me at a party." Therese set the photo on a table and found a place to sit on the arm of a chair. "I'm not surprised you didn't like them. I didn't always get along very well with that group myself."

Joseph snorted in derision. "Right, I'm sure you were such an outsider. No, really, I am. I mean, I'm absolutely sure it seemed that way to you. But you're going to have to forgive me if I don't join the pity party for your white lady tears."

Therese opened her mouth to argue with him, to point out in detail how he had no idea what he was talking about, but she stopped herself. She wanted information here, and fighting wasn't going to get it for her. So she swallowed her anger, tamped down her suspicions, and kept her focus on her goal.

"Okay, so let's just say I understand that they could be jerks—we could be jerks—and then you can tell me what kind of jerks we were, and why you stayed with Oliver even though you hated all his best friends."

"Best friends! That's rich. And so were they, which was the problem. That was Oliver's big weakness—he loved money. Just being around people who had it—the things they bought, the places they went, that was his idea of living. And he'd put up with any kind of shit as long as he could keep that kind of access."

Questions or not, that was about all Therese was going to take.

Joseph might want to put his boyfriend on a pedestal, but her own memory painted Oliver in a different light. Not a ringleader like Jenna, or a bully like Josh, but always ready with a joke that really wasn't funny, or to undercut any moment of sincerity with his own acid cynicism. It wouldn't be kind to try and make Joseph see that after all this time, but that didn't mean she had to let his version of events go unchallenged.

"What shit was he putting up with? Everyone loved Oliver. He didn't get any of the—I don't know what he told you, but he was hardly an innocent bystander in that group."

Ignoring the chair next to Therese's, Joseph stayed standing, prowling around the entrance hall like he was looking for a way out, of the house or the conversation. But he stayed with it, turning on Therese with a ferocity that surprised her.

"No, he was just your performing dog. You want to know what he told me? How about the time you all dressed him up in one of Chloe's mom's suits and had him apply for a job at Walmart? Or when you sent him to buy tampons at the store where the guy he was crushing on worked? Or the necklace Jenna had him wear that said, 'My Gay'? God, that was humiliating. But he wore it, you know? Because it had diamonds in it. Tiny-ass fuckin' diamonds, and that was all it took for him to be that bitch's pet. You and your sad little story of them being mean to you, like that was the worst thing that could ever happen. And then you walked away, because you knew you could. That was a privilege you had, one he never got."

Therese reeled under the force of his anger. She remembered

the stories he was telling, either from being there or hearing about them after, but Joseph's version had no relation to her memories.

"Those were all fun things," she said, realizing as she heard the words how weak they sounded. "Oliver was in on all of it. He even had some of the ideas."

(Had he? Therese had believed so at the time, and for all the years after, but now that she tried to bring up an example the specifics were lacking.)

"Fun for you. He didn't fight it because he knew it was the price of admission. That night—" Joseph stopped and turned away from her for a moment, taking a deep breath. "It was that week he showed up wearing the necklace. I couldn't take it anymore; I said it was them or me. My parents had a place down by Big Sur, and they weren't there that weekend. I told him to meet me there...or I wasn't going to see him again."

Joseph looked back at Therese, his eyes wet. "It was a hell of a thing to say, wasn't it?"

"You couldn't have known," Therese said, but she wondered. Sonia must have had a reason for inviting Joseph here. Maybe it was just his relationship with Oliver, but maybe she had known something more. Something that suggested Joseph hadn't been content to lose his boyfriend to the people he hated without taking revenge on all of them.

Or maybe Therese was just upset that in Oliver's version of history, she was one of the bad guys. Of course, both could be true, Therese reminded herself.

"Hey, what are you guys up to out here? The party's just

getting started." Gil had come into the hall heading in the direction of the bathroom, but stopped when he saw Therese and Joseph.

"Party?" Therese said. "Really?"

"Well, the booze has everyone more relaxed anyway. We can't spend the whole time we're here being mad and talking about the past, can we?"

"I don't know," Joseph got up and walked past Gil toward the living room without looking back. "It works for me."

Back in the living room, the situation had actually developed into a party of sorts. A few more bottles had been added to the bar, and beers were lined up on the kitchen counter. Someone had found a stash of board games, which were scattered on the floor, and the pieces of a jigsaw puzzle were spread out on the coffee table. Adam and Victor were playing foosball, while Wendy looked on and offered suggestions, and Mike and Art stood looking out the window at the rain.

Joseph ignored them all and went back to the kitchen, leaving Therese at loose ends. Not interested in becoming part of the cheering section for the foosball game, she chose a seat near the puzzle and started sorting out pieces of sky.

"You like puzzles too?" Gil was back already, with damp hands and a spot of soap bubbles near his knuckle. Therese moved over to make space for him at the table.

"I used to do them some. I don't really have space in my current apartment." Therese found an edge piece that was a darker blue with a bit of cloud, consulted the box lid, and positioned it near the top-right corner. "I'm hoping we aren't here long enough to finish this one."

"Yeah, me too, of course. But we might as well get started, right?" Gil had grabbed a handful of pieces and tried to force two of them together. He picked up another one and examined it. "Looks like an eye. There's no eyes here, though. Must have gotten in by mistake. So, you live back east somewhere?"

"In DC, yes." While Gil was looking away, Therese took the discarded piece and attached it to another part of the wrought iron gate. "I've been there for about eight years now. Still not used to the humidity."

"Wow, yeah, I can't even imagine. I went to St. Louis in July once, and I pretty much died. I don't know why anyone would ever leave the West Coast. At least where I am in Washington, the summers aren't that bad."

"Well, some of us don't really have a choice." Realizing that was a potentially awkward statement, Therese went on. "My job, I mean. They don't give you a lot of options about where you're going to be assigned. I'm just happy to be able to stay in a city."

It was true enough, but her redirection wasn't successful.

"Things must have been pretty bad for you, after what happened. I heard—I mean, people were saying a lot of shit. Is that why your family moved away?"

"Part of it, yeah. Also the thing where Oliver's dad showed up drunk at our house with duct tape and a loaded gun. That was kind of a catalyst."

"Wow, really? I never heard about that," Gil said, his eyes wide with shock. "I guess that would be something. But you never wanted to come back?" he said.

"Come back to what?" Therese connected two sections of the top edge of the puzzle and centered it as best she could. "Everyone I knew in that town was either dead or thought I was a killer."

"Hey, what's this over here?" Finished with the latest game at the foosball table, Adam approached them, a drink in each hand. "Come on, this isn't a retirement home party. You guys are going to ruin my reputation."

"What reputation would that be?" Therese asked, trying to keep her tone lighthearted. She still wasn't entirely comfortable with the idea of treating their situation as a house party, but it seemed to be the way the others were dealing with the captivity for now. And anyway, with the way Gil was trying to fit a piece of what was clearly the lake into her section of sky, it was all she could do to not grab it out of his hand and put it down where it belonged.

"Don't you know?" Gil said. "Adam is our own homegrown party king. Like the guy in the book, with the light and the pool and stuff."

Adam laughed. "That was just a magazine writer who let their imagination run away with them. I promise, I'm no Jay Gatsby, of Northern California or anywhere else."

"But you do throw the occasional party?" Therese looked at her empty whiskey glass and decided she had better have some water instead. She got up and headed to the kitchen, leaving Gil to puzzle over the puzzle.

"Well, yes, but it's part of my business," Adam explained as he followed her. "I do a lot of fundraising, setting organizations up with companies that can provide exclusive experiences for their donors. It's a very social industry."

"I'll bet." To Therese, who would rather do just about anything other than get dressed up and spend an evening making small talk in uncomfortable shoes, it sounded like a nightmare of a job, but to each their own.

Aloud, she said, "To be honest, I'm surprised that you have a job at all. From the way Jenna used to talk, she didn't seem to think she was ever going to have to work."

"That sounds like Jenna all right. She always had some pretty grand ideas of our family money," Adam said. "Fair enough, back then I didn't think a career was going to be in my future either. But after Dad died and I sold the business, what with the taxes and everything, it turned out there wasn't as much in the pot as we all thought. I mean, I'm not complaining," he said, waving generally at their surroundings. "Plenty of people have it worse. You just never know how life is going to go, you know?"

"Yeah, I know." Therese looked out the kitchen window as she filled her glass from the sink. One of the blackened trees caught her eye, rigid in the wind as the green branches around it waved. "Looks like you had a fire here at some point?" she asked.

Adam nodded.

"Oh yeah, that was a couple of years ago. Really lucky the fire crews managed to save the house. It was started by dry lightning, about a mile uphill from here." He smiled at her and got a glass of water for himself. "At least that's one thing we can be grateful for this storm for—not much chance of a wildfire."

"That's one way of looking at the bright side," Therese agreed, when there was a crash from the other side of the kitchen.

"That is enough! If I hear one more word out of you, you're going to be the next person down that cliff, so help me God."

———

Joseph was standing on the far side of the kitchen island, holding a dripping colander and facing off against Mike and Art. The policeman and the prison guard had a beer each and a shared expression of dislike on their faces, though Art's was tinged with discomfort while Mike's leaned toward belligerence.

"All I'm saying is, if that kid Sean did it for someone else, maybe they seduced him. And he didn't seem like a really manly kid, you know? So I thought the boss man here might have some thoughts about that. You know about seducing kids, right?"

"Whoa, dude, take it easy." Gil left the puzzle behind and got to Mike just as he was reaching across the counter to try and grab Joseph's shirt. The size difference was such that Gil handled him easily, spinning the smaller man away from the kitchen and placing himself between Mike and Joseph. The prison guard made a move like he was going to try to lunge at him, but Gil stared him down from a good six inches above his head, and he backed off, grumbling.

Therese turned to Mike.

"What the hell is wrong with you? You think there's some kind of trophy for the biggest asshole here?"

"I'd say he has something on his mind," Joseph said, setting down the colander with exaggerated calmness. "Like, maybe he knows we're all thinking he had a part in helping Sean kill himself, and he kept evidence away from the police to cover his own ass. Something like that, anyway."

"Oh great, look at this. The queer has got me all figured out. I guess that really puts me in my place!" Mike looked around for anyone to join in his laughter, but got nothing.

Even Art was shaking his head as he placed a hand on the other man's shoulder. "Listen, buddy, dial it back, okay? We're going to get out of here soon, and then you never have to deal with any of these folks again. Nobody's got anything on you. Just relax, have another beer, and let's forget about this whole deal."

Unfortunately, Mike was past the point of being soothed, even by beer.

"Nobody's got anything on me, huh? Like I'm the problem? Yeah, but what if maybe I have something on them? What about that?" He stepped back from the kitchen island, looking at each of the other guests in turn, as though daring them to accept his unspecified challenge. No one did.

"Yeah, you're all a bunch of pussies. I don't even want to waste my time." And with that he turned and left the room, grabbing a bottle off the bar on his way.

The rest of them waited in silence until he was fully out of the room.

"So," Victor said at last. "What are we doing for dinner?"

THE BOYFRIEND

Well, that was embarrassing. Joseph busied himself over the stove, hiding his face so no one could see his anger. He'd been dealing with people like Mike for about as long as he could remember. The guy was a piece of shit, but not in any kind of new way. Normally, Joseph would have been able to brush him off, along with his string of unoriginal insults. But normally he wasn't trapped in a mountain lodge with a bunch of strangers, with a dead body in the basement and giant pictures of Oliver by the front door. There were too many memories, and this was exactly the wrong time and place to try and process them.

Joseph almost laughed. What else was there to do here, except remember? He thought back over the conversation with Therese, wondering what had possessed him to tell her that much. Part of it had been her own revelation, the way she had been expecting them to fall all over themselves at her little story of average high school bullying. As if that was going to impress him, after the sort of shit he had been through. *Some girls called you fat? Cry me a goddamn river*, Joseph thought.

Not that he was entirely without sympathy. Joseph knew enough about adolescent psychology to be familiar with the way relatively minor traumas could carry forward into adulthood, and the fact that the event had been immediately followed by her friends' deaths and her own accidental survival was enough to warp anyone's memory. But Joseph didn't feel like being fair and professional right now. Just the knowledge that this woman had been going through her life believing she had been the one who really suffered, without ever thinking for a moment what she had participated in doing to Oliver, to him, was enough to make him irrationally angry.

And there it was, the anger again. Joseph took a deep breath and focused on stirring the pot on the stove with smooth, controlled strokes. That was his own stress response at work, driving him to lash out as a way of avoiding the fact that he had very little control over his current situation. It was normal, expected even, but it wasn't productive. The anger was of no use to him here, no matter how justified it was.

Step away from the past, Joseph told himself. Everything that had happened with Oliver—the good and the bad, the choices he made, and the way they led to his death—those things mattered, and they always would, but he couldn't let them consume him. Not this time.

He had a life that was his own, with a husband and kids who needed him. They were his priority now. And that meant that Joseph's focus needed to be on doing what he needed to get back to them, back to the way things were for him now, whatever it took.

He tasted the soup and reached for the salt. Not bad, considering what he had to work with. The rest of them would probably complain about it, but at least he'd have something to eat that he liked. Right now was a good time for Joseph to be thinking about taking care of himself.

THE DETECTIVE

A rt hunted around in the cooler until he found one of the remaining Bud Lights. Nobody drank regular beer anymore, just that expensive garbage with the fancy labels. Not that he was against trying some different things; he'd have a Heineken if there was nothing else, and every once in a while when he was in the mood, he'd order a Guinness. But that was as far as any real man needed to go.

This was an ugly situation. He sipped the foam off the top of the bottle and looked around the room. If he had known… But he hadn't known, and that was that. No point beating himself up about it now. The thing he had to worry about was how he was going to get out of this, and what he was going to do after he did. Sonia dying had been unfortunate, obviously. It was going to mean a lot of attention back on that old case, and on his personal history, which he didn't need. That Chinese girl sure hadn't taken long to bring it up, had she? Like she knew anything about it—like anyone did. There was no justice in this damn world.

He took his beer and retreated to the other side of the living room.

This wasn't the sort of place he would have chosen for a vacation. Art's tastes ran more to beachside bars and jet ski rentals, and the kind of restaurants where you knew all the waitresses would be wearing a smile and a bikini top. Not a bunch of rich pricks looking at trees, or whatever they did up here.

And that wasn't even getting into the people he was stuck here with. Art looked up from his beer to see if any of them were paying attention to him, but they had all gone back to their own conversations. Not that he wanted to talk to any of them anyway. Especially not now, with them all thinking they knew all about him, and what happened with Donnie and his idiot wife. He could try to explain, but they'd never understand—that Donnie was a good guy, a good cop, and that wife of his wouldn't stop doing things to make him mad. Of course Donnie shouldn't have done it, but he didn't deserve to go to jail just for making a mistake. And Art always looked after his own; he took pride in that. He didn't regret sticking his neck out for his guy, and he knew the rest of them appreciated it.

The good ones, anyway. Then there were the cops like Brewer, and this Fed daughter of his, who seemed to think they knew better. They didn't, of course; they just got in the way. The only good thing that had come out of that whole mess with the dead kids was that Brewer had taken his family and moved away, and Art hadn't had to deal with him anymore. Good riddance.

And now here was Brewer's daughter, all grown up and acting like she owned the place. It was damned annoying she had been the one who found him down the hillside like that. Climbing on those ropes had looked so easy when she did it, and now she had a funny story to tell all the rest of them.

Not that Art cared what any of these people thought of him. Mike was the only person here who would even understand, and that idiot kept making things worse by running his mouth.

Art took a swig from his beer and thought back to the last time he had seen the prison guard. They had been wrapping up the investigation into the Fletcher kid's death, which in Art's mind should have been the end of the whole thing. Dumb kid gets mad at his popular classmates and goes crazy and kills them and himself. That was what Art had thought then, and he didn't see why it couldn't have happened that way. But the media was all over it, and the brass wanted something better, so he had gone back one more time to talk to Mike, to try and find out if there was anything about the package the kid had gotten that could help them.

There wasn't. The guard had a lawyer, and he wouldn't say anything more than he had included in his original statement—a box had arrived, and he took it to the kid's cell. He didn't know who had brought it, or why he had broken protocol by delivering it. It was just something that had happened. But as Art was walking him out, the lawyer had gotten a phone call, and they had been alone for a minute. And Mike had asked, just kind of like he was thinking out loud, "I bet there were a lot of people who wanted that kid dead, right? Even if you could find someone who did, it wouldn't mean much." And Art had asked him what he meant, but the lawyer came back, and Mike didn't say anything more.

Art hadn't done anything about it at the time. Why should he? The case was over. But now he wondered.

15

In the end, dinner was relatively uneventful. From the contents of the refrigerator and the pantry, Joseph and Lorelei produced a lentil and vegetable soup, a casserole, and a loaf of soda bread. Everyone ate in the lounge, posing awkwardly with plates and bowls in laps, rather than go back into the dining room, which had become forbiddingly dark as night fell and the storm closed in.

The dinnertime conversation avoided their current situation or any murders, recent or otherwise. Instead, talk turned to more conventional topics, to pets and children and jobs. Wendy was enthusiastic about the position she had just started as an internal auditor for a hospital system, and Victor less so about his career in property management. Art was retired, with one daughter who was a nurse in Spokane, and another living with his ex-wife and working part-time as a mechanic. The only other parent was Joseph, with a pair of four-year-old twin boys who were tearing up the Boston preschool art scene. For some reason, that reminded

Wendy of her corgis, and she searched all her pockets for her phone to show their pictures before remembering it was currently in thousands of pieces scattered across the hillside.

That put a damper on the party for a while, as they all thought about how much they might have lost and when was the last time they backed up their devices.

"I still can't figure out what she thought she was going to achieve," Gil said, when it was clear they weren't going to stay off the topic any longer. "Was she really going to set that bomb off with all of us in here? What would have happened?"

"Nothing good," Art grunted into his soup. "Maybe she really was suicidal."

Wendy set aside her empty plate and looked across to the picture windows. "It wouldn't have brought the whole house down though, would it? I mean, this is a lot bigger than—you know, the other place." Wendy seemed flustered by mentioning the cabin where her friend died, which seemed strange for someone who claimed to have kept binders on the event. Maybe her own brush with death had made an impression, Therese thought.

"You're right," said Adam, who seemed less interested in Wendy's embarrassment than her question. "I had a structural engineer out here a couple of years ago for the insurance, and he said the foundation is beyond solid. Not that I'd like to try it, but I think it would take more than what she had in that pot to do any serious damage. Of course, Sonia might not have known that."

"Why do you think he did it?" Joseph asked. "Her son, Sean,

I mean. Even this idea that there was someone else involved, why would he go along with it? Did any of you know him?"

Victor helped himself to another piece of soda bread and nodded. "I knew him a bit, from Cub Scouts," he said through a full mouth. "Me and him and Josh were all in the same troop. Weird kid, kind of quiet. Always had these big ideas of things he was going to do that never worked. Like, he was going to have a business selling pictures of superheroes he drew on his computer, or he would get a million Legos somehow and build a huge tower in his backyard that everyone would pay to come and see. Except his drawings were crap, and even if he could buy all those Legos, why would anybody care? And he pretended like his dad was a rich doctor, but everyone knew he just sold eyeglasses at the mall."

Victor stopped himself, possibly realizing that he sounded like he was endorsing the bullying, and had the decency to look embarrassed.

"Anyway, I guess people were kind of mean to him," he went on. "But it's not like he was the only kid who ever got laughed at. And the stuff he talked about, what did he expect?"

Joseph gave him a hard look. "Were any of those mean kids in the cabin that night?" he asked.

Victor shrugged. "I don't know, maybe? Probably Josh had some jokes, but it was a long time ago. And anyway, Josh was only in the Scouts for one year, because he got caught bringing a girlie magazine on a campout. I quit the den in middle school, so I sort of lost track of Sean, and I don't know if anyone in that cabin had ever done anything to him. But, you know," he said, looking at Therese. "They were the type."

"That was your theory, wasn't it?" Wendy asked Art. "A bullied boy goes crazy and kills the popular kids? That's why you arrested him."

Art glared at her. "Sure, and his car was spotted at the scene, and we found the bomb-building materials in his room," he replied sullenly. "Just some stupid cops making assumptions. Look, Sean Fletcher had the means, motive, and opportunity. Why does everyone need to make this more complicated than it is? And how was this mystery person supposed to have made him help them anyway?"

Gil had been quiet for most of the conversation, staring into his beer bottle like it was a window back in time.

"Do you remember when the equipment shed at the soccer field for the elementary school burned down? That was about six months before it happened, wasn't it? There was a lot of talk and theories, but I don't think they ever found out who did it. I remember Chris talking about it; he'd been supposed to referee a game there that weekend, and they were scrambling to find another field. The cops never followed up on it, but some of the neighbors said they heard something that sounded like fireworks that night." Gil frowned as he spoke, like he was working through the possibilities out loud. "What if it was Sean?"

"Doing a test run before he killed someone? Like how serial killers start small and keep escalating?" asked Wendy.

"Or he did it just because. Teenage boys do dumb shit

sometimes," said Therese, with her more experienced perspective. "But what if the other killer found out and used it to blackmail him into helping them?"

Adam looked up from his soup and raised an eyebrow. "To commit murder, just to avoid a suspension? Come on, I don't think he could have been that crazy."

But Gil wasn't giving up on his theory that easily. "No, but what if Sean didn't know what it was for?" he said. "This other person could have told him it was a prank, a bigger version of the shed thing. And then when he sees what actually happened, he realizes he's in up to his neck, so he panics and confesses."

"That actually makes sense," Therese said. "Then the other killer smuggles him the rope and convinces Sean to use it to kill himself. They couldn't take the chance of him breaking down and giving them away. And him being dead put a nice little bow on the story—all over, nothing to see here."

That got Art's attention.

"Okay, come on. You may not have much of an opinion of us local cops, but your precious Feds were on the case too. You think they just walked away when the kid died?"

Therese started to answer, but Gil beat her to it.

"They didn't find out anything more, did they? None of you did. I remember my aunt Rachel calling her senator, the governor, everyone she could think of, trying to get the investigation to start again so she could get some justice for Chris. Once you let her go"—Gil gestured to Lorelei—"it was like you just ran out of ideas. That's why some of us thought you were protecting someone." He looked at Therese, and she could feel her face getting hot.

With some effort, Therese managed to keep her voice level.

"A lot of people thought that. I don't know if you're aware, but some of the FBI files were released in a public records request a couple of years ago. They did a thorough job of exploring the possibility that I was the killer, and they didn't come up with anything." The material the agency had released had been heavily redacted and generally uninformative, but it had clarified a couple of incidents from after her family had moved to Florida, which at the time had left her confused and her father quietly furious.

She could have gone on, explained all of the avenues the investigators had explored and the ways they had come up empty, but Art jumped in.

"You know, Gil, someone with a record like yours doesn't have much business talking about law enforcement," he said viciously. "If we're talking about boys and violence, maybe you have something to add?"

"What's that got to do with anything?" Gil said, suddenly sullen. "Because I made some dumb mistakes as a kid, I can't ask questions?"

Art snorted. "Oh, so it was just a mistake when you brought that gun to school? Or called in those bomb threats? I wasn't going to say anything, because you seem like you grew up okay, but if we're talking about people's pasts, then I think the others here have a right to know." Art sat up straight in his chair. The rest of the guests stared in silence.

"I remember that," Victor said. "I'd graduated, but my little brother was in school then, and they locked the whole place down. My mom totally freaked out, wouldn't let him go anywhere for like a month."

"It was just an air gun," Gil said, his voice rising. "I wasn't going to hurt anyone. I couldn't have. I was just… Things weren't great for me then."

Art smirked across the table at him. "Got better in juvie, did they? Used to be they'd go easy on boys like you, and look what good that did? Kids killing people all over the place."

"I didn't kill anyone! Not—" Gil stopped to grope for the words.

"Not then?" Wendy completed it for him. "Is that what you were going to say?"

"No!" Gil jumped up from his seat at the table, looking wild. Instinctively, Therese braced herself, ready to get to her feet and trying to make eye contact with the angry young man. "I never did anything! I only thought—I think lots of things. But nobody ever got hurt!"

"It's okay; we know that." Lorelei literally stepped in to stop the fight, carefully folding her napkin by her plate before going over to lay her hand on Gil's arm. "You had a rough time, I bet. I've seen the inside of a couple of juvenile halls, and it's not something I would wish on anyone." Here she gave Art a significant look. "But you said you didn't hurt anyone, and we believe it."

If anyone disagreed, they kept it to themselves. Between the shock of Lorelei taking control and the lingering fear from Gil's outburst, no one seemed inclined to argue. Lorelei sighed. "It's been a long day, and the alcohol isn't helping. I think this is a good time for all of us to go to bed, and we can decide what we're going to do next in the morning. Everything looks better in the morning."

It was too early for Therese to go to sleep, but she didn't mind the bedtime order. She needed the space to think and to plan for an increasingly unnerving set of possible futures.

She had left the heat off in her room, a leftover habit of her money-saving childhood, and it had gotten uncomfortably chilly. Therese turned up the thermostat and went to lower the blinds, to insulate against the cold air that radiated off the giant windows. Before she closed them, though, she stopped and looked out into the storm.

The visibility had been poor in the daylight, and now it was nearly nil. Heavy gray mist crowded up against the glass, which creaked under the force of the wind that was driving the rain against it.

Peering down into the darkness, she thought about the spot where Sonia had landed after she fell. If there had ever been any evidence to be recovered from the site, there was no chance of it now. But someone would have to look; Therese would make sure of that.

Therese stepped away from the window and considered how she would describe the thinking of the woman who had brought them all here. Sonia's plans, bizarre as they were, were almost laughably simple: gather a collection of people with connections to the murders, trap them in a remote house, present them with her accusations, and wait for the results.

Unfortunately, she hadn't had to wait long.

Therese tried to see it the way Sonia might have. She had had twenty years to stew on the wrong that had allegedly been done to her son, to come up with her own narrative of not only what had happened, but what would happen if she had the opportunity to set it right. So blinded by anger and grief that she couldn't see the reality outside of her fantasy, one that had at least one person in it who had a deadly interest in preventing her from achieving her goals.

Sonia had put all her cards on the table, not knowing or caring what kind of player she was up against. But that wasn't Therese's game. No one needed to know about the dead woman's last words, at least not until Therese had figured them out for herself. Only Gil had even been aware that Sonia had said anything at all, and he had seemed fine with her explanation.

Except…Therese had been doing a lot of thinking about how Sonia had underestimated the person she was up against. Maybe it was time to take her own advice.

She left her room, closing the door softly behind her and staying alert. The rest of the house was quiet and dark.

She found what she was looking for in the formal dining room, where ten heavy armchairs were arranged around the table. She chose the one nearest to the door and picked it up, staggering for a moment under the weight. Getting it upstairs was a struggle, with the legs of the chair bouncing off every other step and her arms screaming in protest, but she hurried on, hoping no one would hear the noise and ask what she was doing.

Back in her room, she locked and checked the door, then wedged the chair under the handle. With her suitcase added as a brace, and her book club book to keep her company for as long as she could manage to stay awake, Therese retreated to the bed, to see what the night would bring.

16

The storm was no better in the morning. If anything, it was worse, with a scattering of hail interrupting the sound of the rain on the roof. Therese listened to it for as long as she could bear it, and she was about to try and drown out the noise with the shower when she heard the interior lock on the shared bathroom catch and the water go on. Unwilling to appear in public until she had at least brushed her teeth, Therese settled back in to wait and hope Wendy wasn't the sort to linger in the shower.

Forty-five minutes and three chapters later, she set the book down just before the giant mosquitoes were about to attack Mardi Gras, and let herself into the damp and steamy room, determined to talk to Susan about her choices if she ever made it to another book club meeting.

The smell of perfume in the bathroom air and the pile of makeup-smudged tissues in the trash provided clues about what had taken so much time, as well as where Wendy's mind might be focused. Unsure of how much hot water was left, Therese did her best to be efficient and tried not to wish she had packed something more glamorous than ChapStick.

Most of the guests were already in the lounge when Therese finally made it downstairs. As she passed through the dining room, she noticed that she wasn't the only person who had had the idea to supplement their room security—now a second chair was missing from the table.

After the hostilities of the previous night, Therese had been worried that the tension might flare up again, but a collective gloom had settled over the party, and no one seemed to have the energy to fight. It helped that neither Art nor Mike had appeared yet; without them a lot of the anger had left the group, at least on the surface.

"Breakfast?" Joseph asked. "We found some oatmeal that looks like it's been here for a while, and I'm taking my chances on the milk and sugar. She can't have poisoned everything, right?"

"I hope not. Things are bad enough, us having to eat plain oatmeal."

"Death before blandness?" Adam said, handing Therese one of the two coffee mugs he was holding. "Can't say I disagree with that as a philosophy." Despite the seriously depleted level of the bottle on the counter behind him, he wasn't showing any damage. In fact, in his outfit of dark-wash jeans and a chunky cable-knit sweater, he looked ready to shoot an ad campaign for something manly yet sensitive—cologne, maybe, or low-calorie beer.

Wendy, on the other hand, was clearly feeling the effects of the whiskey. Looking at her glazed expression and the circles under

her eyes, Therese had more sympathy for the time in the bathroom and the makeup.

Not that she had been entirely wrong about Wendy's inten-
tions. Hangover or no hangover, she served herself a bowl of the
oatmeal and took it over to the end of the kitchen island, where
Adam was sipping his coffee.

"When do you think the storm will end?" she asked him, her
eyes fixed on his face as she took a dainty bite of the porridge.

Adam shook his head. "I couldn't tell you. We hardly ever get
rain like this so late in the year. Usually by this time, we'd be loading
up the water skis and heading to the lake. That is, if we had a car."

He laughed and Wendy giggled along. Therese would have
taken this chance to remind herself that she absolutely did not
care, but at that moment Adam caught her eye, and suddenly she
was smiling.

She was thinking about going over to interrupt them, just to
see what would happen, when Gil was suddenly blocking her path.

"Hey," he said. "Can I talk to you?"

"You already are. What's up?"

Gil flushed. "I just wanted to say I'm sorry. Last night, when
I was talking about thinking the cops were covering for you—I
didn't mean that. This whole thing has brought up a lot of stuff
for me, and I think I'm lashing out."

Therese could recognize therapy talk when she heard it,
and she wondered how much was a result of his time in juvenile
detention. More likely a condition of his release, she thought, or
an attempt by his parents to keep it from happening again.

"I get it," she said, avoiding what part it was she thought she got. "I've been hearing variations on that theme for the last twenty years. It's just one of the things people say when they talk about the case."

Gil started to protest, but Therese shrugged it off.

"I said we should be suspicious of everyone, and I meant it. Anyway, not that it matters, but Art and my father couldn't stand each other. No amount of cop solidarity would have made him stick his neck out for a member of my family."

Joseph and Victor were both listening to them, and Therese might have elaborated on that point for everyone's benefit, but Art came into the room, and it was time to change the subject.

"Is this damn rain ever going to stop?"

"Probably," said Lorelei, who was already on her second bowl of oatmeal, slurping it noisily through the gaps in her teeth. "It always has before."

Art was not interested in philosophy.

"Yeah, well, sooner rather than later would be nice. I'm not planning to spend another night in this place."

"I guess we could consider walking it today. It's early enough, anyway," Joseph said, but he didn't sound enthusiastic about the idea.

Wendy made a face. "Out in that? Not me."

"I don't think any of us are looking forward to the trek," Adam said genially. "But Joseph is right. If anyone is going, they had better get started soon to be sure to make it to the main road before dark."

Victor looked up from the puzzle. "I still think it's an

unnecessary risk. We're safe here, and it's only gonna be another day tops before somebody figures out something's happened and comes looking. I know if my mom tries texting me, and I don't reply in under an hour, she'll call."

That turned the conversation to people's texting habits and social media use, and they talked for a while about who each of them knew who would be the first to realize they were out of contact, and do something about it. Therese stayed out of the conversation. There were people in her life and, more importantly, her job who would notice she was gone and would be able to track her down eventually, but if she was going to rely on that to get out of here today, then she would be better off walking.

There was part of her that wanted to do just that, head out the door and keep going until she got to the highway. In a lot of ways, it was the sensible choice, to get away from a place where one person had already died, reconnect with the outside world, and bring in the authorities.

She could, but she couldn't. The first reason was her job. As a federal agent on the scene of a presumed crime, with no other law enforcement available, Therese had a professional responsibility to do her best to preserve the evidence and protect the civilians until such a time as the local authorities could take over. Which meant, barring severe and immediate personal risk, she wasn't going anywhere.

And it wasn't just that, or her honest concern for the other people who were trapped with her. Those were the things she could point to if anyone asked her why she hadn't taken the first opportunity to get herself out of this place. But Therese had another more selfish reason to stay put. Coming here, Therese's main idea had been to try and push back against the narrative that had defined her throughout her life as the girl who ran away. If she did it again, no matter how reasonable or sensible the decision was, that would be the story, and as long as anyone wanted to talk about her, that would be what they said.

So she was staying. But that didn't mean no one else could go. The conversation had moved on to a discussion of whether rental car companies will call the police on you if you don't return on time, which she was about to interrupt with some suggestions, when Gil stopped midsentence and looked around.

"Speaking of going missing, has anyone seen Mike? It's getting late, and if we're going to make any decisions, we should probably at least let him know."

Nobody looked very enthusiastic about the suggestion.

"I guess someone could go knock on his door or something," Adam said reluctantly.

"Really?" said Joseph. "Why can't we just let sleeping jerks lie? As far as I'm concerned, he can sulk up there as long as he wants."

Therese shook her head. "I don't like him either, but Gil's right. Besides, can you imagine what an ass he's going to be if we make plans without including him? We might as well bite the bullet now and save ourselves the trouble later."

She didn't add anything about the feeling of uneasiness that was creeping over her.

Art was nominated as the person most likely to rouse the

former prison guard without starting another fight, but when he refused, Gil volunteered for the job.

"It was my idea anyway," he explained. "All I'm going to do is knock on the door and see if he wants any breakfast while it's still warm. He can't get too mad about that."

Therese wasn't so sure, but it was worth a try. She almost suggested she should go with him, but she couldn't come up with a good reason for why.

She regretted that decision ten minutes later, when Gil returned to the living room, looking concerned.

"I knocked on his door a bunch of times, and he didn't answer. Do you think we should do something?"

This time Therese didn't hesitate. Gil was barely done speaking before she headed for the stairs. If her feeling was wrong, the others could mock her as much as they liked.

Gil was right behind her, and he stood by as Therese pounded on the door.

"Mike?" she called in her best federal agent voice. "We need to talk to you. Can you come to the door, please?"

She pressed her ear against the wood to listen for any sound of movement, but the door was so heavy, she wasn't sure she would have been able to hear anything if there was. She tried the handle, but it was locked.

"Are we going to have to break it down?" Gil asked.

"I don't know. I hope not." Therese knocked on the door again, registering its weight. The hinges were on the inside, so they couldn't remove it that way. "How are you at picking locks?"

Gil flushed. "I don't… I've never done that. I saw a video once."

"Yeah, I think I saw the same video." Therese crouched down and squinted into the lock, but it offered her no hints.

By then the other guests had filtered into the hallway, joining them around the door.

"Do you really think something happened to him?" Wendy asked. "Maybe he's just sleeping late."

"Maybe," Therese agreed. "And if he is, I'll be happy to be wrong. But I think we need to find out."

"How?" Joseph asked. "You're going to need a battering ram to get through that thing."

Adam looked up and down the hall.

"I think this room should have a connecting door to that one," he said, pointing to the next door along. "Those aren't as strong; it should be easier to get through."

"That's my room," said Victor. "I don't remember any door?"

But Victor's memory was faulty, because there was one, and unlike the main door in the hall, it was thin and light, making a hollow sound when Therese tapped on it. There was still no response from the other side.

There was no lock on the door, just a sliding latch. Art, Gil, and Adam were searching the room for things to use to break it down while Victor desperately argued to protect his possessions, and Wendy and Joseph stood back and critiqued his luggage. Only Lorelei remained with Therese at the door, and she looked at her and smiled.

"Might as well try, right?"

"Just what I was thinking." Therese slid back the lock and turned the handle, and it opened easily.

———

The light in Mike's room was off and the blinds were closed tight, but even before her eyes adjusted to the darkness, Therese knew that something was very wrong. The bedclothes were mussed, but the bed was empty. The air in the room was heavy and stale, with a sour smell that made her wrinkle her nose.

The first thing that drew her eyes to the closet door was that the other chair from the dining room was next to it, tipped over on the floor. Then, as she came further into the room and her vision cleared, Therese realized that what was hanging over the door wasn't a pile of clothes.

"Looks like we found Mike," she said.

17

Art insisted on cutting Mike down and trying first aid, even though it was obvious nothing could be done. The former prison guard's body was cold and stiff, his open eyes bulging out of his blue face. Once he was laid out on the bed, the hopelessness of the situation was clear, and even Art quit his half-hearted attempts at revival.

Mike was dressed in what must have been standard sleepwear for him—old sweatpants and a worn-through T-shirt. Both were stained and crumpled, but Therese was grateful, at least, for that level of modesty. What little hair he had was spiky with long-dried sweat, and his slack lips showed a set of badly stained teeth. Oddly, though, death hadn't seemed to diminish him in size. If anything, lying peacefully on the bed, he looked taller than the five-foot-six Therese had guessed for him. Maybe it was the effect of her feelings of guilt for not having prevented his death, but it was the best she was going to be able to do by way of a eulogy.

Therese stepped away from the bed and went back to examine the scene at the closet. The rope looked familiar, and it only took a moment to recognize it as a piece of the climbing rope she had used the day before. The end was frayed, and it was tied to the handle on the inside of the closet door with a simple square knot. Being careful not to touch anything, she examined the length of the rope where it had gone over the door, but there was no sign of damage to either, like you might expect if the weight of a grown man had suddenly put tension on the cord and, in his death throes, shifted it along the top of the door.

The chair was lying in front of the closet, positioned like it had fallen there when Mike pushed it out from under him, though Therese doubted that. She knew how heavy those chairs were and it wouldn't be easy to topple one while standing on it. The whole thing had very much the impression of a stage set, though she didn't know who it was supposed to convince.

Wendy said, "I guess he could have hung himself?" But even she didn't sound like she thought much of the idea, and was only saying it in hopes that someone might agree with her. No one did.

"He could have," Therese allowed, leaving aside her observations. "But two convenient suicides is two more than I'm willing to believe in."

The other guests were standing around in clusters, looking shocked and frightened, and she wished she could think of something reassuring to say to them. All she could manage was, "Let's all try not to touch anything, okay? It'll make things easier down the line."

She didn't clarify who it would be easier for.

"But the door was locked," Wendy said. "How would someone get in?"

"The hallway door was locked," Adam corrected. "The connecting door was only latched on the other side."

Lorelei nodded. "He's right. Therese opened it right up, no problem."

All the eyes in the room turned toward Victor, who was slowly backing toward the door in question.

"What, you think I did it? That's crazy; I never met the guy before this weekend. Why would I want to kill him?"

"Why would anyone?" Gil said. "But he's dead, and you're the only person who could have gotten in here."

"Oh yeah, what about…?" Victor looked around wildly for other options. "What about the window? Or the other key? We've all got two keys now, right? What if someone got one of his?"

They were both decent suggestions, and they were enough to distract the conversation, at least for a while. The room was on the mountain side of the building, so the windows were smaller and closer to the ground than the ones in Therese's room. It wasn't impossible that someone could have gotten in through one of them, but they were all firmly latched on the inside, and the dust on the sills was undisturbed.

The answer to the key question was equally unproductive. Both the keys on the dresser fit the door lock, which showed no signs of having been tampered with.

"Someone could have swapped those," Victor said. "Nobody's

been looking while we've been in here. Or maybe Mike let them in and locked the door after they left."

"Except that he was dead then," Therese pointed out. "How heavy of a sleeper are you?"

"I mean, pretty good, I guess. You think someone could have come through my room, and I didn't hear them?" Victor was clearly considering the value of this as an alibi, and looked to be ready to elaborate on it.

"That, or if he really did knock the chair over himself, it would have made some noise. I don't know if any of you have tried to lift one of those dining room chairs, but they're pretty heavy," Therese said.

"I don't know, I could have—" Victor halted, caught between the twin desires to suggest someone could have made it past him, and that he had heard something to suggest Mike's death had in fact been suicide.

"I don't know," he finished. "But I didn't kill him!"

"Well, somebody must have." Gil had edged closer to the body and was peering at it. "Look at how messed up his hands and neck are." Gil pointed to the broken nails and the scratches on the man's throat, around the spot where the rope had bitten. "If he was fighting, that means it wasn't his choice to do it, right?"

Joseph stepped forward and cast a professional eye over the injuries. "Not necessarily," he said. "A lot of the time, with suicides, the body does everything it can to live, even if the brain has other ideas. And it's pretty common for someone to change their mind once the reality of what they've done sets in."

He straightened up and looked around at the other guests, who were listening to his explanation with varying degrees of skepticism. "Not that I think he killed himself. I'm not crazy. Which is why I'm getting out of here right now."

With that, he turned and left the room.

Joseph's departure barely seemed to register with the other guests, though Therese resolved to catch up with him and find out his plans. But that could wait. While Victor argued with Wendy and Gil about what he could or couldn't have heard or done, she prowled around the room, trying to commit as many of the details as possible to memory.

It was smaller than her room, and without the picture windows, the space felt dark and enclosed. Mike had not been a tidy man; the floor was scattered with crumpled shirts and underwear, and his shorts were draped over the end of the bed. The bedside table held an empty whiskey bottle but no glass.

Unlike Therese's room, Mike's had its own bathroom, and since the door was open, she peered inside. It was dirty too, to a degree that was almost impressive considering they had only been there for two days, but if there were any clues in the body hairs in the sink or the tissues on the floor, it would be up to someone other than Therese to find them.

She came back into the bedroom to find the rest of the guests staring at her, like they expected that she would have found the answer in the toilet tank. Even Art looked like he wouldn't mind being told what to do just then, but unfortunately she didn't have anything to suggest beyond the obvious.

"We all need to clear out now," she said. "At this point the best thing we can do is to leave this room alone so we don't contaminate the scene any more than we already have."

"We're going to leave the body here?" Wendy didn't look happy with the idea, and frankly neither did anyone else. "We could put it downstairs, you know, with the other one."

Therese shook her head. "No. Sonia died outside, and we needed somewhere safe to put her body, so moving it into the basement was the best option. But just being uncomfortable with having his body near us isn't a good enough reason to move Mike all that distance."

Therese was making an effort to say their names, even as her brain was already trying to assign Sonia and Mike the roles of Body One and Body Two. (Or was it Six and Seven?)

"Anyway," she went on. "Maybe it won't be for that long. I think we should go find Joseph and see what he has in mind."

—

As they filed out into the hallway, Therese caught up with Adam.

"Is the door between the rooms usually locked on both sides?"

Adam shrugged. "I guess? There's a cleaning service that comes and does the place between rentals. I don't know exactly how they leave things. Why?"

"Just some loose ends."

The group reached the bottom of the stairs as Joseph strode into the hallway from the kitchen, carrying a backpack.

"Going somewhere?" Therese asked.

"Damn straight. I don't know what the rest of you people are thinking, and I don't care. I'll take my chances in any storm over staying in this place."

"What's the rush?" said Art. "Do you know something we don't?"

Joseph was almost to the front door and not slowing down. "All I know is Sonia and Mike are dead, and I'm not going to be next. Anyway, good luck to the rest of you. I'll send help when I get to the road."

"Are you going to let him do that?" Gil asked, and Therese could see Art bristling at the fact that the question had been addressed to her.

Therese cast an eye over Joseph's supplies. "Why not? It's not going to be an easy walk, but I don't blame him for wanting to do it. If you make it to a coffee shop, can you bring me back one? Two creams, no sugar."

"What if he's the killer?" Gil said.

"Then I definitely want him to go. As far as I'm concerned, far away from me is the best place for a murderer to be."

"But he could get away!"

Therese shook her head. "Not my problem. The U.S. Marshals are pretty good at their job; I don't need to go stepping on their toes."

"Thanks for the vote of confidence," Joseph said, shouldering his pack. "Anyway, I need to get going."

"Hang on. I'm coming with you." No one had noticed that Lorelei hadn't been with them in the hallway, but she came down the stairs now, carrying a bag of her own. "The kid has the right idea."

Joseph looked surprised. "Ma'am, with all due respect, I don't think—"

"I'm not going to slow you down," she assured him. "You'd be surprised how fast these old legs can go. And how much luck do you think a Black guy is going to have hitchhiking out here? If you're by yourself, you might as well plan on walking all the way back to Sacramento." Lorelei smiled and smoothed down her hair. "Now, add a nice old white lady and you might have a chance. Also, you know, I have some experience with surviving in the outdoors."

Defeated, Joseph held up his hands. "Okay, good points. But just so you know, I might be the killer," he said, deadpan.

"Yeah? Well so might I." Lorelei took in the rest of the guests. "You all take care of yourselves, okay? Because if neither me nor Joe are the one, then there's still a lot of danger here."

The two of them turned and headed for the door, against some weak protests from Wendy and Art. They were on the front step when Therese had a thought.

"Wait, just a minute."

Therese reached into her pocket, pulled out her badge, and handed it to Lorelei. "This might help a bit with the cops. I can't promise you'll get white-glove service, but it might get their attention."

It was a risk. ("Agent Brewer, could you please explain again how the fugitive ended up carrying your badge?") But Therese had made the decision not to leave, and even though the stakes were getting higher, her reasons were the same. She couldn't go with them, but she could help get someone to take their crazy story seriously.

"Well, thanks," Lorelei said thoughtfully. "I imagine something like this might come in handy." She turned to Joseph. "Come on, kiddo, daylight's wasting."

18

After Joseph and Lorelei left, a quiet tension settled between the remaining guests. Gil, Art, and Victor returned to the lounge, where Victor paced by the window while Art watched him and Gil sat quietly staring at his hands. Wendy suddenly discovered an interest in some of the architectural features of the dining room and waylaid Adam to explain them to her, asking her questions in a voice that was at least five degrees too sharp and bright.

Therese wandered through the ground floor and eventually found herself in the library. It was one of the smallest rooms, though larger than any library Therese was likely to own, with tasteful rugs on the hardwood floor and deep leather chairs. The library was in the far corner of the building, with windows facing the uphill side of the house, where the trees blocked most of the rain, sending occasional splashes of water against the glass.

Uneasy and doubting herself, she prowled along the bookshelves, trying to find a distraction by reading the titles and guessing how they ended up here. Some of the volumes looked like they had been purchased by the yard (Therese refused to believe that there was anyone, anywhere, who would read *Spirituality and the New England Timber Industry 1826–1897* by choice), while others had probably been left behind by previous renters with more populist tastes. Having set aside a well-read paperback with a glowing hammer and sickle crossed by a DNA strand on the cover, Therese was considering a book where a woman in a ruffled dress was looking away toward a pastel landscape, and wondering if any future visitors might be interested in the giant mosquitoes, when she heard rising voices from the other side of the house.

"I just asked you a question," Wendy was saying when Therese arrived in the living room. "What's the big deal about that?"

"About me being a psycho killer? Don't pretend like I don't know what all of you are thinking." Victor had backed into a far corner of the room, and everything about his posture suggested he was ready for a fight, though none of the others were anywhere near him. Gil looked over and gave Therese a half smile when she came in, and Art pointedly ignored her.

"Why don't you just give us an answer?" Art was saying. "It's a reasonable question."

"If I hated Josh enough to kill him and all his friends? You call that reasonable? Fine, the answer is no. Are you satisfied?"

Wendy clearly was not. "That's what you say. But you were the only one who could have gotten into Mike's room," she said, then turned to Therese. "Can't you lock him up somewhere to protect the rest of us? He's got to be the killer."

"No, I don't!" Victor was frantic now, looking from one face to another in a futile search for support. "Why does it have to be one of us at all? There's a whole forest out there; anybody could be hiding in it."

Adam raised his eyebrows. "As far as I know, the population of mountain psychos has been in decline around here. Are you seriously suggesting there just happens to be a serial killer hanging around out there in the rain, picking us off when he feels like it?"

Wendy laughed at that, but in the silent room it sounded tinny and false.

Having come up with an actual theory of his own, Victor was undeterred.

"No, but what if Sonia had someone working with her?" he said. "Think about it. She had to wait until we all fell asleep, then steal all our keys and phones, and search our rooms to make sure we didn't have any extras, and put the bomb together, all before we woke up. Could she really have done all that by herself? Maybe she got duplicates made of all the room keys and gave them to this other person, and that's who pushed her, and then he came into the house last night and killed Mike."

It was an interesting idea, but Therese had some questions.

She started simple. "Why would that person kill her? Your whole idea is they're on the same side."

That stumped Victor, but not for long. "Sonia was kind of crazy, right? So maybe whoever she brought with her was crazy too. Maybe it was another family member, and they're all like that. Sean must not have been totally together, if he did what they said."

That seemed to inspire something in Gil. At the beginning of the conversation, he had been sitting back in his position on the couch, listening with a concerned expression but not looking like he was interested in joining in. But as Victor spoke, his eyes brightened and he leaned forward in his seat.

"Or!" he said with sudden enthusiasm. "What if Sean didn't die at all, and Mike and his mom faked his death, and he got her to bring all of us up here so he could kill them and get away forever?"

Gil sat back and crossed his arms, clearly pleased with this burst of creativity.

Art was not impressed. "I think this has all gone far enough. There's no reason to think Sonia would have needed anyone to help her. She had all night, didn't she? She came here by herself, and she did things all on her own, and I don't think we need to be going to any crazy theories when we've got a guy with motive and opportunity sitting right in front of us."

"That's what I was saying!" said Wendy, exasperated. "Should we tie him up, or use those drugs Sonia had, or is there a room we can lock from the outside?"

Wendy had found a walking stick in the umbrella stand next to the back door and was holding it in front of her body, as though she intended to defend herself against a nonexistent attacker. Victor looked annoyed, but he gave no sign that he was about to leap into action.

Therese edged around to where she could see both their faces and silently gave thanks that no one had thought of the kitchen knives.

"We can't do that, not without a lot more proof than we have," Therese said. "Now, if everyone wants to take a lot more precautions and not let themselves be caught alone, I wouldn't disagree with that decision. But I'm not going to allow someone to be made helpless on just a suspicion."

Wendy's expression of disgust and the way she crossed her arms and looked pointedly away from Therese showed she wasn't satisfied with that answer, but she didn't try to take on Victor on her own, and no one else seemed like they were in a hurry to help her carry out her plans.

"Thanks for the vote of confidence," Victor said sarcastically, then turned back to Wendy. "Speaking of people who haven't explained things, you've been ready with your information about everyone else, but we haven't heard why you're here yet, have we? What's your reason for wanting to kill them all?"

Wendy looked shocked. "What do you mean?"

"Fair's fair," said Gil. "We have Victor being bullied, my criminal record, Art losing his job, and Therese being the last person to see them alive. You and Adam are the only ones left. What did Sonia have on you?"

While Wendy sputtered, Adam took up the challenge.

"For myself, I honestly couldn't say. I assumed that it was because Jenna was my sister, and she was inviting immediate family members whenever she could get them. But now..." Adam paused, as though lost in thought. "That still could be true. Though, I guess I should admit it, I haven't exactly led a blameless life. Particularly when I was young I—well, let's just say things got a little wild."

"And your sister? Did she get into any of that wildness?" Art asked.

"Jenna? Not hardly. She had her own ways of having fun. No, our dad was a pretty straitlaced guy, and he didn't have much patience for the stuff I got up to. His idea of a good time was to count his money and then spend a wild evening looking for a new way to dodge taxes. Anytime he caught me, you know, painting outside the lines, I'd get the whole 'adulthood and responsibility' speech, and he'd threaten to cut off my allowance. And if he didn't catch me, Jenna wasn't above tipping him off." He shook his head. "Funny sense of humor, that kid."

"That's one way to put it," said Therese. "So, say Jenna found out about some indiscretion of yours, something bad enough to get you in serious trouble with your dad. She might have been planning to tell him, and a person might imagine that would be a reason for you to want to get her out of the way."

"Sure. I mean, nothing like that ever happened, but I can see someone imagining it," he said. For all his cool, even Adam seemed to be getting angered by this theorizing. "But yeah, if Sonia was looking for someone close to Jenna who might have had a reason to want her dead, I guess I would count. Her mom certainly wouldn't—the thing about child support is that you've got to have the child there to collect it."

He registered Wendy's shocked look and shrugged. "Sorry, but it's true. And Dad, well, he's not around anymore, but nothing would have made him turn on Jenna. She was his golden girl who could do no wrong."

He sounded equal parts sad and resentful as he said it, and Therese wondered how he had come to think of his sister over all these years. What happened to memories of a sibling who died so young? But before she could find a way to phrase the question that didn't make her sound like a sociopath, Adam turned the conversation back on her.

"But you don't have to take my word for it. Therese, you were there with Jenna. Did she say anything about this great secret she was about to blow up on me?"

"No," Therese said slowly. Had Jenna seemed overexcited that night? Possibly, but she always seemed excited—it was part of her charm. And there was too much baggage attached to the event for Therese to be sure of any of her memories. "It's definitely the sort of thing she would have wanted to talk about. One thing you could say about Jenna, she wasn't subtle. If she was sitting on something big, she would have been dropping hints at the very least."

"There you go." Adam gestured theatrically. "Saved by my poor sister's own character, or lack thereof. Seriously, though, there's nothing she could have done that would be so bad I would have killed her over it. Not to mention the four other people."

Wendy nodded vigorously. "That's just it. Even if some of us might have hated one person there, that doesn't mean we would have killed them all. You'd have to be a crazy person for that." Wendy gave a significant look to Gil, who ignored her.

Victor, on the other hand, wasn't about to let her off that easily.

"So who did you hate, Wendy? Since that's not a motive, you

can go ahead and tell us. It was Chloe, right? She must be the one you're here for."

Wendy started to protest, then fell silent, possibly enjoying this moment of being the center of attention.

"Okay, fine, I'll tell you. Not that it matters. But sure, I ha—I didn't like Chloe a lot. Not her so much, really; it was her family."

Now that she had the stage, Wendy became more animated.

"It's like you," she said, waving at Victor. "Our families were friends from when we were babies. Only it was through our church; we didn't live near each other. Chloe's family had a big house up in the hills, we were down by the freeway. Her mom was a Realtor, and she always wore these gorgeous suits and drove around in a BMW, and her dad was a dermatologist. My parents owned a corner store by the high school. Chloe got to tour fancy houses and have her freckles lasered, I got expired Ding Dongs on my birthday. I don't think her mom ever really wanted to hang out with us, but there weren't a lot of Cantonese families in the area back then, so we were what they got."

She sighed and went on dreamily, "I loved going to their house. It was so big and nice, and they always had the latest stuff. We didn't even get cable until I was in high school. And Chloe's family was really nice to us. Like they were our friends."

"But they weren't?" Therese asked.

"Depends on what you think a friend is. Is it someone who offers to bring you in on a great real estate investment, only then the dot-com crash happens, and no one needs office space any-more, but that's okay, because there were no buildings to begin with?" Wendy shook her head. "I don't know exactly what happened; my parents never wanted to talk about it. But we lost the store, and I think we almost lost the house, and the lawyer they hired to help them didn't do anything but take the last of our money. My dad was fifty years old, and he had to get a job stocking shelves at Costco, and my mom ended up working at a day care. They tried a couple of times to approach Chloe's parents about it, and after the second time, her mom got a restraining order against my dad and had them banned from their church. That was when I decided to try and talk to Chloe myself."

Wendy's tone had turned dark, and her knuckles were white as she gripped the walking stick, seemingly not aware of what she was doing.

"She didn't answer my texts and she blocked me on Myspace, so I guess I should have taken the hint. But I really believed she was my friend and she'd want to help, maybe even stand up to her parents for me. So one day I waited for her after she got out of school and caught up with her in the parking lot. I tried to explain about what happened, because I thought maybe she didn't really know, but she barely let me get started. She knew all about it, and she didn't care. She said it wasn't her family's fault if my parents were losers, and if they were smart like hers, we wouldn't be poor." Wendy paused and took a deep breath, her eyes focused on a point in the past. "Then she jumped in her car and drove off, and almost hit me on the way out. That was the last time I ever talked to her. She—it happened about seven months later."

She looked defiantly at Victor. "So yeah, I guess someone

could imagine that I'd have a motive. But I didn't do it. And why would I kill all those other people? I'd never even met any of them."

"What about your parents?" Victor asked. "That restraining order must have put them at the top of the suspect list."

"Honestly, we thought it would. They had been at a wedding that night, so they had an alibi, but that doesn't matter if the cops think it was you. But no one ever asked."

Eyes turned to Art, who looked uncomfortable.

"There's a lot involved in running that kind of investigation," he mumbled. "Can't expect us to come across every little thing. Anyway, you heard what she said. They were in the clear."

"That's pretty convenient," said Gil. "It's a good thing you knew that, so you didn't have to ask."

Instead of replying, Art just slouched in his armchair and glowered.

"So was that it?" Adam asked. "After Chloe died and the money was gone, you and your family were able to get on with your lives?"

"Well, pretty much. There was one thing." A smile crept across Wendy's face.

"After it happened, her mom was basically a zombie. You know, just totally checked out from life. And one day she came into the Costco; my dad had been promoted to manager by then, and he got me a summer job, so we were both there, but she walked by like she didn't see us. And my dad, I don't know what he was thinking, but he walked right up to her and said, 'Mrs. Liu, maybe you don't remember me, and maybe you don't care. But I'll tell you something; you might have all my money, but I still have my daughter.'"

Still smiling, Wendy stood up and headed for the door. When she was almost out of the room, she turned back, defiant.

"I didn't kill Chloe or anyone else, but I'd almost say it was worth it, just for the look on Mrs. Liu's face."

It was a hell of an exit line, Therese would give her that. But not everyone seemed to be so impressed.

"How long do you think it'll take Joseph and Lorelei to find someone and get back here?" asked Gil as soon as Wendy was gone.

"Several hours, at least," Adam said. "It's more than ten miles to the main road, and they won't be able to go very fast in this weather."

As if to emphasize his point, at that moment there was a flash of lightning, with thunder following almost immediately. The rain intensified further, pounding so hard on the windows that conversation became difficult. There was nothing for the guests to do but sit in silence, transfixed by the sound and spectacle, and Therese found herself feeling very small and extremely isolated.

The downpour lasted for several minutes before slacking off, back to merely heavy rain. As it did, the spell was broken, and the room came back to life.

"I wouldn't like to be out in that," Adam said.

"I don't think anyone would," Gil agreed, and it wasn't clear if he was being sarcastic or not. "I hope—"

But whatever he hoped, he would have to keep it to himself, because he was interrupted by another sound from outside—a rumble and then a crash.

"That didn't sound like thunder," said Victor, who was standing near the doors to the deck. "Do you think there was another bomb?"

They all went to look.

The noise had come from the mountainside past the house, and the guests gathered at the windows in the kitchen to peer out. It wasn't immediately obvious that anything had happened at all, looking through the rain-spattered windows and into the tangle of scrub. But gradually it came into focus, the mud-covered boulders and uprooted trees that hadn't been there earlier, covering a stretch of ground in the burn scar, about fifty feet out from the deck and extending down the slope.

"Landslide," Gil said. "Oh, brother."

19

All five of them went out onto the deck to get a better look, followed shortly by Wendy. It was difficult to see through the rain and the scrub, and Wendy, Victor, and Art quickly decided the view wasn't worth getting wet. That left Adam, Gil, and Therese to survey what they could see of the damage.

"I knew we used to get them around here," Adam was saying. "But it had been so long, I thought the ground had stabilized or something."

"Yeah, that's not how slide zones work. How do you think the cliffs got like this?" Gil went to the edge of the deck and leaned perilously over the railing. "It doesn't look like it's undermining the foundation, at least. But we should probably get off this deck, just in case."

Therese lingered for a moment as the men went back into the house, looking at the turned-up ground that had been exposed by the slide. It was too much to hope that the missing knife would have been uncovered by the disturbance—with her luck, more likely it was buried now under a couple of tons of rock and mud.

What next? Therese thought as the rain plastered her hair into her eyes. *Or do I not want to know?*

———

Back inside, the atmosphere was barely more pleasant. Gil was explaining the situation with the slide, using metaphors that leaned heavily on baked goods and weren't any more comforting for it.

"So when the underground stream gets too full, like if you have a big rainstorm on top of already higher-than-average snowmelt, that's like the bottom of the cake is undercooked, and it can't hold up all the cake and nuts and frosting on top. And normally the tree roots would stabilize it, but in places where there's been a fire, you've lost that extra bit of help. So if an area like that just starts to shift a little bit, the whole thing can come down. And if the ground above the water is harder, like a crust, then I guess it's more of a pie, but you see how it is; then the whole piece is going to come off together. That's how you get all these big scars in hillsides."

"And mountains," said Adam, who didn't look like he was enjoying this little lecture at all. "So, now that it's happened, does that mean there won't be any more? All the water can just come out over there, right?"

"That's one possibility. The other is some underground structures have been weakened, and now this whole slope is set to go." Gil shrugged. "We won't know until we know."

Wendy, who had been brushing raindrops out of her hair with

her fingers, looked horrified. "So what are we going to do? Do we just sit here and wait until the mountain falls on us?" Her panicked tone grated on Therese.

"You're welcome to try and catch up with Joseph and Lorelei. But, yeah, otherwise I don't know how many options we have," she said, trying unsuccessfully to contain her irritation. Some of which, honestly, was with herself. She was still standing by her decision to not leave, but she wished she had a better plan than to wait here and hope help would be on its way soon. It had seemed like a reasonable choice when the others had left, but that was before an unstable hillside changed the calculations.

But were the only options really to walk out or wait? Something was bothering Therese about that, a question at the back of her mind that she couldn't quite grasp. But the more she pursued it, the further it slipped away.

Gil had more practical concerns. "I don't think there's much point in leaving the house right now," he said. "Unless we could get fully away, there's no reason to think we'd be safer outside than we are in here. And at least it's dry."

"How do you know all this, anyway?" Victor asked. "I thought you just worked in construction or something?"

"Knowing about how the ground works is pretty relevant to building houses," Gil said, bristling a little. "There are ways to learn things that don't involve having your parents buy your way into college."

Victor just laughed and said, "Right, big bribes to get me into Chico State. They paid someone off to get me in as a fencing star."

Gil laughed. "I thought you looked like the musketeer type. Anyway, there's a lot of land like this in the hills around Seattle, and you have to know what it is to build on it. I've done some work for a contractor who kind of specializes in sloping lots, and he's taught me a bunch."

"Okay, but are we going to fall off the mountain or not?" Art asked. "All this theorizing is nice, but I think we would all appreciate a straight answer on that one."

"I hope not, but there's no way of knowing for sure. Life's a big gamble, you know?" Gil said, taking a sudden turn to the philosophical. "Anyway, I don't see how we have a whole lot of options, so I say we stay alert and take our chances." He thought for a minute and then added, "The one thing I'd suggest is we try not to spend too much time upstairs. If the ground under the house starts to go, we aren't going to have a lot of time to get out."

It was a sobering thought, and they hadn't even started drinking.

As if in response to what Therese was thinking, Art went over to the bar where the bottles had been left the night before. He picked one up and examined the level of the liquid before setting it back down, unopened.

"We should be saving these, in case we need them later."

Victor snorted. "What, like we're going to be sterilizing wounds with Scotch?"

"Or maybe we should just keep you so drunk you can't kill any more of us," said Wendy, who was obviously not about to give up on her theory, despite her own revelations. But no one seemed

interested in revisiting that conversation now that there were
more immediate concerns.

"Let's give it a rest with that, okay?" said Therese. "We don't
know who killed Mike and Sonia, and we aren't going to get anywhere just repeating the same accusations at each other."

"Well," Wendy said, glowering, "Maybe I need to come up
with some new ones, then."

She turned to make her second consecutive dramatic exit, but
Adam put a hand out to stop her as she passed him.

"Be careful if you're going upstairs," he said. "There are a lot
of potential dangers here, inside and outside."

From the way Wendy met his eyes and from the warmth of
her smile, a person might have thought he was inviting her on a
yachting excursion, not offering a warning about landslides and
murders.

"Thank you," she said, placing her hand over his on her arm.
"I'll keep that in mind. But the truth is, I'm not really as helpless
as all that."

With that, she left the room again, and this time it seemed to
take.

———

After Wendy left, no one seemed to know what to say. The topics
on everyone's minds—the murders and the unstable ground—
weren't things that could be discussed without conflict, and no
one seemed to have the energy for it. Maybe it was a delayed
response to finding Mike's body and the shock of the landslide,

or maybe the men had just become wary of saying anything that could be used against them, but Therese found the silence stupefying. She needed to be doing something, but she couldn't quite figure out what. There was something—a thought, an idea—but the thunder crashed and it was gone again.

Gil wandered over to the foosball table and spun a couple of the handles, bouncing the ball off the far wall and watching it roll back. Victor joined him and they started a game, playing casually at first and gradually becoming more competitive. Therese took that as a sign that the tensions in the room had lessened, and decided that this was an opportunity to take care of her own concerns.

"I think I'm going to get some of my things and bring them down here. I was thinking about what Gil said, about the chance of another slide. If we have to evacuate in a hurry, I'd like to have a few things to take with me," she said, standing up from where she had been sitting by the window. No one made any move to stop or warn her.

On her way out, she looked back and took in the scene in the room. Four men, two playing a children's game, while Art glowered and picked at a scab on his hand from his adventure on the rope and Adam stared out the window, apparently lost in thought. If she didn't know any better, Therese might have thought this was a completely normal group of people, stuck inside and bored on a rainy day.

But she did know better.

Upstairs, she paused outside the door to Mike's room. Despite what she had told the others, she was deeply tempted to go back in and search the scene again. It would be easier now, without half a dozen civilians breathing down her neck and questioning her every move, to say nothing of the assumptions they were bound to make about her motives. But those assumptions would get a lot worse if anyone caught her in there, and anyway, she didn't even know what she would be looking for. Better to have a clear goal before taking that kind of risk, Therese decided, as she moved on down the hall.

Her room looked exactly as she had left it. She set to prioritizing her belongings while she thought about the situation. Some of the questions she had had before were answered—it was clear now that one of Sonia's motives in assembling her guest list was to put together a group of the most likely people to want to kill the victims in the cabin. Adam with his sibling rivalry, Gil with his history of violence, Joseph's anger at the damage they had done to his relationship, and Victor's and Wendy's motives for harm done to self and family. And she and Lorelei, of course, both on the scene and with very different reasons to raise suspicions.

None of them seemed like great candidates for the role of mass murderer, honestly. But the way things were going, she had no choice but to give some more credit to Sonia's investigative capabilities. She must have known, or thought she knew, something that she believed would lead her to the killer. And whether or not she was right, someone wasn't willing to take that chance.

And then there was Mike. Therese folded her jacket and put it at the bottom of her smaller bag, pressing it smooth as she tried to remember what he had said the night before. There had been something about him having information, hadn't there? Just more of his bluster: easy for her to ignore at the time, but to one person in the room, it must have sounded like a threat. They had already killed once since arriving at this house, and the crime they had thought they got away with all those years ago was now close and present. Why not kill again, just to be sure?

And why not keep on killing, now that they had started? Therese didn't know anything that would be a threat to the killer, but there was no reason to believe they knew that. She looked around her room, painfully aware of how difficult it would be to secure against a truly determined assailant. The main door was heavy enough, but Mike's had been as well. And if there really was a third set of keys floating around, her trick with the chair under the handle wasn't going to do much more than slow them down.

Of course, that was assuming Mike's killer had come in from the hallway. If she accepted the most obvious theory, that Victor had simply passed through the connecting door, Therese should have had nothing to worry about.

She went to examine the only other entrance to the room. The bathroom door was flimsy, in the way of most interior doors, but the simple fact that it latched with a sliding bolt on her side meant it would be difficult to get through without making a serious amount of noise. Of course, any time she was in the bathroom, she would be vulnerable—the lock on the connecting door was the simple button kind that could be defeated by anyone with a paper clip. Not an ideal situation, but manageable—she could go for her remaining time here without taking a shower.

Through the other door, she could hear sounds from Wendy's room—possibly singing? Therese listened for a minute and decided it was none of her business.

Back in the room, it took very little time for Therese to finish packing. She only took the essentials, to keep the load as light as possible in case they had to leave in a hurry and walk out. Her jacket, all her remaining clean socks and underwear, and her useless laptop made the cut; the nice tops and pants she had packed in case of a photo shoot were left to their fates. After checking under the bed for anything she might have missed, she gave one last, regretful look at the pillows. If Therese had to spend another night in this house, she wouldn't be sleeping.

She had almost made it out the door before she stopped and turned back and picked the book off the bedside table. Might as well get some reading done, if she wasn't doing anything else. The mosquitoes were about to take New Orleans and the heroes were desperately trying to call in a warning, after an earlier disaster had knocked out the phone lines. When she had left off the night before, they were looking for other means of communication and had just flagged down a long-haul trucker.

Therese stared at the cover of the book, with its giant electric-green mosquito superimposed over a darkened skyline, and actually slapped herself in the face.

"Of course," she muttered to the empty room. "What kind of idiot am I?"

THE NEIGHBOR

Victor pressed his forehead against the glass and willed the rain to stop falling. If it did—well, they would still be stuck in this place, with all the same problems, but at least it wouldn't be raining.

Behind him, the others were still talking about the dangers of the mountain sliding down. Victor tried to block out their voices; he didn't want to think about that. He didn't want to think about any of it, not the people who had just died, or Josh and the others in that cabin all that time ago. Was that really why Sonia had invited him? Because she had known about the video? Or had she known more? The others had accepted his story at least. It was true, of course—that helped. And it was as much as any of them ever needed to know.

Especially now. That stupid connecting door between their rooms, of course they all thought he had killed Mike. And now Wendy wanted to tie him up, and not in a fun way. Not that she looked like she was very into fun anyway, not with anybody who didn't look like Adam.

Victor ran his hand over his goatee. Maybe it was time to shave it off? He'd grown it years ago and really only kept it out of spite after his brother's wife said it looked like pubes, but even she wasn't paying any attention to him anymore. And it stung that neither of the girls here would give him a second look. Not that he had come here looking to meet anyone, but a man had his pride.

What was left of it, anyway. Why had he told them that story? Okay, so Gil and Wendy had already known, but he could have made something up that would make it not so bad. He could have said that Josh had stolen his bike and told him he had to do this to get it back. At least then he wouldn't look like such a puss. Except that no one would believe that—no one who had known Josh, anyway. He was mean but he wasn't smart, and nothing he planned that far ahead ever worked out.

Victor had never thought about it before, but at that moment it occurred to him to wonder if that was why Josh had turned on him. Not just because he, Victor, had been a fat unpopular kid whose parents were too obviously Mexican for their white-ass suburb, but because he had known how pathetic Josh really was. Victor had been there on the Cub Scouts hike when Josh had seen a garter snake and got so scared he peed his pants. He'd sat up all night after Josh had hit his head trying to do an ollie on his skateboard to make sure he didn't have a concussion so they wouldn't have to tell Josh's parents. And the thanks he got for it was having his whole life destroyed for all of high school. A thing he thought he had finally put behind him, until he was stupid enough to tell everyone here about it.

And now they all suspected him of killing Mike, and probably Sonia too. Well, they could suspect all they wanted, but they couldn't prove anything. Even Therese had said that, and she clearly didn't like him very much. So let them think what they wanted—they would all be out of here soon enough, and it would all be over. For good, this time.

Why had he come here? Stupid question: Victor knew why. Being someone who had known one of the victims of the Memorial Day Massacre was one of the only interesting things about him, and he had been finding ways to work it into conversations for the last twenty years. There was no way Victor could have turned down a chance to be featured in a magazine article about it. He probably would have come even if he had known what Sonia had been planning, whatever that was.

He wondered what Sonia had thought they would be doing right now. She probably hadn't expected this storm or the danger of landslides. Of course, she probably hadn't expected to be dead, either. A lot of things seemed like they hadn't been going to plan lately. Victor stepped away from the window and went to see if there were any beers left.

THE FRIEND

Got lovely Starbucks lovers, they tell me I'm insane," Wendy sang softly to herself. She knew she had the lyrics wrong and she didn't care. In her head she could see exactly the kind of guy she was singing about. He was polished and urbane, maybe a little too slick, but that was part of his charm. He always knew the right thing to say, the right place to go. The kind of guy she deserved, but never seemed to meet. Boys and slobs, that was all that ever crossed her path. Was it too much to ask for a man who thought there was more to life than video games and fart jokes? It was not. But there had been plenty of things in Wendy's life that she had deserved and not gotten, and she had been starting to suspect that this was just one more. But now...

Wendy stared into the mirror as she ran the brush slowly along her hair. She probably shouldn't even be upstairs, not with the way Gil had been talking about the mountainside sliding away. But the time it was going to take to get her hair and makeup back in order after the morning she had had, she felt like it was worth the risk. And it was nice to be away from the other people for a little while. Almost all of them, at least.

Adam probably wasn't interested in her. You could tell the kind of girl he liked by the stories of old girlfriends he told, or the way he kept hanging around Therese. She didn't act rich, but she was an FBI agent, and some guys probably thought that was sexy. And she had been friends with Adam's sister. That probably meant she was more part of his world.

And now she had another song stuck in her head.

The brush caught in a knot in her hair, and Wendy spent some time working it out. As she did, her gaze drifted down to the makeup bag on the dresser. She only bought the best brands now, but for a moment those names were replaced by the discount drugstore labels she remembered so well. She had kept them in a free samples bag her aunt had given her for her birthday (just the bag, not the samples), and the memory of fishing out a half-empty lip gloss next to Chloe, and seeing her friend smirk while she selected from one of the fat glossy tubes of color in her own designer bag, still stung.

They hadn't really been friends—Wendy had known it then, even if she didn't admit it to herself. Maybe once, when they had been little enough that nothing mattered, and a cardboard box was as good of a toy as a Barbie motor home. But by the time they were teenagers, it seemed like Chloe barely tolerated her. They had mostly stayed around Chloe's house, watching movies on cable if her parents weren't around or sitting out on the patio, where Chloe would sunbathe and talk about her summer plans while Wendy tried to stay out of the sun, not willing to risk her mother's wrath if she got a tan.

In fact, Wendy had wondered why Chloe agreed to hang out with her at all, though in later years she suspected it was because she liked being the alpha girl for a change. Wendy had never met Adam's sister, but from everything she had heard this weekend, it sounded like Jenna wasn't the type to let anyone think they could be better than her.

Wendy wondered what that said about her, as she gave her hair a final fluff. The thing was, she hadn't had the opportunity. Some people had more options about what they would put up with; that was just how life was.

And now Chloe had no options at all. Wendy wasn't exactly happy to be here, with the murdered people and the bomb and not knowing if she was actually ever going to get out, but at least she had a chance. She was flirting with a guy who was probably richer than Chloe could have ever imagined, and Chloe was a bunch of ashes in a box somewhere. It was funny how life worked out.

20

Therese found a spot for her bag under a table in the front hall, close enough to grab in a hurry if necessary. Then she went straight to the lounge, where she found Adam cracking open a beer in front of the refrigerator.

"Is there a radio in this place?" she asked.

Adam stopped mid-sip and stared at her, confused. "A what?"

"A radio. When we got here, you said the reason there was no phone connection was because the cellular signal was so good. But this place has to be a hundred years old. What did they do for communication before cell phones?"

Adam's eyes went wide and he set down the bottle. "Holy shit, you're right. I never even thought of that."

"Wait a minute," said Victor, who had been standing with Gil by the French doors. "You mean we could have called for help this whole time, and you just *forgot*?"

"Not exactly." Adam rubbed his hand over his face and looked thoughtful. "What I mean is, there was a radio. There was one when I was a kid; it was a big silver thing that had a special channel to get the weather reports. But that one came out when they did the renovations in the nineties—I remember it ended up at my uncle's house."

"So there isn't a radio, then?" Gil asked. "One that used to be here isn't going to do us much good."

"I know; that's what I'm getting to." Adam circled around the kitchen island to join them. "That was the second radio we had here. That I know about, anyway. Back in the forties or fifties, my grandfather had another one installed; it took up a whole shelf in the library. I know it was taken down at some point, but I don't know where it went. Maybe some parts of it are still here?"

That didn't sound as promising as Therese had been hoping, but it was a start.

"Let's have a look," she said.

———

It didn't take long to find the cabinet where the radio had been, in the wall of bookcases in the library between two sets of shelves. Adam hadn't been wrong about the removal of the radio itself; the only things that suggested it had ever been there were a metal bracket at the back of the cabinet, some wires sticking out of a hole in the top corner, and an old two-prong outlet. The rest of the space was filled with the sort of detritus that tended to accumulate in old houses—papers and printouts, plastic items of indeterminate purpose that might be important for something, and books too irregular in shape or size to go on the shelves.

"What are you all doing in here?" Wendy appeared at the door, looking polished and refreshed, as they were sorting through it all.

"Turns out there used to be a two-way radio here," Art explained. "Adam didn't remember until just now. But he seems to have misplaced it."

"Oh." Wendy looked at the empty cabinet and then back at Adam. "It's so cool you thought of that. Do you think it's still around somewhere?"

Even Adam, who Therese thought must be used to that sort of thing, looked a little embarrassed at her gushing. "Actually, it was Therese who guessed there might be one. I'd completely forgotten about it until she asked. As to whether we can find it, I don't know, but there's a chance. If there's one thing the people in my family have liked more than making money, it's finding ways not to spend it, and it's not cheap to get things hauled away from here. So a lot of stuff no one wanted just ended up being stored."

"Stored where?" Victor asked, though from his worried expression it was clear he had an idea of one of the options.

"Well, the basement, for starters. But there's also some stuff in the shed and the garage." Adam clearly was equally unenthusiastic about making a return visit to the space under the house, where Sonia's body might be guarding their best bet for reaching the outside world.

"It would really help if we knew what we were looking for," he went on. "The radio was mostly my uncle Dave's thing, and I've gotta admit, I always found him kind of boring when I was a kid, so I didn't pay a lot of attention. Now I wish I could at least remember the name. Haley-something?"

Therese had been staying out of the conversation as she sorted through the pile of stuff in the cabinet, keeping half an ear on what was going on while she looked for anything that might help them. Now she stopped and turned to Adam.

"A Hallicrafters SX-73 receiver and HT-20 transmitter?" she asked.

Adam's jaw dropped, and his veneer of cool showed some cracks.

"That's it! How did you know that?" His awe lasted for a moment before dissolving into suspicion. "Seriously, how?"

"Yeah, enough is enough," said Art. "What kind of game are you playing here? Do you honestly expect us to believe you just pulled that out of your ass?"

Even Gil, who had been nothing but enthusiastic so far, looked confused.

"Relax," said Therese, holding up a pair of battered and water-stained paperbacks. "I found the manuals."

***

The basement was the obvious place to start the search, but nobody wanted to go down there. Adam said he would take the shed, and Wendy surprised no one by volunteering to join him, while Art and Victor decided they would try the closets and maybe spend some time looking over the manuals to better understand how to work the things when they were found. That left Therese and Gil.

"Where should we start?" he asked, as they surveyed the basement. It was a good question. The basement was a giant space, running the length of the house, and Adam hadn't been exaggerating when he said his ancestors hadn't thrown much away. One end was filled with old furniture and piles of wooden siding— likely left over from when the house was renovated. That they could probably ignore, but the rest of the room was taken up by stacks of boxes, almost any one of which could hold what they were looking for.

And then, of course, there was the body.

They had left Sonia's corpse near the entrance, just far enough in to not be in the way of the door or the light switch. They had found an old bit of white plastic sheeting to cover her with, so all that was visible now was the colors of her clothing that showed faintly through it. The smell wasn't as bad as Therese had been anticipating, but she didn't entirely blame the others for wanting to avoid the place.

"We might as well be methodical about it," she said, pointing to where the boxes started. "We can go from there and see if there's any pattern in how things were stored here."

It quickly became clear that there wasn't. New Year's Eve decorations from the last decade were stacked on top of midcentury camping gear, next to a collection of nature magazines. Without anything to guide their search, Therese and Gil settled into a routine of her opening boxes and handing off the plainly unpromising ones for him to restack. Anything that looked like it might have a radio, or even part of one, got a closer look from both of them, but even the most hopeful interpretation couldn't turn an old hair dryer or a broken lamp into a way to communicate.

Working that way, they made good progress through the space, and it wasn't long until they had drawn level with the spot where Sonia's corpse was lying. They had left the door open to freshen the air, and as they got closer, a gust of wind came up and lifted the plastic over the body, causing it to flap and expose Sonia's face, blank eyes staring out between streaks of dried blood.

Gil jumped at the movement and cringed away from the sight, then looked behind him, like he expected to find something in the shadows. Therese could understand the instinct; she was mostly glad she hadn't done something similar. Still, she couldn't resist poking him a bit.

"Do you believe in ghosts?" she asked.

"Not yet," he said with a smile. "But I'm keeping an open mind."

They kept going, weaving back and forth across the room and leaving no box unopened. About halfway, Gil stopped by the back wall, where the basement had been cut into the hillside and sealed with concrete. He ran his hand over the uneven surface, looking thoughtful.

"Still worried about more landslides?" Therese asked.

"Yeah. I thought maybe I could get a sense of how the ground is under the house here. But there isn't much to see."

"That's good, I guess." Therese ran her hand over the rough surface. "What are we looking for, exactly?"

"To be honest, I'm not really sure. Sliding, I guess." Gil looked sheepish. "I know the theory, but I don't have a lot of experience with this sort of thing in practice."

"Well, let's hope you don't get more any time soon." Therese looked again at the wall and then back to judge the distance to the door. "If this goes now, we're definitely dying, aren't we?"

Gil followed her gaze, thought for a minute, then nodded. "I wouldn't say *definitely*, but I wouldn't put a lot on our chances. But what else are we going to do? If that radio's here, finding it is our best chance."

"Then I guess we should get back to searching," Therese said.

They did, but Therese had the sense that there was something on Gil's mind, from the way he kept looking at her and starting to speak, then stopping himself. Therese was going to ask him what it was when he closed up a box full of bath toys and took a deep breath.

"I really am sorry about that whole thing with, like, saying you could have done it, and Art was covering up. I was being defensive there, and I didn't think about what I was saying. But I didn't mean it."

"Why not? It's as good a theory as any." Therese opened another box, saw only old shoes, and handed it over. "But I appreciate the thought. I guess it would be your juvenile record that got you on the invite list? Or did you have something against one of us too?"

"Me? No, of course not. Chris was the only person there I really knew, and I kind of worshipped him. He was always so cool, and everyone liked him, and he could do so much stuff. And he was always really great to me. A teenager like him, you wouldn't expect him to want to have anything to do with his little kid cousin, but he'd come over to babysit when my mom was out, and we'd shoot basketballs and play video games and have pizza rolls for dinner." Gil smiled at the memory. "On my twelfth birthday, we all went to Six Flags, and Chris went on all the roller coasters with me, because my mom wouldn't do it. And he didn't tell anyone that I cried twice. I think it was part of why I got so messed up after he died. Like, if he could be gone just like that, what was the point of anything?"

"So you acted out. If you were going to be angry anyway, might as well have something to be angry about," Therese said.

"Something like that, I guess. And I was never going to hurt anyone. But my mom didn't have money for lawyers, so it made more sense to take the plea deal. And I turned out okay in the end. I've got a good life." He joined her in examining a jumble of pieces of plastic and metal that turned out to be parts of a coffee maker, looking at them without seeming to see.

Gil went on. "All these things people are saying about how terrible everyone in the cabin was; that's not how I remember Chris at all. Was he—how do you remember him? Was he really part of all that?"

Therese sighed. "No, I don't remember him that way at all. But I'm not sure I'm a reliable witness. The thing is, I was there too."

"Yeah, but you weren't one of the bad ones, right? You and Chris, you might not have seen what the other ones were like."

"I'd like to believe that." Now it was Therese's opportunity to stare at the contents of a box and get lost in the past. "I think I did believe it for a long time, if I thought about it at all. I never had any illusions about why Jenna suddenly decided to be friends with me—I'd just had the seasons of my life in soccer and track, and I was on top of the world. There was an article in the paper, and my coaches were talking about what colleges might recruit me. And some people would say things about the Women's World Cup and the Olympics."

She laughed. "Even then, I knew I wasn't at that level, but I can't say I didn't like hearing the talk. Anyway, that made me attractive as an item for Jenna to add to her collection, and where she led the rest of them followed. I knew it wasn't real friendship, but it could be a lot of fun. And I don't know, I kind of felt like I earned it? Like I was special, so I got to level up and hang out with the other special people."

Gil started to say something in argument, but Therese had been doing some thinking and now the words began to pour out. "Did I ignore all of the things they did that were cruel, that hurt other people? Sure. I even participated in it. I want to say that I was horrified, that at least I had some kind of crisis of my conscience, but you want the honest truth? I enjoyed it. Even though I knew it was wrong—*because* I knew it was wrong. It was just more proof of our specialness, that I could be on the side of the people giving the pain, instead of taking it."

"And Chris? Was he like that too?" Gil sounded so desperately hopeful that Therese was almost tempted to tell him what he wanted to hear. How much could it hurt, now? But she had started down the path of honesty, and there was no turning back now.

"Chris was..." Therese trailed off, still not sure how much she was willing to reveal. "I wish I could tell you no. The thing with Chris was, he made you feel like you really were important. Like anytime you talked, even if other people were ignoring you, he was listening like he thought you had something interesting to say. And he was good-looking, of course. Everyone liked him, and some of us liked him more than others, including me."

Therese looked away as she made the admission.

"So I'm biased about Chris, and before this weekend I would have said he was just a good person, and he didn't go along with any of the bad stuff. But I also would have said the same thing about myself, and the truth is, I think he enjoyed it too. Not so much to participate, but to watch, and to know at least some of it was for his benefit." She thought about how he had looked while she was fighting with Jenna and Chloe, the way he laughed when she kicked Jenna's leg. "I don't really think it was a matter of it being his preference—if he had gotten in with a different group of people, he would have gone along with whatever they did. I think Chris was someone who liked being liked, and he didn't have the kind of character to push back. I mean, he was seventeen."

"I guess I can see that. I don't like it, but I get it. Nobody's really that perfect, not like I remembered him. He was just a person." Gil looked sad, but less strained than he did before. Illusions were tough to shatter, but it wasn't always the worst thing.

"He was just a kid," Therese corrected. "They all were. No

matter how many mean things they did, none of them deserved to die. And certainly not like that."

"Sure, but—oh!"

Therese had picked up another box while they were talking, one that was significantly heavier than the others had been. The tape that had held it shut was dry and crumbling, and what Therese could see through the flap was already making her hopeful. She had set it back down and opened it the rest of the way, and it was the first glimpse of what was inside that provoked the response from Gil.

"Is that it?" he said as Therese tried to get a grip on the gray metal case inside.

"It looks like it could be," she replied. "Can you give me a hand with this? It weighs a ton."

Together they hauled the object out of the box and set it on the basement floor. There were two handles on the front of the case, framing an impressive array of dials, switches, and knobs. Three hours earlier, Therese wouldn't have known a shortwave radio receiver from a hole in the ground, but she had gotten a good look at the pictures in the manual, and she was confident that was what she was looking at now. What's more, at first glance it seemed to be mostly intact, though a peek inside the case revealed some disconnected wires and gaps where she thought the tubes were supposed to be.

"Come on," she said, suddenly invigorated. "Let's see what else we've got here."

It wasn't hard to find the other parts, once they knew what

they were looking for. There were two similar-looking boxes in nearby stacks, one of which turned out to have the transmitter, and the other, miracle of miracles, containing a nearly full box of vintage radio tubes. They looked for a little while longer, just in case there was more to find, but Therese was starting to get uncomfortable with how long they had been under the house, and from the way Gil kept looking at the back wall, she had the sense he was too. She was about to suggest they move on when he beat her to it.

"You know, I think this might be everything," he said. "And if we find out there's more we need, we can always come back and look for it."

"Good point. Also, my hands are freezing." As if to prove her point, Therese tried to pick up the box with the transmitter in it, and it slipped awkwardly out of her fingers. Gil reached down and caught it in a swift motion, stacking it on top of the receiver box and lifting both easily.

"I've got these," he said. "Can you bring the tubes?"

On the one hand, Therese was mildly annoyed to be left to carry only the smallest and lightest item, but on the other hand those boxes were seriously heavy, and Gil didn't seem to mind them. And anyway, someone had to lock the door.

She gave Sonia's body a last look as she passed. *I haven't forgotten you*, Therese thought. *I just wish I knew what you meant about the picture.*

It was still raining, but for most of the way back, they were sheltered under the deck. Therese took the lead, carrying the box of glass tubes in front of her like an offering, her mind already on how they were going to approach repairing the radio.

"Hey," Gil said as they got to the stairs. "About what you were saying earlier?"

"What?"

"I thought you were pretty special," he muttered, so low that Therese could barely hear.

21

They found the lounge area empty but with evidence of activity—two plastic boxes sat open on the coffee table, with emergency blankets, water purification tablets, bandages, and other assorted necessities spread out around them. The only other open space was the kitchen island, and Therese and Gil were unpacking the radio equipment there when Victor and Art arrived.

"You found it? Wow, that's awesome," Victor said, though he sounded less enthusiastic than you might expect for someone finally seeing a potential way out of a dangerous situation.

"Don't fall all over yourself with joy," said Gil, who must have noticed it too. "Did you guys get anything out of reading the manual?"

"Have you tried to read something like this? It's not exactly for beginners if you know what I mean."

Victor tossed the manuals down on the counter and fiddled

with one of the dials speculatively. "Do you think we can make them work?"

"We're certainly going to try," said Therese. She turned to Art, who had followed Victor into the room and was sorting through the emergency supplies, apparently uninterested in what they had found.

"What about you?" she asked him. "Any thoughts on operations here? I know you guys all had radios in the cars back in the day."

"Yeah, well, that was kind of a different deal, you know? It was all set up there, on the right channels, and anyway, that was a long time ago."

"Right, sure." Therese was remembering a conversation she had heard between her parents one time, when her dad had come home from work exhausted and fed up. "Goddamn idiot," he was saying about his boss. "If he didn't have his lapdogs there setting everything up for him, he'd get lost in his own office."

Or something like that, anyway. It was a long time ago. Here and now, she had a radio to repair, and the only thing she needed to know about Art was that he wasn't going to be much help with that.

At least Victor seemed embarrassed about his inability to contribute. "We found some emergency supplies," he said. "They were in the back of one of the hall closets. We thought there might be some things here we could use."

"Is there a soldering iron?" asked Gil, who had put the receiver on its side and was examining the interior. "Because I'm no electrician, but I'm pretty sure you usually want wires to be connected at both ends."

A closer examination uncovered two wires disconnected in the receiver and three in the transmitter, plus one resistor that was rattling around loose in the transmitter's case.

"Could be worse," Victor said hopefully.

"Could be better," replied Therese.

They were trying to line up the unconnected wires with their corresponding places on the diagrams in the manuals when Adam joined them, wearing a different outfit from when they had seen him last.

He must have caught Therese's surprised look, because he explained, "The shed was pretty dirty, and I figured we might not get another chance to change. Oh hey, you found the radio equipment. Outstanding!"

"Now we just need to fix it," Gil said. "Do you have any tools around here?"

"You think you can get it working? Because we found tools. What do you need?" Wendy must have been doing some freshening up as well, because her hair was freshly brushed, and she was dressed in a new outfit of black slacks and a pale green blouse. Therese was momentarily distracted from the technical problems to wonder how much the other woman had packed for one weekend, before reminding herself that she had several more important things to consider.

"A screwdriver would be a good start," she said. "And if there's no soldering iron, we could make do with some electrical tape."

Adam had already gone back into the hall to get the tool bag, which was the only useful thing he and Wendy had found in the shed. Screwdrivers they had in abundance, but no electrical tape. Gil tried to make do with some masking tape Victor found in the pantry, while Therese worked on making sense of the circuit diagrams. Professing no knowledge or proficiency with technical matters, Adam assigned himself the job of making coffee and offering encouragement. Wendy had been excited about the radio at first, but with no tasks to do, she lost interest and went to examine the emergency supplies.

"It was good thinking, having all this here," she said to Adam, drawing his attention away from the radio. "Did you do a lot of research into what you were going to need?"

"To be honest, I completely forgot we had them," Adam replied. "I think it must have been Deborah's idea—she was a girl I was dating for a while who was kind of a nut about preparedness. I think she moved to Colorado to do the off-the-grid thing."

Wendy made a face. "Ugh. I can't imagine anyone wanting to live like this on purpose. All I want is to get back to civilization as soon as possible. I don't even like camping."

Adam laughed. "Wherever Deborah is, I can guarantee she's not camping. Her family was loaded, like, beyond rich. I think we came up here maybe twice, but it was way too downscale for her." Adam grimaced at the memory. "Anyway, we have her to thank for these supplies, such as they are."

"Better than nothing," said Art. The former detective had been quiet for a while, taking short sips from one of the bottles of water from the emergency kit and looking out the window toward where the slide had happened. If Therese was feeling unkind, she might have said he was sulking over his lack of knowledge being exposed, until he stood up abruptly and turned to face into the room.

"We should try and get those cars started. You guys might be able to get those things working, but we have no idea how long it's going to take, even if you do."

Victor looked up from where he had been watching Gil trying to tape a wire to a bracket. "What about Joseph and Lorelei? They're probably getting pretty close to the main road by now, and then they can find someone and bring them back," he said.

"That's assuming both of them make it to the road." Art gave them all a significant look and then went on. "If one of them is the killer, he or she is going to push the other one down the mountain the first chance they get, and be long gone. Or maybe there was another slide, and the mountain fell on them. What I'm saying is, we need to be able to rely on ourselves."

"That sounds great, but has anyone here picked up the ability to hot-wire a car overnight? Because I don't think I have," Therese said. "This equipment isn't in such bad shape, and it's only been a couple of hours since Joseph and Lorelei left, with a long way to go. I think we should give it a little more time before we start coming up with doomsday scenarios."

Art turned toward her with fury in his eyes. "It's also only a couple of hours since we found a man hanging in his bedroom, in case you have forgotten. Because I'll tell you one thing; I sure haven't. The rest of you may have thought you were coming here to get your pictures in a magazine, but I—" Art thought better of finishing that sentence, but not before the rest of the guests had a chance to guess where it might have been going.

"You what?" Gil asked. "What were you here for, if you didn't think there was going to be a magazine article?"

"I didn't say that. What I was saying was, I thought—that is, at any event that was going to be gathering the principal people involved in the crime, it was important to have someone from law enforcement be present."

Wendy frowned at him. "But you're retired. And how did you know who else would be here?"

"Well, I figured..."

"You know, I've been thinking," Adam said thoughtfully as Art's excuse making trailed off. "When Victor was talking earlier about how Sonia must have had an accomplice, I assumed it was just the best thing he could think of to deflect suspicion from himself. But the more I thought about it, the more I realized he probably had a point. This is a big house, and going through all those rooms plus building the bomb, and doing it all without any of us waking up, even if we were drugged, that's a lot for one lady to do in a night."

"So?" said Art, his nervousness plainly increasing.

"So, I just wondered if maybe Victor had the right general idea, but he was wrong about the mystery guy hiding in the woods."

"I told you!" said Victor.

Therese took the theory slightly more calmly. "I think I see where you're going with this," she added. "If Sonia was going to ask someone to help her, she'd probably want someone who she didn't have any reason to think had committed the crime, but who might have had a strong incentive to get some credit for solving it. Like, say, the disgraced former detective who had been in charge of the investigation."

That got Art to his feet. He approached the counter where they were gathered around the radio and glared at them, his hands planted on his hips.

"You two think you're really cute, don't you? Why would she have blown up my stuff if I was working with her?"

"The same reason she put her own things in the bomb. She wanted us all trapped here, and that wouldn't work if anyone had their keys or phone," Therese said. Art was uncomfortably close to her now. "Come on, you've as good as admitted you knew at least part of what was going on here. Why not fill us in on the rest? Considering all that's happened, it's probably the best thing you can do at this point."

"What's that? Am I being threatened by a government agent? At my age?"

"It didn't sound like a threat to me. It sounded like good advice." Gil left his work on the radio and came to face Art from behind Therese. "Aren't you the one who was just talking about Mike's death? He knew something, or acted like he did. And so did Sonia. That's not a good pattern."

For a moment, Art's resolve seemed to falter. Maybe he was remembering how Mike's bloated face had looked when they cut him down, or maybe it was the flash of lightning that made them all jump, but he eased half a step back from Therese's personal space as the thunder rolled in.

"Okay, so what if I did help Sonia? She had an interest in solving the crime, and she might have had some information, seeing as how her kid was involved." He turned away from where he was facing Therese and addressed the rest of them. "She said she had evidence, but she wouldn't hand it over unless I joined her here. I couldn't get her to tell me what she had planned, and by the time I was here, it was too late to change anything. And she never told me about the bomb. I wouldn't have had anything to do with that."

"But drugging us and stealing our stuff, that was okey dokey with you?" Victor had gone from his triumph over having his theory partially validated to justifiable fury. "You couldn't have let us in on it, so at least we could be ready, have an extra phone somewhere?"

"He wasn't even smart enough to keep a car key for himself," Gil pointed out. "Unless there's more he's not telling us."

Even Adam's air of calm had been disrupted by this latest revelation. "That seems like a distinct possibility, doesn't it?" he said. "He wasn't exactly forthcoming until he got caught just now. Even after two people died, you didn't think that was a good enough reason to fill us in?"

Under attack from all sides, Art backed toward the pantry door. "No! I don't have a key or a phone. Sonia took them all. She didn't say what she was going to do, just that there needed to be no chance of any of you finding them. Look, I had to go along with her. She said she had information, and as an officer of the law, it's my responsibility to do whatever's necessary to see that justice is done."

Therese raised her eyebrows. "You have a responsibility to assist in drugging people, performing warrantless searches, and seizing their belongings for destruction? One that extends past two suspicious deaths? I think you'd have trouble convincing a judge on that one, even if you were still in law enforcement. Which you're not, by the way. Look, we're all stuck here together now, and we're not out of danger. If there's anything Sonia told you that might help us figure out what she knew and who killed her and Mike, the smartest thing you can do is share it now."

Therese thought she was making a reasonable argument but for Art, it was the last straw.

"Oh, you think that would be smart? Well, listen, kiddo, I was investigating crimes when you were just a glint in your daddy's eye, and I don't need your kind of 'smart.' And believe me, I can take care of myself. Because you know what? There's one thing Sonia didn't take from me." Art opened his jacket, revealing a gun in an underarm holster. "So don't you worry about me. And you'd better not surprise me from here on out. I might be a little jumpy, if you know what I mean." He turned and headed for the door. "Now, if you'll excuse me, I have some cars to get started. Maybe, if I'm feeling generous, I'll even tell you when I've done it."

With that, he left, and for a minute no one said anything. Finally, Victor broke the silence.

"I just realized. There were ten people when we got here; now there's only six of us. We're all that's left."

"Don't jinx it," said Gil.

22

"That bastard."

Wendy said it out loud, but the sentiment was universal.

"He knew!" she went on. "He knew, and he let her take our stuff. He helped her!" Her rage was incandescent, and for once Therese felt no inclination to play peacemaker.

"And when she fell, he did nothing to help find our phones, even when it might have saved her," Therese added, in case anyone was overlooking that part. "Makes you wonder what his real priorities were?"

"Do you think he could have killed her?" Gil asked. "You know, maybe we have this all wrong. It would make a lot more sense for Sonia to have had a grudge against the police than that she actually knew who did the murders."

"That makes some sense," said Adam, nodding slowly. "But why kill Mike, then? If there was ever anyone who would want to leave all that in the past, it should have been him."

Gil shrugged. "I don't know, maybe Mike knew something about the investigation that could hurt him if people started looking into it again. Or he might have seen Art push Sonia off the deck."

"That's a thought," said Adam. "I think we've all been assuming Mike was killed because he knew something about what happened twenty years ago, but we've got a potential motive right here and now. He wouldn't even have needed to see the push, he could just have known enough that whoever did it thought he was a threat."

"Yes, because Mike can't have actually known who sent the package, can he?" Wendy asked. "I mean, that person was probably the killer. He would have had to have told someone back then."

Therese, who had been thinking about that question all day, said, "Would he? That would mean admitting that he delivered the box, and probably that he took money to do it. And that would probably have blown his chances of negotiating an early retirement with his pension intact. A decent person would have done it anyway, once he realized what he had been party to, but do you really think Mike was that person?"

"I guess not," said Gil. "But it seems like an awfully big risk to take. For the killer, I mean. To put himself or herself that much into the power of someone they didn't even know. If nothing else, Mike might have been blackmailing them."

Victor had poured himself a cup of Adam's coffee and cringed as he took a sip. "Maybe he was. He didn't say much about where his money was coming from these days, did he?"

Adam shook his head. "Aren't we forgetting something? We're starting from the assumption that this killer is one of us, here in this house. If Mike knew who it was, would he really have held his tongue? Even after Sonia died?"

"Good point," Therese said. "On the other hand, he is dead. So, maybe he didn't know the identity of his contact, and he hadn't been blackmailing them. But he had something, or the hints he was throwing around made this person think he did, to the point that it wasn't worth the risk of leaving him alive."

"But here? Now? Why would they need to do it when there's so much chance of being caught?" Wendy said.

Therese had been thinking about that too. "Was there really any more chance than any other time? Look at all of us—how many opportunities would any of the people here have to get to him? Whatever happens, we're not going to be stuck here forever. Either we get out on our own or someone will come looking, and thanks to Sonia's death, there are going to be a lot of questions asked when we do have contact with the authorities. Maybe the killer thought this was going to be their best shot, before Mike had a chance to reconsider his secrecy in the light of the new investigation."

"And did it from inside Victor's room." Wendy hadn't forgotten her favorite theory, and she wasn't about to let anyone else lose sight of it either.

Surprisingly, it was Gil who intervened this time.

"Come one, we've done this. That's one possibility. You were there when we were talking about the others."

"I was, and I still don't understand why none of you are taking this seriously. Somebody here is killing people!" Wendy threw up her hands. "Fine. Fine! If all of you want to sit around chatting, like we aren't all about to be murdered in our beds or thrown off the cliff, then go right ahead. But I'm not taking any more chances."

"Where are you going?" Gil asked as she turned to leave.

"My room. And I'm going to lock *all* the doors. Is that a problem?"

"I hope not. But I still think we're safer not spending too much time upstairs. You know, if the hillside starts to go, you aren't going to be able to get out from up there," Gil reminded her.

That made Wendy hesitate, but not for long.

"I'll take my chances," she said. "If it's my time to go, then it's my time, but I'm not going to let someone kill me."

———

"I suppose that's one way of looking at things," Therese said as Wendy vanished through the door. Gil laughed, but Adam, who seemed distracted, merely nodded.

Victor didn't even seem to hear her. Clearly upset at Wendy's revival of her accusations against him, he was casting around for other possibilities. "What if Mike killed Sonia, and then he killed himself?" he said. "Like, maybe she was going to expose him for causing her son's death, so he pushed her?"

Therese shook her head. "That part I can believe. But can you really imagine that guy being so overcome with remorse that he would take his own life? Or even thinking about it for five minutes between beers?"

From Victor's dejected expression, she deduced that he couldn't, though he didn't admit it in so many words. Instead, he got up from where he had been sitting on the sofa and looked out the window, like he had just noticed it was raining.

"I'm going to move my stuff out of my room now," he said to no one in particular. "Not like I was going to sleep in there again anyway, with a body right next door."

"What, you're afraid of zombies now?" Gil said, but his heart didn't seem to be in it, and Victor left without responding to the jibe.

Therese went back to matching up the schematics with the wires in the boxes, labeling them with numbered pieces of tape when she thought she'd figured out what went where. She was starting to become cautiously optimistic about the possibility of getting the radios functional—the tape might not be a long-term solution, but it didn't need to be. If they could just get the transmitter and receiver working for long enough to reach someone, then she didn't care if the whole set exploded after that.

Be careful what you wish for, Therese reminded herself. She wasn't exactly superstitious, but this was no time to be tempting fate.

"I really wish we had a soldering iron," Gil said. "Are you sure there isn't one around here, Adam?"

"Sorry. People in my family have never been the DIY types. My uncle was kind of the weird one with the radio thing, but he never built them or fixed them. He was mostly just convinced we'd need it when they dropped the bomb, and we had to hide out up here." He laughed, then shook his head. "I thought he was nuts, still talking about that in the nineties. It doesn't seem so crazy now."

"I don't know," said Gil. "This is pretty bad, but it's not, like, nuclear war bad."

Therese was about to congratulate him on his sense of perspective when the lights flickered and went out.

"Oh, hell no," she said, just in time for them to come back on.

Adam was already on his way to the side door. "I'll check on the generator. It's probably okay—this happens sometimes when it's been running for a while."

He left, and Therese and Gil both held still for a moment, waiting to see if the power was going to fail again. It didn't, and Therese relaxed by degrees, until she could focus enough to go back to reading the part in the transmitter manual about how they were actually supposed to operate the thing.

"I suppose you think it's true, that one of us killed Sonia and Mike?" Gil said. He was trying to sound casual, but he couldn't quite keep his voice from cracking.

"Seems likely," Therese said, avoiding his eyes. "With Joseph and Lorelei included in that, of course."

"Right, of course." Gil thought about that for a while. "If one of them did do it, do you think they'll come back? Or just do something to take out the other one and get away, like Art said?"

"I don't know. Either way, we're safer. Like I said when they left, my priority is staying alive, not bringing anyone to justice."

"Fair enough." Gil fell silent for a while, as he cautiously tested the connection of a wire he had attached to a capacitor with a complicated tape system. "Do you actually think it was one of them?"

"I don't know what to think. All I know is that it's important for us to be careful and focus on getting safely home. Any other questions can be left to the police." It wasn't entirely true, but it was good enough for now. There was still part of Therese that thought that the best chance of the rest of them getting out alive was to answer those questions now of who had committed the murders in the last two days, and that that answer was hiding in the past, in that cabin twenty years ago. And another part that just wanted to know, regardless of what it might mean for her present situation. But both parts were being overruled by her sense and her training, which were telling her that the two people who might have been closest to that knowledge had been quickly and brutally killed, and that the best way to avoid joining them was to not act like you were too invested in the investigation.

They worked for a while in silence until both Therese and Gil agreed that, as far as either of them could tell, they had made all the necessary connections, though neither was confident in their expertise.

"I really wish I paid more attention when Will tried to explain his work," Gil said. "He's the main electrician we work with, and he loves talking about this stuff, but it always just sounds like words to me."

"It's one of many skills I'm wishing I'd brought to this trip," Therese agreed. "But I think we've done the best we could. All that's left now is to hook it up and see if we can find anyone to talk to us."

They got to work putting the cases back on and were almost done when there was a gust of cold air.

"Well, the generator looks okay, so that's some good news at least." Adam came back in through the kitchen door and started peeling off his rain gear. "It's still coming down something filthy out there, though."

"How did the mountainside look? Was there any sign of slippage?" Gil asked.

Adam shook his head. "It seemed about the same. But I wouldn't even know what to look for." He came over to the island where they were working on the radios and peered into the receiver case. "Is it working yet?"

"We're about to find out," said Therese. "I think there was an antenna connection in the library, so we're going to take them in there to set them up."

"Fantastic!" If Adam shared Therese and Gil's concerns about the quality of their work, he showed no signs of it. "I'm so glad you guys were able to do this. I wouldn't have even known where to start."

"Page one of the manual worked for me," said Therese, mildly annoyed. Apparently, for Adam, work was something that was done by other people.

Just as she was thinking that, Adam stepped in to help Gil carry the radios into the library, leaving Therese to trail along behind with the manuals, her mug of coffee, and her preconceptions.

It wasn't hard to figure out where the components went on the shelf, once Gil realized that the brackets on the wall lined up with holes that had been drilled into the sides of the cases. They were trying to figure out how to connect to the antennae that ran up the side of the bookcase when Victor came in, toting an oversized suitcase. His hair was wet and his face pink from washing.

"You guys got that thing working yet? Because I've just about had it with this place."

THE COUSIN

Why had he said that? Had she even heard him? Stupid stupid stupid. "I thought you were pretty special"? What, was he still some infatuated twelve-year-old?

It was a relief to not be alone with her anymore, but he wished it hadn't been Adam who showed up first. Gil liked the guy okay—for a rich dude, he was surprisingly cool. But that was kind of the problem. Adam was the kind of guy who always had the right thing to say, the right way to say it. He never would have blurted out something dumb to a girl he'd had a crush on as a kid.

Therese had taken over trying to connect the antenna—Gil's fingers had been too thick to get into the little gap where it went—and Adam was talking with Victor about Joseph and Lorelei now, how long it would take them to get to the main road and find help. Gil didn't have anything to add to that conversation, and there didn't seem to be anything else he could do, so went back to the other room to check over the emergency supplies. Gil hadn't thought this much about what happened twenty years ago for a long time; he made an effort not to. Thinking about it brought up a lot of bad things for him, not just about Chris. But it really was all about Chris, he supposed. It always had been.

The emergency kit hadn't been stored very well—Gil tried unfolding one of the reflective blankets, and the silver coating cracked and crumbled onto his hands. Even that brought up a memory, of coming home one day in fifth grade after there had been an earthquake drill at school, full of ideas of what he was going to put in his own earthquake kit. The sheet Gil's teacher had handed out had had suggestions like storing jugs of water and a battery-powered radio, but he had bigger ideas, like packing his plaster modeling kit so he could cast broken legs and a whole tub of Kool-Aid mix, to stand in for the astronaut drink he couldn't find. Chris had helped him put it all together, though looking back now Gil was pretty sure his cousin had been laughing at him. He could remember Chris's smile so clearly, but who would smile like that at a kid who thought a bag of watermelon Jolly Ranchers was the number-one thing his family would need in case of an emergency?

That was—well, obviously it wasn't the worst part of this weekend, but it was still bad. Gil's memories of Chris had always been clear, but now he found himself beginning to doubt them. Could his cousin really have not been as good to him as Gil had thought? Were there more realizations waiting for him, situations that his young self had thought were fine, even great, that were really anything but?

And if those things weren't true, then how much else in his life might not really be what he thought it was?

THE ESCAPEES

The two figures worked their way up the road through rain that poured down like it was never going to stop. Neither of them seemed to notice it—the woman walked with her head bowed, keeping her eyes fixed firmly on where she was putting her feet as the water plastered strands of gray hair to her face, while the man held himself resolutely upright, ignoring the raindrops as he watched one side of the road and then the other.

The road had a slight upward slope—the sort of thing you wouldn't notice when driving but had more impact by the second hour of walking up it in the rain. But neither complained, they both just kept moving forward in their individual styles.

Finally, Joseph spoke.

"Maybe we should have made more of an attempt at hot-wiring the cars. How hard can it really be?"

Lorelei chuckled. "A lot harder than you would think. I tried it once, a long time ago. My buddy Bob showed me one time, and later on I tried it on my own, when, you know, I thought it would be handy to have a car. And I'll tell you, you wouldn't believe how many wires there are in there. And that was years ago, when cars were a lot simpler than they are now."

"Yeah, well, maybe it would have been worth a try. If I hadn't been in such a damn hurry to get out of there, I might have done more thinking," Joseph said. "It's going to take forever to make it to the highway at this rate."

"But we'll get there. Which is more than you could say than if we were sitting in one of those cars, shocking our fingers. You should trust your instincts more. Leaving was the right thing, and the nice thing about walking is that we've always got our feet." Lorelei thought about that and amended, "Pretty much always. Anyway, we used what we had, and we're further than we were. Sometimes, that's as much as you can hope for."

"I guess." Joseph walked on, not even looking back at the cracking sound of thunder behind them.

"You mind me coming along with you?" Lorelei asked to his retreating back.

Surprised, Joseph turned around.

"Why would I? I'm not dumb; you had a point about the hitchhiking. And there was nothing special I had in mind to do out here on my own."

"Sure. But you seemed like you were in a hurry to put some space between yourself and the people in that house, and I was one of them, if I recall."

"Oh. Well, yes, but if I'm being honest, you really weren't one of the people I wanted to get away from."

"See, that's where you're making a mistake," Lorelei said. "You don't know who was doing the killing, so you have to suspect everyone. It's just good sense."

Joseph laughed. "So by that logic, you think I could be the killer, and you came along anyway?"

"Sure. I suspect everyone, and since I don't know anything, I suspect everyone the same. You're no more likely than any of the rest of them, and there's only one of you. If I stayed there, I was definitely in the same place as the killer. Out here I've only got one chance out of seven." Lorelei gave him one of her toothless smiles. "I was pretty good at math before I dropped out of school."

A little further on, the road started to level out at a stretch of fresh pavement that made walking easier. For a moment, there was even a break in the rain, and a little sunlight filtered through the clouds. Neither of the pair said anything, but both picked up their pace, and Lorelei even took her eyes off her feet for a moment to look up at the sky. Joseph turned to her, smiling.

"If I didn't know better, I'd say—" he began, but the words died on his lips as they came around a bend.

A giant fir tree had fallen across the road, blocking it completely. It had been growing on the uphill side, close enough to the pavement that the dirt that had come up with the roots spilled halfway across the lane. Moving it was out of the question—each branch was the size of a small tree, and the trunk must have been five feet across. And going around was no better an option, with the upturned roots on one side forming a twisted fence and the other end of the tree extending out over a sheer drop on the downhill side.

"Okay then," Joseph said as he tightened the straps of his backpack. "How long's it been since you climbed a tree?"

Lorelei eyed the barrier with suspicion. "I don't know if that's such a good idea, with it being so wet. Climbing is harder than you'd think, believe me."

"With all due respect, I don't care." Joseph was already working his way in past the foliage toward the trunk, looking for likely branches to support his weight. "My family is on the other side of this tree, and nothing is going to stop me from getting back to them."

He found a branch about two feet from the ground and climbed onto it, steadying himself with one hand on a neighboring branch and the other gripping the rough bark of the trunk. After its short break, the rain was intensifying, gathering in the fir tree's needles and running down in streams and waterfalls that would suddenly change direction.

As Joseph got higher on the fallen tree, the wind began to pick up, but it didn't slow his progress. From where she watched below, squinting into the wind and the rain, Lorelei shouted encouragement and instructions.

"Don't go too fast there, you got it. There's a big gap in front of you; you're going to have to move to the left. Not that one, that branch doesn't look too good. I think you'd better go down to that big one and come back up."

Whether Joseph heard her and decided to ignore her advice, or her words were simply carried away by the wind, it wasn't clear. But the branch he reached for was leafless and long dead, and it held his weight for only a moment before its rotten core gave way, sending him tumbling through the air.

23

W hat do you know about anything, anyway?" Victor said.
"More than you," Adam retorted. "About pretty much
everything, I'd say."

They were arguing about what kind of explosives were used in
pressure cooker bombs, but at that point it could have been almost
anything. The day was dragging on, and the storm was still raging,
and the stress of their situation was quickly turning into anger. To
make matters worse, the radio transmitter and receiver were fully
connected and plugged in, but nothing seemed to come through
besides static and an occasional channel repeating recorded
messages about the weather or just a series of numbers. Therese
turned the knob slowly, inching her way through the wavelengths
to be sure she didn't miss anything, but there didn't seem to be
anything to miss.

To distract herself from her rising irritation, she focused on
where all of the other guests were, and how long it had been since

she had seen them. It was nearly three hours since Joseph and Lorelei had left; surely they must be getting close to the main road by now? And the others—

Gil, who had been repeating their names and location into the transmitter at different frequencies, abruptly set down the microphone and stood up. "I think I'd like to take a look at that burn scar. I'll be back soon."

"Be careful," Therese said absently, her mind half on the radio static and half on who else was missing.

It had been an hour since they had learned about Art's involvement with Sonia, and neither he nor Wendy had returned. Therese wasn't particularly bothered by the lack of their company, but the way things were going, she didn't think it was a good idea for anyone to be separated from the rest of the group for that long. And since she wasn't making any progress with the radio anyway, Therese decided it was worth going to check on the two missing people. Neither of them was likely to be interested in seeing her, so she decided to start with the option that at least kept her inside and dry.

"If either of you guys want to see if you can pull any signal in on this thing, go for it. I'm going to check on Wendy," Therese announced to Adam and Victor. "Just to make sure she doesn't need anything."

"Like a body bag?" Victor replied, joking. No one laughed.

———

Nothing had changed about the upper floor since the last time Therese had been there, but it felt oddly empty and ominous. It was only her imagination, she told herself; there wasn't really that much hazard to being up here, even if it wasn't a good idea in the long term. She was just letting the idea that it was dangerous get into her head.

That and the dead body in one of the rooms.

Whatever it was, the silence in the hallway seemed oppressive, away from the sound of the rain. The thickness of the carpet that had seemed so luxurious when she arrived now swallowed her footsteps and gave her progress a ghostly quality. Therese cleared her throat unnecessarily, just to make it clear she wasn't trying to sneak up on anyone.

Both doors at the end of the hall were shut and locked. Therese took a moment to look inside her room, just long enough to confirm she hadn't missed taking anything she might need. Then she crossed the hall and knocked on Wendy's door.

No one answered.

Therese waited a minute, then knocked again. There were plenty of reasons Wendy might not have come to the door. She could be napping, or in the bathroom, or listening to music on headphones. Or she could be lying in a pool of her own blood, or taking her last breaths as she struggled at the end of a rope. She was on her way back to her room to assess the relative strength of the connecting bathroom door when the handle on Wendy's door turned and the other woman looked out.

"What's going on? Did something happen?"

Therese willed herself not to feel foolish.

"No, I was just checking on you. It's been a while and I wanted to keep tabs on people."

Wendy made a face like she'd been called to the principal's office. "Well, I'm here and I'm fine. No tabs needed."

It was the sort of line that might be followed by a door shutting in her face, but since Wendy stayed where she was, so did Therese.

"We got the radio hooked up, but we haven't been able to reach anyone yet," Therese said conversationally. "And we should probably start thinking about dinner at some point. There's no telling when Joseph and Lorelei are going to get back, if they even make it today."

"Or ever." Wendy gripped the edge of the door, so hard that her knuckles and fingertips were turning white. "Seriously, what's your deal? Did you really come all the way up here to talk to me about food, when we could all be killed anytime?"

"I came up to check on you," Therese repeated. "Just because I don't talk about it at every moment doesn't mean I'm not aware of the danger we're in."

"That most of us are in," Wendy corrected. "There's one person here who has nothing to be scared of, because they're doing the killing."

"True. Though, in a way, I suspect they're the most afraid of all of us. That's what makes them so dangerous."

Wendy didn't look convinced, but she also didn't close the door.

"But not you, right? You're not dangerous, because you're a cop," she said.

Therese smiled. "There's a couple of problems with that line of reasoning, but sure. What else would I say? But you shouldn't take my word for it. Or anyone else's, for that matter. The only person any of us can be sure of is ourselves."

"So what are you doing, being alone up here with me?"

"Taking my chances, I guess. Anyway, I'm not sure it's a good idea for you to stay up here, even if you are keeping your door locked. The rain isn't letting up, and landslides are no joke."

"Yeah? Well, maybe I'm taking my chances too. Two people are dead, and it's not from the house falling down."

Therese nodded. "Fair enough. We'll be down in the library or the lounge if you change your mind. I'm going to get that radio working if it's the last thing I do."

Wendy stared at her like she wasn't quite sure she had heard right, then burst out laughing.

"You're just totally crazy, aren't you?"

Therese shrugged as she turned to leave. "Wouldn't you be, if you were me?"

———

Back downstairs, Therese was steeling herself to go out to see what Art was up to, and wondering if it would be a good idea to take someone with her, when she was distracted by the sound of voices raised in yet another argument. She slowed her steps as she approached the door, stopping to listen beside one of the resident taxidermied bears.

"How would you know that if you weren't there?" Victor was saying. Gil mumbled something indistinct, and then Adam's voice came through clearly.

"Well, I was there, not that night but plenty of other times. And I can tell you that it's not possible."

"I didn't say I knew anything; I just wondered," Gil said, having apparently recovered his voice. "And if there was a way for someone to have been hiding in the cabin, who didn't get hurt in the explosion, wouldn't that explain how they were able to time the bomb just right? Otherwise, how would they even know anyone would be in there when it went off? Everyone might have gone out to watch the fireworks or something."

Therese had heard enough. This was, at least, a topic on which she could claim to be an expert. "It's not a bad point, but you couldn't see them from there," she said as she came into the room. "Honestly, there wasn't much reason to hang out outside of the cabin at all, especially at night. And Adam's right—the whole place was just one main room and a bathroom. There was nowhere for someone to hide."

"Not like here," added Victor, who clearly didn't want them to lose sight of his theory of an outside killer stalking the premises.

The work on the radio must have lost its appeal, because none of the men were paying any attention to it. Gil, back from his trip outside with the wet hair and clothes to show for it, was pacing around the library, while Adam sat in an armchair and Victor hunted for something in his suitcase.

"Still no luck with the radios?" Therese asked, hoping to head off another round of argument.

Gil and Adam at least looked embarrassed. Victor seemed to only be annoyed that he wasn't able to push his pet idea.

"They started to smell," Gil explained. "We thought maybe

the tape was getting too hot, so we unplugged them for a bit to cool down. But it's probably been long enough now."

"Okay, then let's get to it." Therese didn't like the idea of the smell, and when she got closer to the receiver, she could pick it up too—a faint whiff of too-warm paper.

She hesitated for a moment after plugging the devices back in. But nothing happened, and the smell seemed to be growing fainter, so she went back to her slow survey of the channels while Adam took over Gil's job of transmitting their location over random wavelengths. He was using a loud, clear voice, as though his personal volume could boost the signal, and Therese was about to ask him to turn it down when she caught something through the static on the receiver.

"Wait, listen!" she said, holding up her hand. Adam fell silent, and the conversation Gil and Victor had been having about house wiring ended abruptly.

"There it is again, listen." Therese leaned closer to the receiver as the others gathered around her. Sure enough, it was a man's voice, though she couldn't hear what he was saying through the static. But it sounded like a live person was talking to someone, and if they could talk, maybe they could listen.

"It's just over eighteen megahertz," she said, squinting at the dial. "Maybe eighteen point seven? Try tuning to that, maybe we can talk to them."

Adam turned the knob, trying to match the frequency where Therese had found the voice.

"Hello? Emergency, SOS. SOS, emergency," he repeated, getting louder again as he went on.

Therese leaned down and put her ear next to the speaker, trying to catch some indication that they were being heard. She put her hand on the side of the receiver to support herself, which was why she was the first to be aware of the heat coming from inside.

"Oh shit," she said, at the same moment she and everyone else smelled the smoke.

Therese jumped up and pulled the plugs out of the outlet, then grabbed a blanket that had been folded on the back of one of the chairs and used it to smother the radio. Adam ran out of the room and came back with a fire extinguisher, and a few sprays from that seemed to solve the immediate problem.

What it left them with wasn't much better.

"Maybe they heard us?" Victor said.

"Heard what? Someone saying it was an emergency?" Gil shoved his balled-up fists in his pockets and looked deliberately away from the rest of them. "I guess there's probably a reason people don't usually do electrical work with masking tape."

Therese wasn't having any of it. "We did the best we could with what we had. Next time we'll do better."

Adam gestured at the foam-spattered equipment. "How is there going to be a next time?"

Therese didn't blame him for his frustration. Rationally, she should have found the situation hopeless too. But something in her wouldn't accept that. They had come so close; to stop now would be what a quitter would do.

She found herself caught up in a memory, not of being a

teenager but of her time at the Academy. The instructor, a grizzled veteran with thirty years of service in the agency, had been leading them through a hypothetical investigation to a point where it seemed like they were out of options. One of her classmates had said as much and the instructor had smiled, like he was expecting this.

"There's always something," he'd said. "It may not be a good option, or an easy one, but you'll be surprised how far you can get by not taking 'It can't be done' for an answer."

"We'll let it cool down completely, clean it up, and try again, maybe use foil or something for the wires." Therese was aware that she was giving orders again, and that reminded her of what she had meant to be doing when she came into the room. "In the meantime, we should check on Art."

"Why? He said he wanted to sit outside, let him sit outside," Victor said. "There's still some of that whiskey left, right? As long as he's out there, more for the rest of us."

"No," said Therese, her earlier sense of foreboding returning. "It's been too long. He can either hot-wire a car or he can't, but it's no good leaving him to sit out there on his own. And if he really did succeed and drive off, I'd like to know."

As if to punctuate her point, the rain suddenly intensified, and a flash of lightning was followed much too quickly by the thunder. Therese wasn't sure, but she thought she saw one of the tallest trees down the hillside split under the strike.

"I think we need to check on Art," she repeated.

24

Therese was relieved when the three men fell in behind her. She didn't like the idea of letting herself be caught alone, and Art's warning about shooting anyone who surprised him was still on her mind. Not that she really thought he was serious, but when approaching an armed man, there was at least comfort in numbers.

At least there was no question Art had been busy. As soon as they came out the front door, it was clear that an attempt had been made on almost every car, with broken windows being Art's entry method of choice. That he hadn't succeeded was demonstrated by the fact that all of the vehicles were still in the driveway, in various states of damage. Only Adam's Tesla had been left unmolested.

But, once again, she didn't see the man himself, until she took a closer look at her own rental car. The last to arrive, she had parked the furthest down the driveway and it was hard to see much more than an outline, but from the bulk of the silhouette, Therese assumed it must be Art. He was bent over like he was working on something under the dashboard—or napping—so she led the way toward the car, calling out to him as she went, her fear rising with every moment he didn't move.

The second time she called Art's name and there was no response, Therese broke into a run. Ignoring the rain that spattered her face and flattened her hair, she kept her focus on Art's figure in the car, willing it to sit up, to yell at her, to wave that stupid gun around. But he didn't and as she got closer, Therese noticed several things, and one of them caused her to take a sharp, involuntary breath.

"What is it?" asked Gil, who was right behind her.

Therese slowed back down to a walk and tried to control her voice. "He didn't need to break in twice."

"What?"

But they were next to the car now, and Therese didn't have to explain. Not with the clear pattern of blood spattered on the driver's side window, and the spiderweb of cracks that were not caused by Art trying to get in, but by a bullet on its way out.

Art was slumped forward in the driver's seat, his forehead resting awkwardly on the steering wheel. The passenger side window was broken, and the door on that side was unlocked, so Therese opened it with her jacket wrapped around her hand. She had little hope of prints at this point, but procedures had to be followed. As she did it, she noticed fragments of glass on the ground, not where they should have been for a window that had been smashed inward.

Art's face was tilted toward them, slack-jawed, sightlessly staring, and half-coated with blood. The entry hole just left of center in his forehead was tidy enough, but the exploded matter on the window behind him left no question of a miracle miss.

It was obvious what had killed him. Art's gun was on the seat next to him, awkwardly cradled in his limp hand. The three men had all gathered around the door behind Therese, and despite the horror in the other seat, she could tell they were all staring at it.

"Could he have shot himself?" Victor asked, the hopeful note in his voice faltering even as he said it.

Gil snorted. "Are you crazy? Like that could have happened three times? Do you think there's some kind of curse on this place that makes people commit suicide as soon as they're alone?"

"He didn't shoot himself." Therese pointed, drawing their unwilling gazes up to the dead man's face. "Look at where that bullet hole is. Nobody holds a gun like that. He was shot by someone sitting here next to him, who put the gun in his hand, hoping we might be stupid enough to think he did it." She looked around at them with finality. "And we're not."

Therese took the silence that followed as an opportunity to examine the rest of the car. The passenger seat was soaked with rain, and most of the broken glass that wasn't on the ground had been swept off onto the floor. Art might have done that when he got into the car, to keep the shards from cutting him as he slid over into the driver's seat, but it was more likely it had been done by his killer. Therese wished she had been more observant of the people who had come and gone from the house that afternoon—a memory of someone turning up with a bit of glass on their pants would be very useful right now.

She didn't have that, but at least she was sure whoever had shot Art was someone he recognized. Therese hadn't really believed his threat to fire at anyone who got close to him, but she couldn't see him staying calmly in his seat as a stranger carefully brushed aside the glass before sitting down next to him and taking his gun. In fact, she could see no signs of a struggle at all.

Therese was pondering the implications of that when there was a cracking sound, and she looked over at the house just in time to see a tree branch fall and tumble down the hillside. When she looked back, Adam was holding the gun.

"What do you think you're doing? That's evidence," she said, shocked and furious.

Adam was unmoved. "It's also a weapon. And there's no way in hell I'm going to just leave it sitting here where anybody can pick it up and start shooting the rest of us."

"But we're supposed to trust you with it?" Gil asked. "Not a chance."

"Then who?" Adam said. "You? At least I've never spent time behind bars."

Therese sighed. "Looks, there's no one the rest of us is going to trust to have a weapon at this point. Let's just throw it down the hillside. The police can go find it when they get here; it can't get much more contaminated anyway. Nothing about this situation is going to be improved by adding a gun."

Now it was Victor's turn to be outraged. "No way, not a chance. What if I'm right, and there really is someone else here? That gun might be our best chance to defend ourselves."

Therese was too cold and wet to feel like arguing.

"Okay," she said. "We'll split the gun up. I'll take the ammunition magazines, and Adam can keep the rest. That way, no one can use it on their own, and if we need it, we can use it."

"And let the rest of us get killed while you're putting it back together?" Victor said. "What kind of stupid plan is that?"

"This isn't up for debate. Look, your imaginary outsider obviously doesn't have a gun, or they would have used it by now. And, if they existed, they probably would have taken this one." Therese looked around at the three men and said, "The way I see it, it makes a lot more sense that the killer left it behind because he or she knew the rest of us would be looking for it on them."

That finally shut Victor up, so Therese took the magazine out of the gun (noting as she did that only one bullet had been fired), ejected the round from the chamber, and handed the body of the weapon back to Adam. Then, with some reluctance, she ducked into the car and crawled across the passenger seat to hunt through Art's pockets until she found the spare magazine and his room key. She didn't like the idea of having to explain her actions to any future investigators, but not as much as she disliked not being alive to talk to them.

While she was there, Therese took the opportunity to get a closer look at the corpse, which had gone cold and stiffened in its slouched position. Art had slid the seat all the way back—the better to get at the dashboard, probably—and some wires from under the steering wheel had been pulled out and ineptly disconnected. His face was blank and gray, and his faded button-down shirt was crusted with blood, but other than that he looked almost peaceful.

A closer examination confirmed Therese's impression that Art hadn't done much to fight his attacker—in fact, it looked like he hadn't even tried to move out of his seat before he was shot. So either the killer had been very fast, or Art had handed over the gun willingly. Given the choice between a killer with superhuman speed and Art having been kind of dumb, Therese knew where she would put her money.

Having gotten all she could out of the scene for now, Therese backed out of the car before anyone started to ask questions.

"This is probably it for the ammunition, but we should check Art's room just in case," she said, holding out the magazine so they could see. "I don't think there's anything more we can do here."

The men either agreed with her or were as sick as she was of standing out in the rain because they followed her back to the house without any further arguments.

———

"What happened? Where have you been?"

They had barely gotten through the front door when Wendy came hurrying down the stairs.

"Art is dead," said Therese. "Someone shot him while he was out trying to get the cars started. With his own gun."

She let Adam finish the explanations, including what had happened to the radio, while she peeled off her sopping jacket and transferred the ammunition to her pants pockets. As Adam described the arrangement with the gun, Wendy turned to stare at her and Therese could see the distrust in her eyes.

Therese didn't blame her. The gun was another potential flash point in an already volatile situation, and the more she thought about it, the less she liked the idea of there being a weapon on hand, even if it was in pieces.

"What are we going to do now?" Wendy asked. She hadn't meant her question literally, but Therese answered it anyway, because she didn't know what else to say.

"We're going to search Art's room, in case he had any other weapons." She finished wringing out her hair and started up the stairs, then stopped and looked back. "I think we had all better go together."

25

Art's room wasn't as much of a mess as Mike's had been, but it did suggest a man who had lived most of his life with someone else to clean up after him. Clothes spilled out of the open suitcase, and the top of the dresser was littered with detritus—a couple of pens, a belt, some crumpled receipts that must have been pulled out of emptied pockets. The bed was unmade, with only one pillow dented, the other side left waiting for an absent companion.

Therese started her search in the drawers of the bedside table, while Adam and Wendy made straight for the suitcase, and Gil peered at the receipts. Victor stayed in the doorway, looking nervously down the hall.

Coming up empty on the tables, Therese did a quick search around and under the bed, to make sure she hadn't missed anything. She didn't really expect to find any additional weapons or ammunition—Art had struck her as the type who liked to keep that sort of thing close at hand—but considering the stakes, it was worth being thorough. Adam was working his way through the man's limited wardrobe, shaking shirts and turning out pockets, and Therese was about to ask what he thought he might find when Gil turned from his spot by the dresser with something in his hand.

"Hey, look what I found." Gil held up a small clothbound notebook. "It was in the middle drawer here. Do you think it was Art's?"

"Must have been," said Victor, emboldened enough to come all the way into the room. "My room didn't come with a free book."

"It's not one of the features of the house rental," Adam agreed. "And the cleaners are supposed to put anything that gets left in the lost and found. What's in it?"

Gil laid the notebook out on the bed, and they all gathered around as he started flipping through the lined pages. The first few were unremarkable: lists of household tasks, names and numbers for local plumbers, a reminder to get an oil change by the fifteenth. Based on the dates that showed up on the pages, it seemed the book was something Art had meant to use to improve his organization, but only occasionally followed through on.

There were a couple of blank pages, and for a moment Therese thought that might be it, but Gil kept going, and about a third of the way in, the writing resumed.

The first page had the dates of the present weekend, and the address for the lodge, with directions. These looked as though they had been copied down hastily, possibly from a phone call.

At the bottom of the page was the note "background check Sonia Fletcher."

The information from the check must have come back good, or at least not bad enough to overcome Art's curiosity, because the next several pages were filled with more notes relating to the weekend. There was a list of the bedrooms, with instructions for him to take the one they were in now, next door to Sonia's, and a reminder to not eat any of the food except for the tortillas and the chicken. ("No salsa" was underlined twice.)

"I guess that settles that," Gil said. "He was working with Sonia, and she told him not to eat the poisoned food. Can you believe this guy?"

"Unfortunately, yes." Therese thought back to all the times her dad had come home from work, enraged about yet another way the brass had arranged things for their own benefit, and to hell with everyone else.

Victor, on the other hand, was still incredulous. "But what was he going to get out of it? Say he helps Sonia, and she tells him what she knows, then what? He'd still be in trouble for what he did to us."

"He probably thought it was worth it, if it meant solving the case," Adam said. "Think about it. Here's a guy who lost his job because of his own wrongdoing and had to resign. And now he gets another chance at the biggest unsolved case of his career—don't you think that would be worth some risk?"

"But probably not as much of a risk as he ended up taking," Gil pointed out.

Wendy, who was straining to read over Adam's shoulder, showed less interest in the outcome of Art's decisions than his planning. "What do you think 'four knocks' means? Is that a drug reference?"

Adam shook his head. "More likely the super-secret signal Sonia was going to use to tell him it was time to go. I'm not getting the impression this was a really sophisticated operation."

"Yeah, but they still managed to steal all of our stuff," Therese pointed out, but her heart wasn't in it. Gil had started to turn the page before Victor stopped him because he was still reading, but she had gotten a glimpse of what was on the other side, and she was impatient to see more.

Finally, everyone had gotten what they could out of the current pages, and with one last expression of regret for the deliciousness of the carnitas, Gil flipped the page.

Here, Art moved on from his practical preparations to what he clearly saw as his role as investigator. The top of the page had the date of the first murders, with the victims' names and ages written beneath and a code that Therese recognized as the original case number, which she had seen in public records requests over the years. Below that was Sean's name and date of death, with some notes about his background and schooling, and one about the equipment shed fire that showed the authorities hadn't completely dropped the ball on that one, though a parenthetical lowercase "feds" suggested that Art's people couldn't take the credit.

But it was on the facing page that Art really got going. At the top he had written "SUSPECT LIST" in block printing, and below were their names, in approximate alphabetical order. Therese read through it first with alarm, then increasing amusement, ending at frustration and disgust.

Amy Therese Brewer—there that night/got away just in
    time/dad might have covered?/not likely
Adam Reynolds—sister killed/something creepy there?/
    knew the cottage/too attractive
Victor Aguilar—jealous unpopular/immigrant/no girl-
    friend/something about a video? ask S
Joseph Boden—deviant/dangerous/works with kids/
    prob obsessive
Gil Morley—young kid then/violent-crazy?/boys like
    bombs/might hate cousin
Lorelei Hughes—junkie/nuts/prob still using/we elim-
    inated but S thinks she can get something from her
Wendy Zhao—poor family/S thinks parents could have
    set it up/shifty
Mike Swift—does he know something?/could be bad/
    talk to him first

"Shifty?" said Wendy. "It's a good thing I didn't see this until after he was dead, because I'd definitely be a suspect."

Therese didn't bother pointing out that she already was. Though, honestly, if the killer believed the former detective was enough of a threat that he had to be put out of the way immediately, Therese thought they might have miscalculated.

If this list was a good representation of how Art's mind worked, and she had no reason to think it wasn't, it was no wonder the case had never been solved. In fact, it was amazing that anything might have been, though thinking back over her childhood, Therese couldn't remember any criminal investigations that involved less than three eyewitnesses ever having been settled. Her father had once described his boss as dumber than a sack of hammers, and right now Therese was thinking that might have been unfair to the hammers.

But where intelligence had failed Art, luck seemed to have come through for him (at least until it ran out in the driver's seat of Therese's rental car). Everything in his notes indicated that Sonia had done all the work of putting together the guest list and arranging this weekend, for all the good it had done her. But there must have been some things she hadn't shared with her confederate before he had arrived, which were made clear by the next page, the last to have anything on it. The writing here was in a different pen, a failing ballpoint, and seemed to have been written quickly, in a state of agitation. There was no header, and the words spilled down across the lines.

she has knife?? need to examine knife
had to give up phone, see about theft charges when back
who is Lenny? talk to him

And then, at the bottom of the page, written in all capital letters and underlined twice:

GET THAT SHIRT

Gil frowned at the page, like he had been expecting something more. "What do you think he means about a shirt? Seems like a weird place to have that."

"Are you sure it says *shirt*?" asked Victor. "It looks like *short* to me."

Adam snorted. "Like that makes any more sense? Was he planning his investment strategy or something?"

Therese wasn't really listening to any of them. "He must have written this after he got here. Like these are things Sonia told him to get him to give up his phone when he didn't want to. And it makes sense—if he'd known she had the knife before, he would have sent his buddies from the force to get it. So maybe this shirt is something else she had."

They all looked back at Art's suitcase, its contents spilled onto the floor by Adam and Wendy's hasty search. None of the shirts looked at all remarkable, but it was the obvious place to start.

Art's clothing choices were not what you would call inspired. For the three days of the weekend, he had packed four shirts (plus the one currently worn by his corpse), none of which was substantially different from the others. All were cotton, button front, worn at the collar and the wrists, and all in shades ranging from dark to light blue. No amount of scrutiny could turn up any clues within them, and more to the point, there was no indication that any of the shirts had ever belonged to anyone but Art.

"It makes sense," Therese said. "Why would he have a note about getting the shirt if he had brought it with him?"

Adam nodded. "It must have been something Sonia told him about. But I guess we'll never know."

Therese wasn't so sure about that last part, but she didn't say so. There would be time enough for that when she was trying to convince whatever agency ended up with the case to turn Sonia's house inside out, looking for any and all shirts she might have in her possession. Art had obviously thought it was important, and as little respect as she had for his intelligence, she was going to give him that one.

But to do that, she was going to have to survive for long enough to tell someone, and that was anything but a given. First Sonia, then Mike, and now Art were all dead, all because they knew—or maybe just appeared to know—something about the long-ago murders. How much would the rest of them have to learn before they were threats too? Were they already there?

Even the weight of the ammunition in her pocket, which ought to have been reassuring, only increased her anxiety. In her experience, guns didn't make a situation better; they just increased the opportunities for them to get worse.

She was going to have to do something about that.

⸺

They moved on from the suitcase to searching the rest of the room, and as Gil got up from where he was kneeling on the floor to check under a chair, Victor reached out a hand to stop him.

"Wait a minute. What's that on your shoe?"

Victor pointed at the bottom of Gil's sneaker, where something small and clear glittered in the treads.

"It looks like glass," Wendy said.

"Safety glass," Victor corrected. "Like the kind that was all around the car where Art was shot. How did that get onto your shoe, Gil?"

Gil's face clouded over with anger.

"What do you mean? It got there when we were all out looking at the car, obviously. You probably have some too."

But Victor didn't, and neither did Therese or Adam.

"Okay, but that doesn't prove anything," Gil argued. "We were all out there, you saw the glass on the ground. I must have gotten it then, because I wasn't there before. When could I have gone?"

"When you left the room to check the hillside," Adam said. "I don't think any of us were in there for the whole time. Wendy was mostly in her room, Victor went to take a shower, and Therese left to check on Wendy."

"And you went out to check on the generator," Therese finished. "So none of us have an alibi."

Adam nodded. "True enough. So what are we going to do about that?"

"We could start by not throwing around accusations without good reason," Therese said. "And we could also resolve to keep a better eye on each other."

Therese thought that point might finally get through to them, and was immediately proved wrong.

"Okay, fine. But these arguments aren't getting us anywhere.

I'm going to go downstairs and see if I can find anything we can use to fix that radio. If Lorelei and Joseph don't get back soon, that may be our only option," Adam said as he headed for the door.

Wendy jumped up to follow him. "I'll help you. There's got to be something around here we can use."

Victor and Gil both left the room too, and Therese sent up a silent thought of sympathy to every one of her colleagues who had to deal with civilians in an emergency. It wasn't all bad, though— the search of Art's room had reminded her she hadn't had a chance to go through Sonia's possessions since all they were looking for were the keys and phones, and she wouldn't mind being able to do this one on her own.

No one was in the hallway when Therese stepped out, and she made her way to Sonia's door in quick strides, her footsteps muffled by the carpet. As she opened the door, Therese could hear Wendy's voice fading down the stairs. "I mean, *shifty*? Seriously?"

26

The last search of Sonia's room had been more thorough than detailed, with every potential hiding place torn apart and anything that couldn't hide keys or a phone discarded on the floor. For the first few minutes, Therese just looked around and took in the destruction.

The mattress was off the bed, the furniture was moved away from the walls, and all the bureau drawers had been pulled out and emptied. On the floor the contents of Sonia's suitcase were spread out, with the suitcase itself disassembled down to its metal structure. Sonia's purse, a large black bag made of cracked faux leather, had suffered the same fate. Even the bathroom hadn't been spared—Therese wasn't sure how much could possibly have been hidden in the towels or the toilet paper rolls, but she appreciated the thought.

But all anyone who was here before had been seeking were their own keys and phones; now that Therese knew those were gone, she looked at the scene with new eyes. The first thing she did was to go through all the shirts she could find, though she wasn't surprised when this search was no more productive than the last. Whatever had made Art write about a shirt in all caps with two underlines, Therese didn't see it having been a synthetic-blend blouse in one of three colors or a surprisingly lacy pajama top. So she moved on to find out what else Sonia had seen fit to pack for her weekend of trying to prove her son hadn't acted alone in killing five people twenty years ago.

The answer, it turned out, was "not much." Therese found printouts of the rental agreement for the house, which confirmed what Adam had said about there only being one extra set of keys and listed an eye-watering price for the weekend. (Therese wasn't sure how popular a place this remote would be, but if Adam was able to rent it for even a quarter of the year at those prices, he must be doing all right. Though it was possible the events of this weekend would change that.)

She was contemplating the receipt from a Mexican restaurant in Sacramento when she heard the door open behind her. Willing herself not to move quickly, Therese straightened up from where she was bent over the items she had spread out on the bed, placing her hand over the pocket with the ammunition with what she hoped was a natural motion.

"Hey," said Gil. "Sorry, I didn't mean to surprise you. I just heard someone moving around in here, and I wanted to see what was going on. Are you looking for the shirt?"

He smiled at her, but Therese wasn't happy with the situation.

After Art's death, the one thing she had set as a priority was to not be alone with any of the other guests, and now here she was, with Gil blocking her path to the door. Her size disadvantage meant it wouldn't be much good trying to get past him, so the best she could do was to play it cool and hope for the best.

"Yes, but no luck. Whatever that note was about, I don't think it's here." It was the truth, and Therese didn't mind sharing it. She wasn't happy with the results of her search, but at least finding nothing meant she had nothing to hide.

Therese tried to measure the distances between herself, Gil, and the door as subtly as possible as she returned the rental agreement printouts to the pile on the dresser and said, "If Sonia did have anything, it was probably in that briefcase where she had the knife."

Gil brightened up but made no move to get out of her way. "Oh yeah, I saw that downstairs. I was going to ask about it, but I forgot. Something must have happened."

"Several things have," Therese agreed. "Well, if anything's still there now, it can wait a little while longer. I'm going back to my room to freshen up and change into some dry clothes. I don't know about you, but all that time we spent out in the rain has me soaked to the skin."

If Gil was surprised by her sudden outbreak of fussiness, he didn't show it, and Therese passed him easily on her way to the door.

"That's a good idea," he called after her retreating back. "Maybe I'll do the same. See you downstairs?"

Therese paused and unbent just enough to smile at him.

"Sure. I won't be long."

——

With everything that had been going on, Therese hadn't been paying much attention to the state of her clothes. But now that she had mentioned it, she couldn't help noticing how cold and wet she was, and though she had long ago stopped believing the myth about getting sick from being out in the rain, she couldn't quite convince the scratchy feeling in the back of her throat.

She had taken most of her practical clothes downstairs already, as much as she could fit in her smaller bag in case she had to escape, so the options left in her room were limited. But she didn't want to waste any time, so she went with what she had on hand. Which meant that she ended up wearing her best silk blouse and the skinny jeans she only wore when she knew she wasn't going to be sitting for very long.

And anyway, she hadn't really come back to her room to change. As soon as Therese was decently dressed, she cleared a space on top of the dresser and got to work.

It took her more time than it should have, because as familiar as Therese was with the theory, she had never actually tried what she was doing now. As she worked, she could hear Wendy moving around in the next room—either the search had been successful, or they'd decided the radio was beyond fixing after all. Whatever Wendy was up to, Therese hoped she wasn't planning to stay upstairs long—recent events might have pushed the fear of landslides into the background, but the oversaturated ground didn't know that, and nobody should be upstairs for longer than they needed to.

She was aware that she needed to take her own advice, and she planned to, but she thought she had time for one more stop before she took on the next step.

Her hand was on the bathroom doorknob when she heard the shout. It was followed by a series of thumps and then silence, but by then Therese was already out the door.

———

The sound of groaning was coming from the staircase. Therese raced down the length of the hallway and found Gil lying halfway down the stairs, hanging onto the railing and cursing.

"Are you okay?"

Gil looked up at her, scrabbling to get his feet back on the steps. "Yeah, I'm fine. Ow, dammit, I think I hit my elbow."

He got himself to a sitting position and flexed his arm a couple of times.

"Seems okay."

Adam appeared in the doorway from the dining room, carrying a dish towel. "Did something happen? I heard shouting?"

"It was nothing," Gil said sarcastically. "Just someone pushed me down the stairs. No biggie."

"Somebody pushed you?" Wendy asked. She and Victor arrived at the top of the stairs at the same time, both looking shocked and concerned.

Gil, who really must not have been seriously hurt, merely looked pissed.

"Yeah, somebody. Somebody who came up behind me and put their hands on my back and pushed and then ran away. And unless Victor's mystery man has a secret hidey-hole in one of these rooms, then I think it had to be one of you."

Wendy looked shocked and Victor stammered a denial, and even Therese, who had expected nothing less, found herself feeling defensive.

Only Adam, safely downstairs, was able to respond calmly.

"Well, at least you're not hurt. But maybe it's time now for us all to come down, and stay where we can see each other?"

It was what Therese had been trying to suggest for two days without success, but she noticed no one took any issue with the idea when it came from Adam. On the other hand, it was the right thing to do, so Therese decided to stow her outrage for the time being.

"I'll be right there," she said. "I just have to grab a couple of things from my room."

She didn't need to take much, just her shoes and the ammunition magazines, which she had left on top of the dresser.

The good news was that her shoes were still there. Therese stood for a long moment looking at the blank space where the magazines had been and thinking. Then Therese took a deep breath.

"All right," she said. "Here we go."

27

The others took the news of the missing ammunition about as well as could be expected. Which is to say, not very.

"You let them get stolen?" Victor said, "You, Miss 'I'm an FBI agent so I'm in charge'? Why the hell did we ever listen to you?"

"You didn't, mostly," Therese pointed out. "But yes, I'm sorry. It was a serious oversight." She looked around at the other three who had been upstairs with her. "I don't suppose the person who took them would like to own up? Let's just say you were doing it for safekeeping, because I was clearly not to be trusted, and someone else can hold on to them instead."

No one took her up on her offer, and the silence grew awkward. They were back in the open lounge area, with Adam and Wendy in the kitchen, and Victor and Gil sitting on the sofas, as far apart as they could get. Therese stayed near the door to the dining room, awkwardly leaning on a side table.

"Well, the gun's safe anyway," Gil muttered. He hadn't looked straight at Therese since his fall down the stairs, which made her wonder if he suspected her of doing the pushing. It wouldn't be unreasonable—after all, she had been the first to arrive on the scene.

And Gil couldn't have been the one to take the ammunition, since at the time the magazines had vanished, she had been looking right at him, lying on the stairs. Of course, that didn't prevent the entire episode from having been a setup, designed to get her out of the way so Victor or Wendy could make the grab.

Therese shook her head. The suspects were narrowing down, but she didn't see how it helped her. If anything, the danger would only increase as the list got shorter.

Victor stood up.

"I've had enough," he said. "I should have left with Joseph and Lorelei. But who knows if they're ever coming back, so I'm going now."

"The hell you are," said Gil. "What's to stop you from sneaking around and getting back into the house, so you can kill the rest of us? From right now until help gets here, I say nobody leaves this room."

"That's crazy; I'll—"

But whatever Victor was going to do about Gil's proposal, they never found out. He was interrupted by a roaring sound and a crash that shook the building so hard it knocked Adam off his feet and sent Therese stumbling into the couch where Gil was sitting.

"What was that? An earthquake?" Wendy made a move like she was about to duck under the table, before thinking the better of it.

"It sounded like something hitting the house," Victor said. "Over on the other side."

Adam was already on his feet and heading for the door, and Therese scrambled to follow him. She didn't want to know what kind of new disaster had befallen them, but she was damned if anyone else was going to get to it first.

As they crossed through the house, the air got noticeably colder, and the sound of the rain intensified, and once they reached the library, the reason became clear. A wall of rock and mud had slammed into the building, bursting through the mountain-facing windows and splitting their frames. Rivers of rainwater streamed down it, pouring across the buckled hardwood floors into the hall, and the rain itself pounded in through the gaping hole where the outer wall had been. The chairs and table that had been next to the window were buried under the slide, to which the entire room had lost half its space.

Not everything was completely covered. At least half of the radio receiver was visible under the mud, and the transmitter was only mostly smashed by a huge rock.

You might never run out of options, Therese thought, *but sometimes they run out on you.*

Almost all of the bookshelves along the far wall had been crushed under the slide, but one was still standing, tilted on its side with its contents tumbled out onto the floor. Therese was wondering how it got propped like that when she looked up and realized the ceiling was a lot lower than it had been. She followed its slope to where she found the point of failure, then took an involuntary step back.

"That's a structural post, isn't it?" she said, pointing to a heavy piece of timber at the far end of the room that had bent and split up in the middle.

"I think so. I mean, it was," said Adam, wiping the rain out of his eyes. He looked stunned and pale, and Therese hoped he wasn't going to faint.

"Definitely structural," Gil said. "And badly compromised. I think we had better get away from here."

Gil might have been the voice of experience, but the rest of the group had already come to the same conclusion, and before he had finished speaking, they were already retreating down the hall. Therese brought up the rear, mostly because she didn't like to have anyone behind her, and as she took a last look back at the library, the broken beam gave way. She stared, frozen, for just long enough to see the outer wall begin to collapse and the remaining bookcase splinter to matchsticks, and then she ran.

By the time the building had stopped shaking, they had made it to the front hall. Gil had his hand on the door but before he opened it, he turned to count the people behind him.

"Where's Adam?" he asked.

Victor pointed toward the living room. "He went that way. Said he'd be right back."

"Idiot." It wasn't clear if Gil was more frightened or impatient, or something else, but he stepped away from the door.

"If we go anywhere, we all need to go together," Therese reminded him. "Are we safe to stay here until he gets back?"

"I guess so." Gil ran his hand along the nearest support beam, then looked into the powder room that was on the uphill side of the hall. "It looks like this was all pretty isolated from what happened to the other side of the house. As long as the whole mountain doesn't fall on us, we should be all right for a bit."

Wendy crossed her arms and sat down on the bench by the front door. "And if it did, how much better off would we be outside? At least here we can be dry."

Therese wasn't sure about her reasoning there, or her priorities, and as she was casting about for a way to make the point, her eye was caught by one of the oversized photographs. Oliver, Chloe, and Jenna, laughing on the sofa in the cabin—three of five people who would have been a lot better off if they had gotten out of the building. Was that what had drawn her attention? A warning from her subconscious that she had had the right idea last time? But no. She looked again and she saw it.

It was on the wall. The picture.

Sonia's last words. Of course.

She needed time, to look more closely and figure out what it all meant. And more importantly, to come up with a plan. But she had barely gotten her thoughts in a row before Adam came back into the hall from the dining room door. He was carrying one of the bags that had held the emergency supplies, and he looked worried.

"The gun is gone," he said. "I put it in here for safekeeping, in case we had to evacuate, and it isn't there now. I looked all over. Someone must have taken it."

"Jesus fucking Christ," said Victor, and there wasn't much anyone could add to that.

28

S o who has it?" Gil asked the question like he expected an
answer, but didn't wait for one. "Because I know it isn't me.
For one thing, when the bullets went missing, I was flat on my ass
down a flight of stairs."

"That's true," Therese agreed. "And Adam was down here. So
unless there's a hidden staircase, then both of you are out for that one."

She left a quiet emphasis on the second half of the sentence,
but no one seemed to pick up on it.

Wendy gripped the fabric on the bench as she leaned forward.
"So, what, you're saying it has to be me or Victor? Is that it?"

"Or her," Victor added. "We only have Therese's word for it
that the ammo vanished at all. What if she just kept it so she could
steal the gun later?"

Therese gave him a sideways look. "Why would I do that? I
already had the ammunition, so why make a big deal of stealing it
from myself?"

"Because we all knew you had it." Adam hadn't said anything since announcing the loss of the gun. He had been standing by the entrance to the dining room, but now he came down the hall and placed himself firmly in front of the door.

"If the gun had vanished before the ammunition," he went on, "there'd be no question who was the most dangerous. Now, it's all up in the air."

"That's a good point," Therese said evenly. "I guess you all should add me to the suspect list."

"I think we can do more than that."

Adam was staring hard at Therese now. "We've been dancing around this for long enough, don't you think?"

A gust of cold air rushed down the hallway from the destroyed part of the building, passing through Therese's wet hair and plastering a strand against her cheek. The rest of her was feeling cold for an entirely different reason.

"Why don't you tell them?" Adam asked. "Tell them about the pills."

"The pills?" Therese hadn't expected that.

"You had pills that night. Jenna told me about them. She said you were going to bring something your dad had stolen from the evidence locker at work. She didn't want to go along, but she said she was going to, so she could catch you and turn over the proof." Adam looked around at the rest of the group. "I didn't want to say anything earlier, because I wasn't sure. The kids weren't drugged after all. But I was talking to Art earlier, and he said they found a bottle of oxy at the scene, but they left it out of the report because they didn't want to smear the names of the dead kids." Adam gave Therese a significant look. "So I didn't bring it up. But now he's dead, and so is everyone else with any connection to what happened that night. And the gun is missing, so I'm thinking it's time I stopped holding anything back."

As Adam spoke, the air seemed to crystallize around Therese, locking her in place under what felt like endless sets of eyes. Not just Gil's and Victor's, looking respectively confused and wary, or Wendy's, whose scared but triumphant expression from her spot behind Adam's shoulder filled out Therese's set of theories—even the glassy stares of the taxidermied animals that decorated the walls seemed suspicious. But the gaze that caught her attention was none of those. Directly across from Therese, Jenna's picture looked down on her, smiling, vibrant, and powerful.

You wanted to be her, Therese thought. *Now is your chance to be something more.*

Therese took a deep breath and tried to keep her voice level.

"I don't have the gun, and I didn't bring the pills. I did take them away, though." Therese looked steadily at Adam as she spoke, tracing the muscle next to his eye that had begun to twitch. "You're right, Jenna did have pills in her purse. I found them when I was looking for the bottle opener she sent me to get. And I recognized them as oxycodone because my grandma had a prescription when she had cancer. But the reason there was nothing in the police report about them at the scene was that they weren't there. I emptied out the bottle and swapped them with my allergy medicine."

"What? Why?" Wendy's confidence showed a sudden flicker, and Therese wondered how much she thought she knew.

"Because I didn't want Jenna to be able to give those pills to anyone, but I did want to know what she was up to. I thought I would wait and see what she did with the pills, and once she did, I could call her on it and show everyone the proof. Should I have told someone about it right away? Absolutely. I should have told everyone there. I should have known this wasn't something for me to take on and try to solve by myself. And I should have realized Jenna might not have even known what really was in that bottle." Therese smiled bitterly. "For all her posturing, she really was pretty straight arrow. She didn't even like beer. That's where you were different, wasn't it, Adam? Actually, I wouldn't be surprised if she stayed away from the stuff because it made her look good in comparison to you."

Adam sneered, his curling lip spoiling the perfect symmetry of his face.

"Nice story, Amy," he said, putting deliberate emphasis on the syllables of her first name. "None of this gets past the fact that you had those pills, or is going to convince anyone you didn't take the gun. I think what really happened is, you tried to get your friends in on your drug scheme, and you had a plan if they didn't go along with it. No witnesses, no trouble for you. Get your little buddy Sean to blow them all up, and you finish them off, then move to a new state to start over. Tell us something that proves that's not true."

Water was running down the hallway now, pooling around Therese's feet. Everything was coming into focus now, and if she had enough time to get her thoughts together, she might just make it.

"I'm telling you the facts as I know them. I can't do anything more." Therese shifted slightly, testing the Oriental rug in the middle of the hall to see if it would provide firmer footing. It didn't, sliding away under her shoe, and when she looked up, she saw Gil watching her.

He glanced down at how she was positioning her feet, and she knew he had noticed what she was doing. *All or nothing now*, Therese thought.

"And there's at least one person here who knows I don't have the gun. Not all of it, at least. Wendy, why don't you tell the others how you stole the ammunition from my room and gave it to Adam?"

If Wendy was going to look more like a deer in headlights, she would need antlers. Eyes wide, she clutched at Adam's sleeve and stammered, "But it doesn't matter if you have it; what he's saying could still be true. Can you prove it's not true?"

"No, but you can prove I don't have the bullets. Which I think would go a long way to convincing everyone else here that I'm not enough of a threat for them to do what Adam was about to suggest next."

Adam's eye twitch had gotten more pronounced, and his nostrils flared, but he didn't say anything to that.

Probably recalculating his next move, Therese thought. *I don't have much time. Here goes everything.*

Aloud, she said, "Adam gave you his theory about why he

thinks I'm the killer, so it's only fair I share my own about why I think it's him."

Between the sound of the rain and the rocks that were still tumbling in through the open wall, it wouldn't be fair to say a person could hear a pin drop, but there was an intensity to the silence that Therese didn't expect would last.

"We talked about theories for all of us," she went on, looking at Adam. "And the best we could come up with for you was some secret that Jenna was going to tell your father. But she didn't need to tell him anything; he already knew. He was fed up with you and your antics, the amount of money you were costing him. Your father was sick; he didn't have much time left. And he decided he wasn't going to let you be his legacy."

Adam was about to speak, so Therese hurried to go on. She took the risk of turning away from him, and looked up at Jenna's picture on the wall.

"Jenna even told me herself, that night. 'I get everything.' When she said that, I only heard it from my point of view. But she wasn't talking about boys, or clothes, or friends. Her father was dying, and you were being written out of the will. Everything was going to her."

Adam snorted.

"What a sharp memory you have. And it proves what? Even if my sister did say that, it means nothing."

Therese turned to the next picture, the one of the group on the couch, and pointed. Not at the laughing teenagers or the drinks in their hands, but at the decoration on the wall behind them.

"Does that look familiar to anyone? The thing that's sticking out behind that plate on the wall, behind Oliver in the photograph."

It was a risk, drawing everyone's attention away from Adam and toward the picture, but it was one she needed to take. Even Adam turned to look, maintaining his sneer even as a touch of worry crept into his expression.

"I don't see it," said Victor. "What are we supposed to be looking at?"

Gil frowned and came closer to the picture. "Is that what you mean? Some kind of stick that's, um, sticking out behind that plate? With something wrapped around it and studs down the—oh."

Wendy gasped. "It's Sonia's knife!" She was still tucked close behind Adam, apparently unaware that she had wound the fabric of his shirtsleeve between her fingers. He gave her an irritated look and pulled it free.

"So what?" he said. "Maybe it is. Maybe you used it to kill them all, and now that you're caught, you're trying to pin it on me."

Therese was ready for that one. "Except that I had never been to the cabin before. How was I supposed to know it was even there? Since we're doing theories, I'm going to tell you mine. I think when you found out Jenna was going to inherit your father's estate, you decided you had to kill her. But to do it outright would put too much suspicion on you, which is why you came up with the plan to hide her death in a mass killing. You knew about Sean and his bomb-building and manipulated him into helping you, and you gave Jenna the pills on the pretext they were some kind of harmless prank. The idea was that she would get us all to take them, maybe even including her, and then when the bomb went off, we would be too out of it to do anything."

Therese smiled grimly. "That one was my fault. If I had known what I was doing… Well, if I had known, I would have done a lot of things. The fact is, that part of your plan failed, and you were left with at least some of your victims still alive and able to call for help. So you went with your backup plan, using the weapon you, and only you, would have known was at hand. Because who else would have had a chance to plant a deadly knife in the wall decorations? But you couldn't be found with it, so you handed it off to Sean. Along with, I'm guessing, the shirt you were wearing, which would have been covered in a lot of blood. You must have told him to get rid of them, but it looks like he didn't."

She looked around at the group gathered in the hallway. Gil and Victor were to her right, looking like they might believe her but weren't going to put their lives on it. Wendy was still behind Adam, trying to get his attention and looking angry, scared, and confused. And Adam faced Therese, as handsome as ever, his clothes still wet from their time outside and his hair hanging loose, curling as it dried. He looked confident and aloof, but the muscle by his eye was twitching full-time now.

Therese went on, meeting his gaze dead on. "And I don't think it matters what I say now, because at this point you can't let any of us leave here alive."

29

S he's crazy! Come on guys, we have to stop her." Wendy had picked her side, and she was staying with her choice. She looked pleadingly up at Adam, from where she was holding on to his arm.

Adam looked at Wendy, sighed, and shoved her hard into the wall. She cried out and tried to catch herself, only managing to knock over a stuffed deer head on her way to the ground.

"Yeah, not really. Thanks for your help, though."

In the time it took Therese to look from Adam to Wendy and back again, he had the gun out and was leveling it at Therese.

"Pretty neat how you managed to put all that together. Especially the part about none of you getting out alive. I had a better plan for that, but this is going to have to do. Come on, let's get moving."

Adam waved the gun toward the hall, back in the direction of the library. Gil—who had jumped forward to help Wendy, stumbled over his own feet reversing course, ending up in a crouch—looked up at him.

"Go where? Why?"

"You'll figure it out soon enough, genius. Now hurry up, before this entire shithole falls down."

Victor started to obey, backing up slowly with his eyes wide with fear, but he was the only one. Wendy was still leaning against the wall, sobbing, and Gil shifted his weight like he was about to stand, but looked undecided. And Therese tucked her thumbs into the excessively tight pockets of her jeans and faced Adam squarely.

"Nope," she said.

Adam returned her stare calmly as he raised the gun to point it at her forehead. His eye had stopped twitching, Therese noticed.

"Fine," he said. "Your funeral."

"No!"

At that moment, three things happened, and one didn't. Adam pulled the trigger, Gil leaped at him, and Wendy let out an ear-piercing scream. And the gun didn't fire.

Gil slammed into Adam, and they both went down in a struggling heap. Adam held on to the gun, making several more attempts to fire it, and when that didn't work, he used it to hit Gil in the face. Gil was doing his best to defend himself, keeping close enough that Adam couldn't get any force behind the blows, and working at pinning his arms. Therese was trying to find an angle to get in and help without making things worse, but she lost the opportunity to an unexpected combatant.

That was Wendy, coming up behind the pair, swinging the deer head by the antlers and, with the full force of her fury, bringing the wooden base down on Adam's skull. He crumpled and went limp in Gil's arms, who looked shocked for a second and then dropped him to the floor.

Wendy stood over him, her face wet with tears and the deer head dangling from one hand. "You absolute bastard."

———

They tied Adam up with the remainder of the climbing rope, and on Wendy's insistence, Therese added a gag made from one of the bathroom hand towels. Gil suggested that they should move outside after all, and this time there was no argument, particularly as the rain had slackened to a steady drizzle. The still-unconscious Adam was left on the front step, and the gun remained where he had dropped it in the hallway.

The four remaining guests, damp and shell shocked, congregated around one of the cars—Lorelei's, because it was the closest to the door. Wendy leaned against the driver's side, alternately looking at her feet and back to the house. Victor and Gil found seats on the hood, and Therese positioned herself at the front corner, in a spot from where she could see both Adam and the road.

It was late in the afternoon, and the low sunlight slanted through the clouds. It would be dark soon, but for now Therese wasn't going to worry about that. There had been nights before, and she would get through this one somehow. Besides, she was feeling optimistic for a change.

"Why didn't the gun go off?" asked Victor, who had been mostly silent so far.

Therese could have answered that, but Gil got there ahead of her. "Because Therese broke it, right? I should have known that's why you weren't scared," he said sheepishly. "I thought you were just being cool. Guess I was pretty dumb there."

"Dumb, but brave," Therese agreed, smiling. "And yes, I did break it. Specifically, I bent the follower, the part of the magazine that sits over the spring, so it would jam when the gun was fired. Probably."

"Probably?" said Wendy. "So you didn't know? Why not just get rid of the bullets?"

That was a good question, and one that had definitely occurred to Therese when Adam had her handiwork pointed at her head. But that was over now, so she shrugged and said, "Calculated risk. I knew someone here had killed three people, and I didn't think they were done yet. And I figured a gun would be pretty tempting to someone like that, and if they had it, or thought they did, they might end up doing something stupid."

"Stupid like believing a man." Wendy looked over at the front door, where Adam was starting to stir; then she turned to Therese. "I'm sorry, by the way. He told me he had evidence you were the killer, and he was just being nice to keep an eye on you. Then when you split up the gun, he got me alone and said we had to get your part away, and I could do it better than him because my room was next door. And I just totally fell for it. I always did have the worst taste in men."

Therese might have had some choice words for that particular apology, given what could have happened, but considering her own plan had used Wendy as well, she decided to let it go.

"We all have our blind spots," she said. "And I've gotta say, you swing a mean deer head."

Everyone laughed. Out of the corner of her eye, Therese could see Adam shifting—she was fairly sure he was awake and playing possum now, but she wasn't very concerned. If he thought he could get out of her knots and make a run for it, well, he was welcome to try.

She wasn't the only one who had noticed.

"I think he's awake," Gil said. "Should we do something?"

Therese shook her head. "Just stay alert and keep an eye on him. If we're going to be here longer, we'll have to come up with a plan, but he should be fine for now."

The mention of staying caused the group to fall silent, thinking about what their immediate future might hold. At least, that was what Therese thought they were thinking about. Gil, at least, seemed to have the past more on his mind.

"Did he really do that? Kill all of them so he could inherit his dad's money?" he asked.

"That's the theory, yeah," Therese said. "The police should be able to follow up on it when we get back. It's funny—so many times over the years I've thought about what Jenna said, about her getting everything, and it never occurred to me to wonder what she really meant. But we had been talking about the cabin and her father's business for some reason—it must have been on her mind."

Victor raised an eyebrow. "It seems kind of obvious, now that you say it."

"It does now. But back then, well, let's say I had a more limited range of interests. If I'd thought—anyway, I didn't think, and that's a big part of the problem. So here we are."

"Here we are," Gil agreed. "The question is now, for how long? We could start walking, but we aren't going to get far before dark, and there's still the question of what we're going to do about him."

They weren't referring to Adam by his name, Therese noticed. That was fine with her; she wasn't very interested in acknowledging him either. And Gil did have a point, though she was starting to have some hope there.

"Worst-case scenario, we can lock him in the basement with Sonia," she said.

From the way his body jerked around, there was no question that Adam was awake now. Therese went on.

"But I don't think that's going to be necessary. Call me an optimist, but I think things are about to get better here."

In fact, it wasn't optimism that inspired her. It had stopped raining, and in the distance Therese thought she could hear the sound of chainsaws.

30

The first cars to arrive were from the California Highway Patrol, followed shortly by a delivery van that seemed to have been assembled from pieces of other, long-dead vans and painted with a variety of colors of house paint. Not far behind it were a few more police cars, an unmarked sedan, and a Cal Fire forestry truck that Therese suspected of being along for the gossip.

She figured the sedan should be her first stop, but she waited long enough to see Lorelei and two other women of about Lorelei's age who she didn't recognize come tumbling out of the van. Joseph followed behind them, his left arm in a sling, carrying a paper coffee cup in his good hand.

"Two creams, no sugar, right?" he said as he handed it to Therese. "Sorry it took us so long. The coffee might be a bit cold."

"Sounds perfect; good to see you." She took in Joseph's

injured arm and the bruises and bandage on his face. "I'd say you missed all the excitement, but it looks like you had some of your own?"

Joseph gingerly touched his cheek where it was starting to swell up. "You could say that. Nothing serious, though. I can tell you the whole story later, but I'll just say, you could do a lot worse than having Lorelei as your spotter. That woman is some kind of goddamn superhero."

At the moment, the hero in question was hugging Gil and offering him an apple, while the two women with her peppered Victor and Wendy with questions.

"I don't doubt it for a second," Therese said, as she spotted a man getting out of the unmarked sedan. She gestured at the house, with the hillside slid into half of it and Adam tied up on the front step. "Things have been busy here, too. I'll let the others fill you in. Looks like I have to take a work call."

The man had the look of having put on his suit in a hurry, but he was clean, well-dressed, and holding a cell phone, none of which Therese could say for herself.

"Special Agent Brewer?" he asked perfunctorily as she approached his car. Therese was about to ask how he was so sure who she was when he handed her back her badge.

"I believe this is yours."

"It is, thank you." Therese ran her finger around the edge of the plastic and then looked up at him. "I imagine you have a few questions for me."

"Just a few."

By the time Therese's interview was finished, Adam had already been taken away, and the others were scattered among the various law enforcement vehicles, giving their accounts of the weekend. Three CHP officers were gathered around the car with Art's body in it, looking concerned and talking into their radios, and another group had already left with the keys to the basement. The forestry crew was examining where the slide had hit the house, making concerned faces and shaking their heads.

Therese's colleague—an agent from the Sacramento office by the name of Jones—had some calls to make, and though he had told her to stick around, he didn't seem to need her at the moment. So she wandered back over to the van, where Joseph and Lorelei were sitting in the open side, chatting with the strangers.

"These are my roommates, Ruth and Patti," Lorelei said when she approached. "It's thanks to them we were able to get back as soon as we did. There was a tree down across the road that caused us all kinds of trouble—would have been all night if we'd had to go the whole way on foot. But while we were dealing with it, they turned up on the other side, and it was a damn good thing."

"They came to find you? But why?" Therese asked.

"Let's just say we're of a suspicious turn of mind." Ruth was probably in her midsixties, with her hair dyed a shocking pink and a full set of teeth that were definitely not her own. Sipping from a battered water bottle covered in stickers, she went on.

"It just seemed a little too neat, you know? Lorrie getting invited like this to a trip to the mountains by some journalist with an unlimited budget. And you know, I've known some reporters, and they don't get to expense hardly anything these days. So I made sure that Lorrie gave us all the information about where she was going and who invited her, and then, when her phone stopped responding yesterday, we knew something was wrong. But it was Patti who figured it out."

Lorelei picked up the story there, beaming with pride.

"That's right. She picked up what none of us did, which was that the L in 'Atlantic' in that so-called reporter's email address was actually a capital I. That's how Sonia tricked us into coming here, and that's how Ruth and Patti knew something was up."

Patti was a short woman, under five feet tall and round in every direction. She was clearly pleased with her achievement, but she tried to sound modest about it.

"For all the good it did us," she said. "We tried going to the police, but no one had any interest in what we had to say. So then when it had been another day, and we still hadn't heard from Lor, we decided there was nothing for it but to come up here ourselves and see what was going on."

"And I, for one, am extremely grateful," said Joseph. "I have to admit, once I tangled with that tree, I was really starting to think that walking out hadn't been such a good idea." He looked over to where Art's body was being photographed by some crime scene techs who had just arrived. "I'm revising that thought now. So, what actually happened?"

Therese sighed deeply. "Maybe I should start at the beginning."

THE SURVIVOR

Early Wednesday morning, Therese pulled her second rental car into the lot at the main cemetery in her hometown. The last two days had been long, full of questions, phone calls, more questions, emails, questions from people who didn't care for being called in on a holiday, and a lot of time spent on hold with her cell phone service provider. And there was still more to come, she knew, but while she had a little bit of time to herself, there was something she needed to do.

The grocery store had just restocked its flower selection when she got there, so Therese had had her choice of the bouquets. She picked one with pink daisies, because Jenna would have liked them, and some sprigs of eucalyptus. The store was one she must have shopped at a hundred times as a kid growing up in this town, but the layout had been completely changed, and it was like she had never been there before. Which was fine—Therese had had enough nostalgia for a while.

Almost enough. The memorial was easy to find—all the parents had contributed, but Jenna's father had been the one to make sure it was in a prime location at the end of the entry path to the cemetery. Not that any of them were buried here—the memorial had initially been planned to be on the grounds of the high school, until the county objected. The families had been outraged at the time, but Therese thought it was better suited to this spot, shaded by trees and surrounded by grass, rather than just another surface for successive generations of teenagers to write their names on and make out behind.

Therese laid her flowers at the base and stood back to look at it. The memorial was simple, minimalist even: just a huge slab of granite with five names and their dates of birth, and one date on the bottom. Something was written in Latin across the top—Therese had known what it said at one point, but she couldn't remember now.

"How well you live makes a difference, not how long."

Therese hadn't heard Gil approach, but now here he was, standing behind her and looking up at the stone.

"Aunt Rachel insisted we come out here once a month, and she read it every time. At least I think that's what it says. I'm pretty sure Aunt Rachel doesn't speak Latin."

"Close enough, probably," Therese said. "Interesting choice."

"Yeah." They both fell silent, thinking about lives of different lengths and impacts.

At least, that was what Therese was thinking about. She had thought she could read Gil pretty well before, but now she wasn't so sure. Whatever was going on, they both seemed to finish with it at about the same time, and as Therese turned to walk on down the path, Gil fell into step next to her. The cemetery was empty now, but it must have been busy over the long weekend, and patriotic decorations were scattered around on many of the graves.

"Are you done with the police?" she asked.

"For now," Gil said. "They have more questions for me and asked me to hang around for a couple more days. They can't make me stay, though, can they?"

"Not without arresting you," Therese confirmed. "Why, do you need to leave?"

"Well, I do have a job to get back to. My boss has been pretty good about it so far, but I can't stay away forever."

They had passed into an older part of the graveyard, where the flat, lawn mower–friendly plaques gave way to taller gravestones, mostly worn away to illegibility. There were fewer ribbons and flowers here, just the occasional fading plastic bunch. Gil stopped to pick up a fake rose and put it back in its stone base.

"Oh, and I found out who pushed me down the stairs," he said. "It was Victor. He came and apologized after we got done with the police. He said he thought for sure I was the killer, because of the glass on my shoe, so he figured you'd all be safe if he could take me out. But then when the bullets got stolen from your room, he didn't know what to think, so he didn't say anything."

"Nice of him."

For someone who had been pushed down a set of stairs, Gil didn't seem too bothered. "We were all pretty freaked out at that point. At least he apologized."

The path they were on turned uphill, and Therese paused under an oak tree to get her bearings. The cemetery was located on a prime piece of real estate overlooking the valley, but Gil didn't seem interested in the view.

"I heard Adam got a lawyer," he said. "A really good one."

"Of course he did. He can afford it."

"Do you think he'll get away with it?" Gil sounded truly worried, and Therese regretted being so flip.

"I don't know, maybe? People do. And there isn't a lot of direct evidence for any of the murders. They're looking for the knife, but I think the landslide is making it harder."

"Oh. Well, I guess that's how the world is, isn't it? Some people get to do whatever they want."

Therese didn't entirely disagree with that, but she wasn't going to say so. Besides, there were advantages to knowing people in law enforcement.

"It's not all bad news. For one thing, remember how Art had a line in his notebook about finding someone named Lenny? Well, the cops were able to find him, and he was happy to talk. Turns out Lenny is a cousin of Sonia's who'd been helping her do some work on her house. According to him, about six months ago, he pulled up some floorboards in what had been Sean's room, and he found a stained man's shirt wrapped around a knife. He showed it to Sonia, and she freaked out, took it away, and made him promise not to tell anyone."

"And you think it was Adam's shirt?"

"That's the idea. Best guess is it was the one he was wearing when he went in to kill them, and he gave it and the knife to Sean to hide."

Gil frowned. "That seems like a big risk. Why would he let someone else have that kind of evidence?"

"Good question. Maybe he panicked, thought the police were going to search him before he'd have a chance to get rid of it. Or maybe he didn't realize at the time how dangerous it could be for him. After all, DNA technology has come a long way in the last twenty years. Back then, there wasn't much chance of getting enough genetic material from the skin cells in the fabric to prove the shirt was his."

"They can do that now?"

"In theory. And then there's Mike's evidence."

Gil looked surprised. "What did Mike have? Did he know it was Adam all along?"

"Not exactly. At least, nobody seems to think so. But he did save the email message he got offering him fifty grand to deliver the package, and he managed to get a partial picture of the license plate of the car that dropped it off."

The path ended at the top of the graveyard, where a bench had been positioned to take in the view. Therese sat down, doing her best to avoid the old gum and bird poop, while Gil took the seat next to her with less care.

"Fifty thousand dollars, wow. No wonder Mike was willing to keep it secret. He would have been in plenty of trouble if people found out."

"He would," Therese agreed. "Plus it was being paid over five years, at ten thousand dollars a year, so he needed to sit tight if he wanted to see all the cash. Aside from any potential DNA, that money is probably our best way of tying the crime to Adam, but tracing it is going to take some time."

"That's something, I guess." Gil sat for a moment lost in thought, and they both watched a turkey vulture riding the thermals over the valley.

"So, what happened at the house, then?" he said at last. "Adam didn't know what was going on, but he showed up anyway? And then Sonia did her act, so he killed her? And then…" Gil trailed off, lost in the bizarreness of his own recent experiences.

"Something like that, yeah." Therese understood his confusion. No matter how many times she went over the events, they still barely seemed real to her. "I think he honestly believed there was going to be a magazine article, and he wanted to be there to have a hand in controlling the narrative. But when Sonia showed up with the knife, he knew Sean hadn't gotten rid of the evidence like he wanted, and if that was the case, then he couldn't be sure how much Sean's mother might know. And I think he was probably running on pure panic once he killed her, so when Mike started hinting that he might know things, and Art revealed he had been working with Sonia, they had to go too."

Therese shrugged. "And then we saw the notes in Art's book, about the shirt in particular; it wasn't safe for any of us to leave there alive. I don't know what he would have done, probably something to make it look like we all died in the mudslide, or I shot the rest of you and then he killed me. Either way, there had to be no one left who knew Sonia had that evidence."

She looked over at Gil and found him looking pale, staring down the path back into the cemetery. He swallowed hard and turned back to her.

"I guess I knew that," he said. "It's just kind of a shock to hear it out loud. But he's going to be locked up for good, right? All that evidence, they'll have to convict him."

"Well, it's never going to be a slam-dunk case. Adam's a rich guy, and twenty years is a long time. But on balance, I think they're going to get him. After all," Therese said with a smile, "he's not nearly as smart as he thinks he is."

Gil laughed. "I guess that's where I'm lucky. I've never thought I was that smart. Good thing you were around to do the thinking."

"I could have been better at that myself," Therese reminded him. "And you came through when it counted."

"So maybe we make a good team?" Gil crossed his arms and leaned back on the bench. "Let's never do it again."

"Deal." Therese knew it wasn't really over, but for this moment, sitting in the sunshine with Gil smiling back at her, it was nice to pretend for a moment that it was.

They had run out of conversation, so they stayed there on the bench, looking out at the view in silence. Across the valley Therese could just make out the wooded hillside of the park next to where the cabin had been. She brushed her hair out of her face and smelled eucalyptus, and wondered for a moment if she was being haunted by the memory, until she remembered the bouquet, and the oil that had rubbed off the leaves onto her hands.

"I think we might as well go back now," she said. "There's nothing more for us here."

THE END

READING GROUP GUIDE

1. Twenty years after the death of her friends, Therese is invited to a mysterious event alongside other people connected to the crime. If you were in Therese's position, would you have wanted to go?

2. Why did Amy/Therese leave the party the night of the Memorial Day Massacre? What do the other characters think about her story? Would you have left too?

3. Describe each of the characters and what you learn about them from their brief vignettes. Who are they, and what are the motivations that they have for attending this reunion? Were there any characters that you connected with or found suspicious?

4. The story touches on the consequences media might have when covering crime stories. How did Therese have to change

her life after the murder of her friends because of the stories that were being written about her? Discuss how you feel about true crime media. Do you think it's always ethical?

5. At one point, Therese says she wanted to stop defining herself as "the girl who left." What does she mean by this, and how did she try to do that? Do you think she was successful?

6. How does the theme of memory come into play throughout the story? Discuss how the characters remember the same events differently and what implications this had on their motivations to be at the reunion.

7. Therese may be considered an unreliable narrator. Why is that? In the end, do we learn the truth about what she remembers of the night of the murders?

8. Discuss the end of the story. Were you surprised by this outcome?

A CONVERSATION
WITH THE AUTHOR

This is a twisty mystery with a closed circle element. What made you want to write this kind of story? What was your favorite twist to create and why?

I love to read classic and Golden Age mysteries, and in writing this story, I wanted to capture some of the things I enjoy most about them—the limited cast of characters who could all be the potential killer, the investigator who's just a little bit smarter than everyone in the room, and the tension of never quite knowing what's going to happen next.

As far as the twists, I love them all, but my favorite is probably what happens with the cell phones. It's the eternal problem of the modern mystery writer: How do you keep the suspense high when anyone can just take out their phone and call for help? I think I found a creative way of dealing with it, and I hope the readers will think so too.

How did the novel evolve over the course of writing? Were there any major changes?

I started with the opening scene, which was the first thing in my head before I even came up with the rest of the novel. Aside from some editing, that hasn't changed much, but everything else was fair game! Typical for me, I wrote some opening chapters that had to be cut, and I even had an early draft that was written in first person, which I ended up changing to third. But the biggest edits were in the middle third, which was largely rearranged and had a whole section added! So, yes, there were a few changes made.

Each of the characters gets their own perspective in the form of vignettes. What was it like to write from the perspective of so many different characters?

That was one of my favorite parts of writing the book. It was really interesting to try to get into the heads of all these different people—especially the ones I don't find very sympathetic. Because, of course, each of them sees themself as the main character, and no one believes they're the villain.

What does your writing process look like? Are there any ways you like to find creative inspiration?

My writing process mostly looks like me staring out the window and/or playing Candy Crush for several minutes on end, followed by a short period of furious typing. More generally, I used to make the plot up as I went along, but over time, I've come to see the value of doing at least some planning before I get started. I don't think I'll ever be a true outliner, but you never know.

What do you hope readers experience while reading this book?

I hope they have fun! I wrote this book to be exactly the sort of thing I want to read when I'm sitting on a lounge chair on a summer afternoon or curled up on the couch in the winter. But beyond the entertainment aspect, when I was writing *She Left,* I was thinking a lot about how we see ourselves when we're young, and the positives and the flaws in hanging on to those feelings as we get older. So one thing I would like is if readers were to reflect on that in their own lives, with empathy for the kid they were but also with the adult understanding that things may not have been as straightforward as they thought.

What are some books you've read that have influenced your writing?

Obviously, the biggest influence on *She Left* has been *And Then There Were None* by Agatha Christie. And many of her other books have influenced me as well—*Sparkling Cyanide* in particular. But I also love modern writers, and I'm very excited about the things that are going on in mystery and thriller writing right now! The initial seed for the inspiration to write this book came from reading *They All Fall Down* by Rachel Howzell Hall, which reminded me how much I like an "island book" (which this technically is not, but the spirit is there). I was also inspired by the structure of Lucy Foley's *The Guest List* and the atmosphere of *In a Dark, Dark Wood* by Ruth Ware. And though the real-world setting of *She Left* couldn't be more different from Terry Pratchett's *Discworld*, I like to think that a little bit of the spirit of Samuel Vimes and Granny Weatherwax have made it into these pages.

ACKNOWLEDGMENTS

No book is an island, and there are many people to thank for helping to launch this one and save it from sinking under the weight of disastrously mixed metaphors. Thank you to my marvelous agent, Abby Saul, for pushing me to achieve the things I'm not sure I'm capable of and getting me back on track when I have quite literally lost the plot.

Thank you to Anna Michels for recognizing the potential in this book and using her editing powers to help to realize it. And thanks to all the team at Sourcebooks/Poisoned Pen for their great work in making the manuscript into a book.

Thanks to Laurie, Tammy, Michelle, and all the NorCal MWA write-in crew for keeping me on track when I actually manage to show up. Thanks to Sisters in Crime writing partners Jen and Susan for all their useful feedback. And a special thank-you to all the Larkies for their advice, encouragement, and GIFs.

Thank you to Cameron for your support and your patience,

even when deadlines are making me panic. Thanks to Mom and Dad for introducing me to reading mysteries and being my biggest boosters. And to the rest of my family for your cheers and encouragement. And thanks (in the form of treats) to Zaphod, for being the nuttiest labradoodle to ever zoomie around the living room.

And thanks, I guess, to Daisy Bateman, for whatever it is she brings to the party. (Cheese, mostly.)

ABOUT THE AUTHOR

© Andrea Sher

Stacie Grey is an author and fan of mysteries who lives in Alameda, California, with her husband and dog. In what passes for normal life, she works in biotech research. She mostly posts to Instagram and Mastodon, and occasionally writes a newsletter.